TEDDY

Elite 8 Studios Book 5

Emmy Sanders

Beta Reading by Christie, Georgia Johnson, Jen & Maxie of Smut Readers Society, and Lauren

Special thanks to Genevieve and Marie-Pierre for Québécois French translations

Editing by M.A. Hinkle

Proofreading by Ky

Cover Design by Natasha Snow Designs

ISBN: 9781967130047

Content Warning: This book contains homophobia and family conflict.

For the wild ones. The big-hearted and brightly chaotic.
Crumple up that ill-fitted box. You don't need it.

Contents

Chapter 1
Kipp

"I love dick!" I shout.

My dance partner's eyes flick to the dildo crown atop my head. "Honey, I can tell."

"Wanna lick?" I ask, holding out my candy necklace. It, too, is made of dicks. Tiny ones in all sorts of colors.

The guy grins, but before I can feed him one of my sugar penises, I'm spun away.

"Shit," I mutter, stumbling a step before strong hands steady me. Recognition kicks in immediately. "Teddy! I know you. Hey, open up. Not for anything weird, I swear. I just wanna put a dick on your tongue."

"You're wasted," Teddy says, his tone stern even as there's a smile on his face.

"You're lovely," I counter.

Teddy's eyebrows rise, and he grabs hold of my hand, leading me off the dance floor. The guy I was twerking with tries to come along, but Teddy shakes his head in a clear *nuh-uh* gesture.

I'm pretty sure the cockblock should irritate me, not make me all warm and gooey inside, but I can't find it in me to care.

Not when Teddy's big hand is wrapped so securely around my own.

"Why haven't we fucked?" I ask him.

Teddy glances at me over his shoulder, but he doesn't have time to respond before we're arriving at the bar. Teddy plops me onto a stool and flags down the bartender, and a minute later, there's a cold bottle of water in my hand.

"Drink," he says.

I do. Not because Teddy told me to, but because I'm thirsty. That's the only reason.

"You didn't answer my question," I point out when my water is gone.

Teddy leans close, something spicy and sweet hitting my nose with his proximity. He smells good enough to lick several times over. "We're not having this conversation while you're drunk," he says.

"Boo," I reply, but then I notice how low-cut his shirt is. "Your chest is *so* nice. I like it a lot."

"That so?" he asks. I get the sense he's laughing at me, but it feels like a nice laugh, so I roll with it.

"Mhm. I like your cock, too, even though you've never let me have it." And *whoops*. Niko would call that an *inside thought*.

Teddy leans close again, causing my pulse to hitch. "You've never asked."

"What?" I practically shout. "That can't be true."

I've known Teddy for over a year and a half at this point, even though we've never been particularly *close*. He works with my bestie Niko, aka Adonis, at Elite 8 Studios, hence my having seen his very nice cock. The man makes beautiful porn. That thick frame, hairy chest, his massive arms, even bigger thighs, and the long, cut dick that could easily fuck me into next Thursday? Yeah, sign me up.

"Surely I've asked," I say. Why wouldn't I have? Teddy is plain hot, and I've had a lowkey crush on him since we met.

He shakes his head, his face so very close to mine. Probably because of how far I'm leaning off my stool.

"But you're so pretty," I say, stroking his beard.

He snorts, his big brown eyes crinkling at the corners. "And you're drunk."

"Not *that* drunk," I defend, nearly slipping off my perch. Teddy catches me before I can fall to the floor.

"Yes, that drunk," he says, shaking his head. His voice is almost too low to hear when he adds, "What am I going to do with you, Kipp?"

I open my mouth to tell him anything with his dick and my face would be fine, but then a drink is being set in front of me on the bar. "From the guy in the red shirt," the bartender says before walking off.

I turn and, upon finding Mr. Red Shirt, wave exuberantly. "Thanks!" I call.

The man grins, but when I turn back to my drink, it's gone.

"You're cut off," Teddy says.

I gape as he downs the drink himself, setting the empty glass on the bar top once he's done. "*Dude*, you can't do that. You're not my *dad*."

The look Teddy gives me has me stilling in my seat, my hair standing on end and every muscle in my body freezing. It only lasts a second, that searing gaze, and then Teddy blinks and looks away. But that one second is enough to have my breath coming short.

"Hey," a voice says near my ear. I turn, and Mr. Red Shirt is standing there. "I saw your friend take your drink. Can I buy you another?"

"He's not interested," Teddy says, unceremoniously tugging me off my stool and dragging me away from the bar.

I follow, voice lost and dick confusingly hard.

"Kipper!" someone calls. A second later, a small, blonde human collides into me. I grab hold of Alex, another Elite 8 performer who goes by Tink, and laugh when he snags a dick off my necklace.

"Mind your teeth," I tell him.

He grins rakishly at me, chomping down on the candy. "I was looking for you guys. C'mon. We're doing blowjobs."

"We're doing what now?" I ask, grinning wildly as I follow. Teddy's hand pulls against my own for a second before he walks after me.

Alex sends me a wink. "Shots, boo."

As promised, there's a large tray of whipped-cream-topped shots on the table Alex leads us to. The rest of our party is already there, most of them porn stars. We're out celebrating Cas's—or Himbo's—departure from the studio, as well as his boyfriend, Jason, becoming a nurse. Honestly, I don't know either well, but I heard the words *party bus*, and I was in.

Niko sends me an up-nod when we reach the table, and I lean across Dixon, his boyfriend, to give him a hug. Dixon, who goes by Dix, grumbles the entire time.

"Having fun?" Niko asks when I step back, his eyes smiling.

"*So* much fun," I assure him just as Alex calls out a toast.

"To swallowing!" the blonde says.

There's a collective cheer, and everyone goes for their shots. Before I have a chance to show off my incredible blowjob skills, Teddy snags my drink right out from under me.

I watch, eyes wide, as he swiftly downs the shot, followed by his own.

"You're gonna be drunk soon, too, if you keep that up," I say, reaching over to run my finger along his lip where a small dollop of whipped cream lingers.

Teddy's chest rises as I bring the sweetened finger to my tongue. Our eyes catch. Hold.

"Time to dance!" Alex shouts.

Heart thundering, I break Teddy's gaze and grab a spare shot off the table. Before he can stop me, I toss it back and take off after Alex, snickering all the while. My mind is wonderfully hazy as I get lost in the sea of bodies on the dance floor, ignoring everything but the undulating wave around me and the music pulsing through my ears. It doesn't even register at first that the big hands holding tight to my hips are familiar.

When I open my eyes, Teddy is watching me with a hawk-like intensity. He leans close, his lips brushing my ear. "You need a keeper."

"You could keep me," I suggest, grinding a little—*maybe a lot*—against Teddy's leg.

His fingers spasm on my hips. "Don't tempt me, Kipp."

"I want to tempt you," I counter, past the point of caring about my loose tongue. "Why haven't we fucked?"

He closes his eyes for a beat, looking almost pained. "I don't want to fuck you, Kipp."

"No?" I ask, disappointment hitting hard. I could have sworn...

"I want to *own* you."

What little breath I have left in my lungs punches free, leaving me dizzy. *And painfully aroused.* "No one's stopping you."

Teddy shakes his head, the intensity in his gaze fading like a sunset. "Tell you what. Ask me again when you're sober."

"I will," I promise.

"We'll see."

I don't know what to make of that—any of it—but I see a tray of neon-colored shooters nearby, and my attention gets waylaid. "Fuck yeah. Tiny science experiments." I wave down the server, and after forking over some cash, she hands me a shot. Teddy grabs it from my hand, downing the bright pink liquid before I can utter a protest. "*Dude.* You can't keep that up all night."

"Watch me," he says, setting the empty shooter back on the tray.

Well, *fine* then. If Teddy is so determined to be my watchdog, I'll give him a show he won't forget.

The muscles in his cheek twitch as I take a step back and start dancing again, tugging up my shirt enough for him to see the bottom of my stomach. I raise an eyebrow in invitation, one Teddy easily accepts. He closes the distance between us and spins me around, holding tight to my stomach as his crotch nestles against my ass.

Yesss.

This is good. Very good. I'll drive Teddy so wild he won't be able to resist me the next time we meet. He won't keep a respectable distance like he usually does at these Elite 8 gatherings. I won't catch his eyes on me only for them to slide away in indifference. He'll *want* me; I'll make sure of it. And then, maybe, he'll keep me. Or, no, *fuck* me. Yeah, then he'll fuck me.

I give myself a mental high five. It's a brilliant plan. Absolutely bulletproof. And okay, maybe I am a *little* drunk, but people get drunk in Vegas all the damn time.

Seriously, what could go wrong?

Chapter 2
Kipp

A thousand tiny daggers stab into my retinas the moment I wake up.

"*Noo*," I groan, closing my eyes and face-planting onto a hard surface. "Ow."

"Fuck," the surface mutters. "Why are you shouting?"

"Why are you?" I hiss, pushing myself upright and blinking a few times.

Slowly, my vision comes into focus. Dark sheets. A broad, hairy chest. A room that is most definitely not my own.

"Where am I?" I ask, trying to think past the pounding in my head.

"My place."

"And who the fuck—" *Oh.* "Teddy?"

The man snorts, rubbing his face. My eyes drag down his bare chest before I grab the sheet at his hips and tug, revealing...*jeans*. I frown.

"Did we fuck?" I ask, trying to piece my memories together. I remember being at the club. Drinking a lot. I remember Teddy, his hands on my body as we danced. I remember feeling really happy. But past that, it's all a blur.

"No, we didn't fuck," Teddy says, sitting up.

"Are you sure?" I ask, checking myself over and then looking around. I'm in briefs, and the rest of my clothes are on a chair in the corner of the room.

Teddy makes a sound that could be incredulity. "I don't fuck drunk men, Kipp. Not even you."

Not even me? What does that mean?

"Okay, but you were wasted, too," I point out. "So you might not remember. And *fuck*. Why is my voice so goddamn loud?"

Teddy huffs a laugh, running his hands through his hair. *Christ*, the man has nice arms. "You'd know if we fucked," he says simply.

My eyes skitter down to his crotch again. And yeah, I guess he has a point. The man is definitely packing, and considering my ass isn't remotely sore...

"I need water," I groan, rolling off the bed and nearly falling on my face.

"Bathroom is right through there," Teddy says, pointing to his en suite.

"Thanks," I mutter, walking that way on shaky legs. I close the door behind me and grab the counter, breathing for a second before turning on the tap. After ducking my head and drinking a few mouthfuls of water, I splash my face, hoping the wash of cold will bring some clarity. When something hard drags across my cheek, I pull my hand away. "What the..."

Oh, no. Oh, *no, no, no*.

"Teddy?" I call a little weakly.

His voice comes muffled through the door. "Yeah?"

"Do, uh... Do you actually remember last night?"

Teddy has his head cocked when I open the bathroom door. "Not much," he answers.

"Yeah," I say, swallowing. "I was afraid of that. Um, can I see your hand?"

His brow furrows, but he holds up his hands, palms facing me. A gold band glints on his left ring finger, something Teddy notices immediately. His right hand falls lax at his side as he stares at his left, his face turning uncharacteristically blank.

"So, uh," I say, huffing a slightly hysterical laugh as I hold up my own hand, gold ring included. I wiggle my fingers. "I guess congratulations are in order."

Teddy blinks.

"*Yaaay?*" I cheer meekly.

He opens his mouth, but a vibration cuts off whatever he was going to say. I head for my phone, grabbing it off my pile of clothes and cursing when I see the barrage of notifications onscreen. The call from Alex goes to voicemail. There are a few other missed calls, too, including one from...my brother?

I frown, and the screen lights with Alex's name again. This time, I answer.

"Hey," I say, going for casual.

"Hey?" he asks, voice high. "I've been calling you and Teddy all night. What the hell happened, sweets? Jason said he saw you two heading into a chapel, but no one could find either of you. Don't tell me what I think happened *happened?*"

"Um." I rub my neck, my ring catching on my skin again. I look at it, noticing Teddy doing the same to his. "I suppose I could lie."

"Oh my *God*," Alex hisses. "You two got *married?*"

Teddy's head lifts at that. I'm guessing he could hear Alex's ungodly screech.

"Alex, look," I say, my gut falling as Teddy gets up, tugging a shirt on over his head. He looks upset. "I'll have to call you back." Alex sputters something, but I end the call, dropping my phone on the chair. "Teddy?"

He turns to me, expression dimmed. It's not what I'm used to seeing on the man. He usually has a smile on his face, but not right now.

"I'm sorry," I tell him seriously.

A flicker of confusion flashes in his eyes. "What for?"

"For dragging you into this. If we *are* married, it's my fault. You were just trying to keep me safe last night."

He shakes his head. "It's not your fault, Kipp."

"Do you remember what happened?"

"Well, no," he admits.

"Then it's likely my fault," I say, grabbing my pants and tugging them on. "If you haven't noticed, I'm a bit of a mess."

I'm also nearly thirty years old. Shouldn't I have my life figured out by now?

"Kipp," Teddy says gently.

This time, it's me shaking my head. "Don't defend me," I say, grabbing my shirt. "I went overboard last night, and I dragged you down with me."

I startle somewhat when warm fingers touch my chin. My gaze snaps up to Teddy, who looks a lot less surly than he did a minute ago.

"It took both of us to get married," he says. "If it's your fault, then it's mine, too. We'll figure it out, okay? I'm sure we can get the whole thing annulled. It'll be like it never happened."

"Yeah, okay," I mutter, not sure, for some reason, if that makes me feel better or worse.

Teddy gives my chin a squeeze before letting go. "I need to use the bathroom."

I nod as Teddy retreats into the en suite, and then I pick up my phone. "Who even lets people get married when they're that drunk?" I say loudly. "I mean, I was wearing a dick crown, for Christ's sake. That should have been a dead give-away. Oh, hey, where is that thing? Hopefully, I didn't lose..."

My voice sputters out when I open my Instagram. There are two new pictures posted on my account from early this morning. In one, Teddy and I are practically falling over each other, my arm around his neck and his lips pressed to my blush-red—or maybe booze-red—cheek. We're standing in front of a chapel. I labeled it, simply, "Hubs." The next is a close-up of our joined hands, gold bands clearly visible. Below the picture is "We did it!"

"*Fuuuck*," I groan. Suddenly, my brother's phone call makes a lot more sense.

"What's wrong?" Teddy asks, emerging from the bath-room.

I swing my phone screen his way. "I don't think we can pretend it never happened."

I leave Teddy's apartment in a funk. I don't bother respond-ing to my missed calls or messages. I simply grab a rideshare home and silently berate myself for being so utterly reckless. Twenty-nine and gearing up for my first divorce. *Annulment.* Whatever.

"I need to send him a gift basket for putting up with this crap," I mutter.

"Pardon?" my driver asks.

"Oh." I huff a humorless laugh. "My husband. He deserves the biggest apology basket ever. Which one do you think says 'I'm sorry we got drunk and made major life decisions together'—muffins or fruit?"

The guy mumbles something I can't make out, and I slump in my seat, keeping my mouth shut for the rest of the drive. He drops me off in front of my building, and I head inside, eyes catching on my ring again as I stand at my door. My stomach rolls with something not entirely unpleasant, but I shake it off and turn the knob.

My roommate pounces before I've taken two steps. "Holy shit, did you seriously get married?"

I give Brodie a rueful smile. "Signs point to yes."

Although, technically, we've yet to find paperwork confirming it. But the rings and pictures are pretty damning.

"I didn't even know you were serious about someone," Brodie says, following me into the kitchen as I fill up a glass with water and chug it down. I'm fucking *thirsty*. "If I'd known, I would have talked to you sooner, but this is actually pretty great."

"Wait, what?" I ask, setting down my empty glass.

Brodie holds his hands together, giving me a big, pleading smile that has me more than a little concerned. "Well, Xavier and I have been getting serious, too."

"Yeah?"

My roommate and I aren't exactly close, even though we've lived together for over a year. We get along fine, but Brodie works the graveyard shift, whereas I have a typical nine-to-five office job. We rarely ever see each other, and the times we do, it's usually in passing. Frankly, I don't even know who Xavier is.

"Uh-huh," Brodie says. "And I was trying to figure out a way to ask if we could have the apartment. But *now*, I don't have to, right? What's your husband's name again?"

"Oh, uh, Teddy."

"Right," he says. "Well, I assume you're moving in with Teddy? Honestly, the timing is perfect. Win-win all around." He grins as my gut does a nosedive.

"The thing is..."

"Oh, and congratulations!" he practically shouts, coming in and wrapping his slender arms around my shoulders. He bounces a little, bringing me along for the ride. "I'm so happy for you."

I cough, my wince going unnoticed. "Thanks."

"This is so great. We're all going to be so happy," Brodie says.

"Yeah," I mumble. *So happy.*

I leave my apartment in a daze, a duffle bag over my shoulder. I feel a bit like a zombie as I walk down the sidewalk toward my car. Maybe I'm sleepwalking, and this is all just a dream.

When my phone vibrates, I stop and pull it free.

"Yeah?"

"*Bro.* Why didn't you tell anyone at the office you were getting married?" Jacob asks. "You know we would've all come to your wedding."

Fuck. My coworker must have seen the pictures, too. Has everyone?

"It was kind of a spur-of-the-moment thing," I say a little numbly.

"Well, congratulations. Pretty sure Carly is already planning a party, so get ready. Will I see you at work on Monday, or are you going on your honeymoon?"

"Um, I'll be at work," I mutter, rubbing my face.

"All right. See ya, man."

Jacob hangs up, and I look down at my phone. A text comes through from my brother, his simple message more ominous than the words warrant.

Vaughn: Mom and Dad aren't happy.

Shit. Motherfucking—

"Excuse me," someone says, walking around me on the sidewalk. I mutter an apology and head toward the parking garage.

Once inside my car, I slump forward, my head hitting the steering wheel with a thunk. I let myself wallow for a good long minute before dialing the one person who never fails to have my back.

"Kipp?"

"I fucked up, Nik."

Niko says something quietly, probably to Dixon, before addressing me. "I was about to call. I'm guessing this has to do with those pictures you posted?"

"Yeah," I say, throat clicking when I swallow.

"Did you two really get married?"

There's no judgment in my friend's tone, and that simple fact has my eyes pricking.

"Think so," I whisper.

He hums, a thoughtful sound. "Have you been fucking?"

Again, zero judgment.

"No," I say around a pained huff. "We barely talked before yesterday."

Sure, I've seen Teddy at Elite 8 events or at the club, Sublime, where the cast and crew hang out on Friday nights. Not the same club we were in yesterday for Cas and Jason's party. But we've crossed paths numerous times before. Yet we've never had so much as a full conversation prior to last night.

I don't know what changed.

"What are you going to do?" Niko asks.

"I don't know. Get an annulment, probably." I rub at the ache in my chest. "Tell me it's going to be okay, bro-friend."

Niko huffs a small laugh. "It will be. Teddy's a good guy. He'll help you get out of this."

"Yeah," I mumble. That should be a good thing, right? "Um... I might be out an apartment, too."

"What?" Niko asks, more alarmed this time.

I explain what happened with Brodie, to Niko's apparent frustration.

"Kipp," he groans. "Why didn't you speak up?"

I flounder. I might, possibly, *maybe*, have a little bit of a chronic people-pleaser problem. My response is a murmured, "I didn't know what to say."

Niko sighs, but it's not an unkind sound. "Come stay here."

"No," I say immediately. "I'm not going to crash with you and Dixon. I already have a plan."

"You do?" he asks.

"Yeah, I do. I'll be *fine*." Hopefully.

"Okay, but come here if your plans fall through," Niko says. "You're always welcome."

"Thanks, Nik," I say quietly.

"Always. Call me later?"

I agree, and, after hanging up, I blow out a long, *long* breath. Then I start my car.

Thirty minutes later, I'm walking back through the lobby of Teddy's apartment building, my hands overfull. The doorman lets me through, presumably having remembered me from this morning. Or *earlier* this morning. Juggling the items in my possession, I head up to the third floor and find the door I walked through only a few hours ago. Duffle heavy on my back, heart weighted with something I don't quite have a name for, I knock.

Teddy opens the door, his eyebrows nearly hitting his hairline. "Kipp?"

"*Heyyy.*"

"What are you doing here?" he asks, expression shifting to concern as his gaze rakes over me. "And...why do you have so many muffins?"

I let the baskets in my hands fall to my sides. "I have a *teeny* tiny favor to ask."

Chapter 3
TEDDY

Kipp looks at me with wide, blue eyes, and I can't do a thing other than usher him inside.

"Give me just a second," I tell him, shutting the door and walking a few paces away. I bring my phone back to my ear. "Maman?"

"Yes, mon chéri."

"I have to go. Give my love to Papa, all right?"

"Of course. Bisous."

"Kisses," I repeat.

When I hang up, I realize Kipp is still standing inside the door, holding on to everything he arrived with. Mainly, a bunch of muffins, although the large duffle bag slung over his shoulder doesn't go unnoticed. I focus on that instead of the relief I feel at having him back so soon.

"Here, let me get those," I say, grabbing the baskets.

"Thanks," he says appreciatively. "That was your mom?"

"My grandma, actually. But I call her Maman," I explain.

"Is that French?"

"It is." I bring the muffins into the kitchen, and Kipp follows. "My birth mom was from Saudi Arabia, but my dad was French

Canadian. I grew up in Canada speaking both French and English."

From Kipp's expression, I can tell he caught the *was* portion of that explanation in regards to my parents. He doesn't ask, though. "I didn't know that," he says, taking a seat on a chair in front of the island. His bag falls lightly to the floor with a *thump*.

"Frankly, there's a lot you don't know about me," I say, which is true. But I regret the words immediately when Kipp's face pinches. It wasn't meant to be a criticism. "What's going on, Kipp? You mentioned a favor?"

Barely a beat passes before he starts speaking, his words tripping over themselves. "I lost my apartment, my parents found out we're married, my coworkers know, and I don't know what the hell I'm doing, Teddy. I'm going to disappoint everyone. How the fuck do I get myself into these situations?"

"Hey," I say gently, rounding the counter to reach him. I thread my fingers through his hair, tugging his gaze up to mine. "Breathe."

He does, expelling a big breath, eyes wide and looking so lost that I feel it like a physical thing. A *tug* inside my chest, urging me to do something. To make it better.

"Good," I say slowly, that hook digging deeper when Kipp's eyes lose some of their tension. "Another."

He blows out another breath in time with mine.

"Okay," I say, massaging his scalp for a moment before I force myself to let go. "One thing at a time. You lost your apartment?"

He nods as I take a seat beside him. "I was living with this guy, Brodie, to save on the cost of rent, you know? But he saw our wedding pictures and was so excited because he assumed

I'd be moving out, and he wants his boyfriend to move in. And I couldn't say no."

Couldn't or wouldn't?

"Where does that leave you?" I ask, already knowing the answer.

Kipp offers a weak grin.

"You'll stay here," I confirm. "What's next?"

"Really?" he asks, perking up, but then he rushes on. "Okay, my family. That's...complicated."

"How so?"

"Do you want a muffin?" he asks, stretching across the counter to snag one of the baskets. His t-shirt rides up with the movement, and memories from last night assault my brain. The feel of that skin under my fingertips. The way Kipp couldn't stop *rubbing* himself on me like a cat in heat. There's something else, too, but it flits away too quickly for me to grab hold of. "Blueberry or chocolate chip?"

"I don't need a muffin, Kipp."

"Here," he plows on, handing over a blueberry muffin and righting his shirt as he sits back down. "I tried one on the way here. They're good."

I raise a brow, doing my best not to be charmed by this man. *And failing spectacularly.* "You're avoiding the subject."

He huffs in a way that has my blood running hot. *Christ*, if he were truly mine...

"They don't approve of my lifestyle," Kipp answers, dousing me in cold water.

"Being queer?"

"Gay, in my case. But yes," he says. "They're very...traditional."

"So what did they say about you marrying a man?" I ask, not taking Kipp's bait as he nudges the muffin closer to me. "Kipp," I warn.

"I don't *know*," he huffs out, dragging a hand through his hair. It musses the dark brown strands, which usually sit so neatly styled atop his head. Right now, they're falling every which way. "I haven't talked to them yet. I don't know what I'm supposed to tell them."

"What do you *want* to tell them?"

"Nothing?" he says, like a question. "They're staunch believers in marriage—the heteronormative kind—so they're going to be disappointed in me no matter what. I haven't actually spoken to them in over a year, and now, not only do I have to tell them that yes, I married a man, but I also have to admit I'm getting a divorce? It's not going to go over well."

Kipp ignores my frown.

"And my coworkers," he says with a groan, leaning onto his elbows and dropping his head into his hands. "They saw my posts, too. I'm fucked."

"Look at me."

He does, slowly, his head turning in his palms. For the briefest of moments, I'm hit the same way I was the first time I laid eyes on Kipp. Like a shockwave is going off right in the very heart of me.

Kipp isn't a delicate guy. He's nearly six feet tall, has a leanly muscled build, and his face could be on the cover of a magazine devoted to elegant masculinity. The five-o'clock shadow. The piercing blue eyes. The straight eyebrows and full, dark lips set in contrast to pale skin. He's not delicate, no.

But he is damn beautiful.

"It's going to be okay," I tell him, hoping he hears the truth in my words. "We don't have to make any decisions right away. Stay here, and we'll figure out the rest."

"And what—you'll just stay married to me in the meantime so I can save face?" he says incredulously.

I shrug. "Sure."

His mouth falls open. "Wait, seriously? Why would you do that?"

"I'm not in a relationship," I point out. "And I'm not planning on *being* in a relationship anytime soon. So why not? We could always amicably split down the road once this whole thing blows over, no harm done."

He blinks several times, gears turning. "So, I'd call you my husband?"

My pulse kicks. "Sure."

"And we'd live together?"

"For now," I say, trying to ignore that *tug* in my chest.

"And what would you get out of this?" he asks, pushing up from his slouched position.

"I don't need anything out of it, Kipp," I tell him, which is really only a half-truth. I would get something. The chance to take care of *him*.

I don't tell him that, though. Barely want to acknowledge it myself. It's been a long damn time since I've had someone to care for. And it didn't end well for me last time.

"Okay, fine," Kipp says, blowing out a breath. "But if this creates any issues for you, you have to tell me. I don't want to be a bother."

"You couldn't be," I assure him.

"Fuck," he says, hands scrubbing through his hair. "This is ridiculous. I can't believe we got married." His laugh is a little strained. "Oh, fuck. I'm *married*."

"Breathe," I remind him, sliding to the edge of my seat and bracketing his face in my hands again.

He nods, breaths coming out in choppy increments. "I think... you're the best husband... I could have asked for."

It takes everything in me to hold back the sounds that want to climb out of my throat. The whimper. The *growl*. "You barely know me, Kipp."

"Yeah, but Niko trusts you. Which means I trust you. Actually..." He shakes his head. "That's not even the full truth. I just trust you, too. I always have."

I let my hands fall away, standing up before I do something I can't take back. "Come on. Let's get you settled. Is the one bag all you have?"

Kipp grabs his duffle off the ground. "For now, yeah. I told Brodie I'd be back for the rest."

"All right," I say, waving him forward. "We'll make space for whatever you have."

"Thanks, Teddy," he says, his words sounding like a sigh.

"Don't mention it."

When we reach the hall, Kipp walks ahead of me, strolling right past the bedroom and bathroom and going for the final, closed door. I watch in amusement as he throws it open, stopping just inside my office and looking around in confusion.

"Um," he says, stepping back into the hall. "Where's my bedroom?"

I snort, grabbing him by the shoulders and leading him to my room. He stutters a step at the entrance.

"Oh," he says, swallowing hard as his eyes meet mine over his shoulder. "So there's only one bed."

I bite my tongue hard before answering. "Yep."

He purses his lips and nods. "So, uh... I don't suppose you sleep naked?"

My lips twitch at his hopeful tone. "Guess you'll find out."

"Teddy," he groans.

I keep my laughter to myself and give him a small nudge into the room. "Dresser's there. Closet's there. Unpack wherever you want."

He makes a small sound of acknowledgement, and I leave him to it, heading back to the kitchen to store the muffins. I don't realize Kipp has followed me until I hear his voice close by.

"Teddy?" He's standing at the entrance to the living area, hands on either side of the narrow hallway. "Why haven't we fucked? I'm asking sober."

My stomach tumbles over, and I ease out a breath. "You never asked before."

His brow furrows. "And if I'm asking now?"

I grab a storage container to buy myself a few seconds. "We're not having sex, Kipp."

"Why not?" he says, just short of a whine.

"Because we're married."

His mouth opens and closes once. Twice. "I fail to see the problem."

My lips twist, but I shake my head quickly. "We can't get an annulment if we have sex," I point out.

"We could get divorced."

When a bark of laughter leaves my mouth, Kipp grins, his blue eyes bright.

"You want us to fuck so we can get a divorce?" I check.

"I mean, shit, when you say it like that..."

"Kipp, we're not fucking," I say, trying to keep my voice firm. *And my resolve.* "It's a bad idea."

"Says who?"

"Me."

"What about a *little* fucking?" he asks, holding his thumb and forefinger an inch apart. "Just the tip?"

I snort before clearing my expression and glaring as best as I can, which isn't very good at all. Kipp continues to grin at me. "Kipling, go put your things away."

His mouth falls open. "How the hell do you know my real name?"

"I know a lot about you. Now go."

"*Dude,*" he complains, spinning around.

"I'm not your dude," I call.

"My husband is mean," he shouts from the bedroom.

I laugh before clearing my throat. *Don't get attached,* I remind myself firmly.

Less than a minute later, there's a yelp of happy surprise. Kipp reappears at the end of the hall, eyes wide.

"Holy shit," he says. "What is *this?*"

He waves the massive dildo my way, as if I couldn't see it.

"You went through my nightstand?" I ask, amused despite myself.

He waves me off. "I'm your husband. I'm allowed. Do you *use* this?"

"What do you think?"

He presses a button on the base of the dildo, jolting when it starts to move. "Teddy," he says in awe, flicking the part at the bottom that stimulates the perineum. "Can you give me a demonstration?"

I raise a brow. "Sure," I say evenly. "Drop your pants and bend over."

He blinks at me. "What?"

My grin is all wolf. "I never said I use it on *myself.*"

He visibly gulps, looking down at the dildo, contemplating, if I had to guess, whether or not he actually wants said demonstration. It's a huge toy. Not at all for the faint of heart.

"Do you...have something smaller?" he finally asks, carefully turning the dildo off like it might bite him. "You know, something a little less likely to eviscerate me?"

My lips twitch. "Put it back in the drawer, Kipp."

"Teddy, *nooo*," he whines, coming to the edge of the kitchen and holding the dildo between his flattened palms. The tip hits his chin. "Please. Fuck me with the Dildo of Death. I beg of you."

"Not happening."

"I can take it." He eyes it again dubiously. "I think."

I point down the hall. "Drawer."

Kipp curses, wheeling around and heading toward the bedroom. "Worst husband ever!"

"Love you," I yell after him.

His laugh has me grinning from ear to ear.

Shit. I'm in so much trouble.

Chapter 4
Kipp

Teddy cooks us dinner. Like, a whole meal. There's chicken breasts, sauteed vegetables in some sort of brown sauce, and rice.

"I take it back," I moan. "Best husband ever."

Teddy snorts, something he's been doing a lot of, like he's trying hard not to laugh outright. But he's smiling again, and that makes me feel a lot better, despite the whole *invading his house and his life* thing.

We're eating at the island countertop, which also serves as his table. He could probably fit a dining table in the space next to us, but instead, he has some gym equipment set up there. Between us and the hallway that leads back to the bedrooms is the living room. Even with the gym equipment in plain sight, his apartment looks nothing like a bachelor pad. It's thoughtfully decorated, with black-and-white canvases along the walls and a rather comfortable-looking sectional opposite the large TV.

"How old are you?" I ask.

Teddy's eyebrows lift. "Thirty-six. Why?"

"Just wondering," I say, waving my fork. "You seem so...put together."

He huffs a laugh. "Thanks."

My phone takes that moment to vibrate from inside my pocket, but I ignore it. "Where's that?" I ask, pointing at the canvas closest to us. It looks like a small town, the houses crammed together, flowers hanging out windows and trees squeezed into the empty spaces along the sides of the cobbled street.

"Quebec," he answers. "I grew up there."

"Is that where your grandparents still live?" I ask, piecing two and two together.

He nods, drinking some water before speaking. "Did you grow up here?"

"In Vegas? No. Born Midwesterner. My family lives in Indiana."

He hums, and my foot taps against the bottom rung of my chair.

"Is this weird?" I blurt, setting down my fork. "It's weird, right? Like, we barely know each other, and suddenly, we're sitting down to dinner, talking about our pasts, and playing house as if we're married."

We are. We are married.

"It's not weird," Teddy says calmly. "It's nothing different than what people do on a date."

"Yeah, but we're not dating," I say slowly. "Are we?"

"No," he says, shaking his head. "We're not."

"Okay, so..."

"Stop overthinking, Kipp."

I huff. "Do you even know me? Overthinking is what I do."

Teddy eyes me then, something unnervingly focused in his gaze. Sometimes, I swear the man is two people. There's genial, teddy bear Teddy, whose mouth is always turned in a smile and who speaks soothingly, like he has a degree in setting people at ease. And then there's the hawk-like Teddy, who goes still and silent, a predator hunting prey.

I probably shouldn't enjoy being the potential mouse in this scenario, and yet I can't help but wonder what would happen if I run.

"Try not to worry over this," he says, sharp expression clearing. "Do you need help getting the rest of your things?"

"Nah, it's not much," I tell him. "All the furniture and stuff came with the apartment."

He nods. "Done with dinner?"

"Yeah, all set," I say, my plate practically licked clean. "Thanks again for cooking."

He squeezes the back of my neck as he stands, and I have to work *real* damn hard on not making a sound. His hand is so *big*.

Teddy picks up my plate and loads our dishes into the washer. Reluctantly, I pull my phone from my pocket. There are a barrage of comments on my Instagram posts, congratulating me and Teddy. I don't know why I haven't taken the pictures down. I *should*, but... They're so nice. So normal, almost, despite the circumstances that led to our drunk wedding and the fact that the whole thing is a sham. But we look happy, and even if it is fake, I can't quite make myself get rid of the lie.

"I'm going to take a shower," Teddy says, rousing me from my phone. "Feel free to look around or watch TV. There are a few streaming services to choose from."

"Thanks," I mutter, my mind stuck on the *shower* part of what he said. I don't think I truly considered what living in close proximity to this man would mean. "Can I watch *you*?"

Teddy laughs as he disappears down the hall, and I groan to myself.

"It was a serious question," I mumble.

I do busy myself with TV, but my thoughts won't stop running wild. Again and again, I go over the implications of staying married. *For now*. Surely Teddy will tell his coworkers it's not real, so no problem there. I'll be lying to my family, but it's either disappoint them now or disappoint them later. I'd rather deal with it later. And when it comes to my coworkers, what's the harm? People get married for all sorts of different reasons, and love doesn't always factor in. It's not like I have to pretend to love Teddy. I'm just pretending to be his husband. I *am* his husband, so it's not even a lie. Right?

When Teddy plops down next to me and a waft of spicy vanilla *something* hits my nose, I groan. "What *is* that?"

He looks at me curiously.

"The..." I wave my hand his way, trying to ignore his wet hair and the small damp spot between his pecs on his low-cut tank top. "*Jesus*. The, uh, that smell. What is it?"

His lips hike up on one side as he sets his heel on the coffee table, affording me a rather nice view of his crotch. "Tom Ford."

"Uh-huh," I mutter. "And, uh, how'd you get into porn?"

Teddy huffs a laugh. "I needed to get away from a job and a partner, and it seemed like the perfect fit."

His words are said with a casual air, but there *has* to be a story there. "Well, you're good at it."

He gives me a smile. Not quite a smirk, but close. He knows he looks hot while fucking. He looks hot all the time, frankly, but *especially* then. When his light brown skin is dappled in sweat, the muscles in his thighs and ass flexing. When his hands are spread over hips or ass cheeks, his eyes focused and smoky dark. When his cock—

Nope. Shut it down.

I adjust myself as discreetly as possible.

"What time do you usually go to bed?" Teddy asks.

I swallow down my moan. "Eleven or so?"

"Same. That'll work well."

"Uh-huh," I say weakly. "So good."

By the time bedtime arrives, I'm contemplating jumping out a window.

"Maybe I should just take the couch," I say as Teddy brushes his teeth in the en suite.

"If you want," he responds. "The bed is more comfortable, though."

"Sure, sure. Um, what if we have the same side, though?"

He sticks his head out the door. "I don't have a side."

"What?" I ask in shock. "That's not a thing."

"It is for me," he says, spitting into the sink. My mind immediately jumps to him spitting *other* things, and—*No.* Bad Kipp.

Refocusing, I ask, "You just, what, sleep wherever the hell you want?"

"Why is that so odd?" he replies, coming out of the bathroom. He strips his tank top over his head without a care in the world, utterly confident in his body. It's sexy as hell. *He's* sexy as hell. "Kipp?"

"Uh, yeah," I manage. "It's just...*everyone* has a side."

"Not me. Any other reasons?" he asks.

"Reasons for what?"

"You to avoid sleeping in my bed. You didn't have a problem with it last night."

"Right," I say slowly, hoping my blush doesn't show. This whole *sleep with but don't fuck your husband* thing is throwing me. I'm not used to spending nights platonically in someone else's bed. "It's fine. I like the left side."

"Left side in or left side looking from the footboard?"

I huff a laugh. "Left side in."

He waves me on, as if to say *have at it.*

"I'm just gonna piss," I say, heading for the bathroom. I do pee. And then I brush my teeth. And then I wash my face. And *then* I contemplate at what point Teddy will think I'm in here taking a shit. Before I reach that point, I head back into the bedroom.

The lights are set low, the overheads off with only a soft glow emanating from beneath the top of the headboard. It's nice. I've never seen a headboard like that. I get undressed without a word, opting to wear only my briefs like I normally do to bed. I'm not sure what Teddy's wearing under the sheet.

It feels odd, slipping in beside him. Despite knowing Teddy for well over a year, closer to two, I don't *know* him, not really. These past twenty-four hours have been like a small crash course into Teddy 101. But we're still only acquaintances at best. Maybe, given a little time, we could be friends. And then eventually, we'll get divorced. So, a pretty natural progression, all things considered.

Somewhere in the recesses of my mind is a manic laugh.

"You're overthinking again," Teddy says, eyes dark yet warm in the limited light.

"Yeah," I admit.

Teddy reaches forward, fingers sifting through the hair at the side of my head. My eyes slip shut as he scratches there, like a tiny head massage.

"It'll be okay, Kipp," he says softly. "Whatever you think is best, we'll do. If you want to get an annulment, we can go file the paperwork on Monday."

"No," I say, not yet opening my eyes. "I'd rather wait. I just…"

"It's a lot," he says. His thumb presses near my temple, the pressure strangely relaxing.

"Yeah," I breathe out.

"Sleep," he says. "We don't have to take care of anything tonight."

I nod, and Teddy's hand slips away. I open my eyes in time to see him turning off the light, and then it's dark once more. It's not quick, but eventually, I do drift to sleep.

Hopefully, everything will make more sense in the morning.

Nothing makes sense.

I blink my blurry eyes, wondering if, *maybe*, I'm still dreaming. But the vision before me doesn't clear.

Jesus, Mary, and Joseph.

"Do you, uh…" I swallow down my spit, holding on to the wall for support. "Do you do this often?"

Teddy lifts his head, looking down the length of his body at me. His arms are stretched above him, hands holding loosely to the barbell that's now resting in its cradle at the top of the weight bench. He's wearing gym shorts that are gaping around his substantial thighs, and his furry chest is on full display.

"Yeah," Teddy answers. "I do some reps most mornings. Why?"

I won't survive this.

"No reason," I lie. *Can* one die via blue balls? "I think I might go for a run."

"Want some company?" he asks, sitting upright.

"You run?" I ask, the surprise of that overriding my current brain melt situation.

He shrugs. "Sometimes."

"Um, okay, sure. Maybe you could show me around the area?"

Teddy gives me a beaming smile that makes me feel like I did something right. "I'd be happy to."

"I'll just go change," I mumble, reversing course for the bedroom.

Ten minutes later, I'm running beside Teddy, regretting every single one of those shots I drank Friday night. This is torture. Absolute torture.

Teddy is wearing a tank top now, but it's drenched in sweat, I can see his nipples, and— "*Jesus Christ*," I cry, narrowly avoiding the mailbox I almost ran into.

"All right?" Teddy asks, his hand steadying me.

I nod, wheezing out a breath. "I'm not normally this clumsy. Or winded," I assure him.

"We can slow down," he offers.

I shake my head. "No, it's fine. Honestly. I just need to focus."

He smiles before looking forward again, and my eyes drop to his ass. *Fuuuck.*

I nearly clip a tree.

The run is the longest of my life, and when we get back to the apartment, I go straight for the bathroom in the hall as Teddy heads for his en suite. I lock the door, strip out of my clothes, and jump into the shower before the water is even hot. It doesn't matter in the least. My cock is painfully hard despite the brief semi-frigid dunk, and I take it in hand, my heart beating like a drum as I jack myself off furiously. It's over embarrassingly fast, all my pent-up sexual energy from the past couple of days needing an outlet. To be honest, I'm proud of myself for making it this long. My hand slaps the tile wall as I come, and a particular furry-chested man lingers in my mind's eye.

"Fucking hell," I groan, dropping my forehead against my arm. How long have I been living with Teddy? Fifteen hours? "My husband is going to be the death of me."

Chapter 5

TEDDY

"All right, spill," a certain tiny blonde orders as he unceremoniously plops himself onto my lap, his intent not remotely sexual, only—I'm certain—to keep me from running.

"Afternoon, Alex," I reply, reaching around him for my water. At least I'm done eating.

"Don't *afternoon* me, Teddy Bear. You're in trouble."

Alex's crossed arms and frown have me biting back a laugh. The man is a sprite, not nearly as threatening as he pretends to be.

"Am I?" I ask.

He huffs. "Don't play coy with me."

"All right. Well, this was fun, but I should get going," I say, standing up and tossing Alex over my shoulder. He yelps.

"Put me down, you big, furry—" Alex's hand comes down hard on my ass, and he goes still. "Ow, *fuck*. My *hand*. What are you smuggling in here, a boulder?" He gives my ass a softer pat, yelping again when I deposit him onto a couch. He hops up to his knees in an instant. "Theodore!"

I raise a brow, but as soon as I register the genuine concern on Alex's face, I sigh and drop into a seat next to him. "What do you want to know?"

He huffs, but the sound has lost its ire. "You and Kipp. What the fuck, Teddy?"

"We were drunk. We got married. It doesn't *mean* anything. End of story."

"But you like him," he says quietly.

I don't bother asking Alex how he knows. He's observant. He must have noticed the way I look at Kipp, even though the man himself seemed oblivious before this past weekend.

"Doesn't matter," I say. "You know I'm not looking for a relationship."

"Which is exactly why you went and got married," Alex says with all the sass of a porn star twink.

"I honestly don't know how it happened," I admit, even though there's not a single part of me that's surprised. I can't remember what led us to that chapel, no, but I was clearly too inebriated to fight the pull that's been anchored on one side to Kipp ever since I met the man. "Regardless, we'll file for an annulment at some point, and then Kipp will move out. Simple as that."

Alex cocks his head. "Move *out?*"

The arrival of Dixon in the break room saves me from Alex's questioning.

Dixon stops, crossing his arms. "You and Kipp."

I hold back my groan. "Apparently."

"Niko is concerned," Dixon says, arching an eyebrow.

I understand why Kipp's best friend would be worried about him, but surely he and Dixon know I didn't go out of my way to impulsively marry the man? I mean, for fuck's sake, I've been doing everything in my power to be *good* around him.

But I'm only human. Slip-ups happen.

Even ones as big as this.

"There's nothing to be concerned about," I assure Dixon, knowing my message will be relayed if he sees Niko before I do. "We're handling it."

Dixon grunts, heading over to the fridge to grab a drink. Our break room at Elite 8 Studios is always stocked, both with beverages and snacks for the performers and crew. Porn is hungry work.

"Grumpy Bear," Alex muses, eyeing Dixon in a way that has my guard going up. "When you first met Niko, didn't you adamantly deny your attraction to him?"

Oh, here we go.

"Pretty sure you know the full story, you meddlesome pixie," Dixon answers.

We all do. Dixon and Niko fucked on set long before they started dating. In Dixon's case, it was annoyance-at-first-sight when it came to our Greek costar.

Alex, undeterred, says, "Yeah, but you were *so* determined to hate him, remember? Until you realized how nice it is to have someone there for you. Someone who has your best interest at heart."

Dixon pops his drink open, raising a brow.

"And *now*," Alex goes on, "you're in love and all happy, and everything's just great, right?"

"Sure?" Dixon says slowly.

Alex's grin turns my way.

"I see what you're doing," I inform him. "It's not going to work."

Alex pouts so dramatically, it's a miracle I don't laugh. "*Teddy*. But you *like* him. I know you do."

I shrug, getting up.

"Why are you fighting this?" he asks softly. "What happened?"

I gather my trash from the table, dumping it on my way to the door. "I found out hearts can be broken."

Alex doesn't say anything to that as I leave the room, but I can feel his frown following me out the door. I shake it off as I stroll down the hallways of Elite 8 Studios. Lights are on outside Studio 2 and 3, indicating filming is underway. A few crewmen pass, Raylin waves from inside her small cosmetology den of horrors, and Nathaniel, the assistant producer, gives a nod as he talks on the phone. I swear the man owns more argyle sweaters than any one person should. But hey, I'm not one to judge.

Since I'm done filming for the day, I head out the door with the intent of going home. I'm halfway to my car when my phone rings. I don't recognize the number, but it's local.

"Hello?" I answer.

"Were you going to tell me?"

I stop still, letting my phone drop down to my side as I look heavenward and sigh. *This.* This is why I don't talk about it. One word to Alex, and it's like I breathed the man into existence. I bring my phone back to my ear, not bothering with niceties. "You changed your number."

"Because you blocked me."

"For a reason."

Antoni doesn't care. "He's pretty."

I heave a breath I can feel throughout my entire body. "What are you doing?"

"Catching up," my ex responds. "I'm hurt. You didn't invite me to the wedding."

"Why would I possibly do that?" I ask, unlocking my car with the key fob.

He makes a short sound. "Well, that's rude. We used to be close once upon a time. *Daddy.*"

"Don't," I grit out. "Don't you fucking dare."

He sighs, the sound quiet beside the pounding of my pulse.

"Why are you calling, Antoni?" I ask, my voice surprisingly controlled considering how I feel inside. "Truly, for what reason? Are you not happy with my brother anymore?"

"I love him very much," he answers.

"Then why are you calling *me*?"

He's quiet for a moment, and I have half a mind to hang up. I blocked Antoni's number for a reason. It's been over five years since we broke up. Over two since I last talked to either him or Cameron. Neither has a place in my life anymore.

"I miss you, Theo," he finally answers. "We could be friends, you know. All of us."

"Yeah, no, not happening. Bye, Antoni."

"Wait," he says, his tone making me pause. "You could sell your shares. Then I'll stop calling."

I huff a bitter laugh. Of course, it always comes down to money with Antoni. More money, more prestige, more power.

"I helped build that company," I reply, tone clipped. "I'm not selling."

With that, I hang up, not giving Antoni a chance to respond. I block his new number, and then I get into my car, gripping the steering wheel so tight my knuckles ache. I breathe in and out slowly, forcing my heart rate to calm.

It's *fine*. They can't hurt me anymore.

So why does it still ache so fucking badly?

I expect the apartment to be empty when I get home, but it's not. The door is cracked open, and Kipp is standing just inside, a couple of boxes on the floor in front of him.

He looks over at me with a soft smile that instantly has my tension dropping. "Hey."

"Hey," I reply, closing the door and stepping out of my shoes. "Why aren't you at work?"

Kipp brushes his hair back, the strands disheveled. "I was, but Carly insisted I take the afternoon off to finish moving, so I've been doing that. My coworkers, uh... They sent me home with a cake."

He waves his hand toward the kitchen, where what can only be described as a miniature wedding cake sits. The three-tiered structure is covered in white frosting and pink flowers, and Kipp's face blooms just about the same rosy hue.

"I told them no gifts," he says. "That would have been too much, considering—you know." He motions between us. *Considering our marriage is fake.*

"I understand," I assure him before pointing at the boxes near his feet. "Need any help with those?"

"I'm on the last one," he says. "Question. Do you wanna keep separate sex toy drawers or consolidate?"

I bark a laugh, unable not to. "You want your toys in with the Dildo of Death?"

"I mean, sure," he says with a grin. "It's not like it'll rub off on them." He pauses, considering his words. "You know what I mean."

"Put your stuff wherever you want," I tell him, shaking my head in bemusement. "I'm not picky."

Kipp's head tilts to the side. "There you go again, being decidedly laissez-faire about your space. Don't you, I don't know, like to be in charge of your possessions?"

I still, my entire body prickling with awareness before I shove the feeling away. *Far* away.

"With certain things," I admit, heading past Kipp toward the bedroom. He follows, watching as I clear a drawer in my dresser. I go to the closet next, pushing everything to one side. "Better?"

"Yeah, thanks," he says with a sheepish smile.

I nod, and Kipp walks with me back toward the kitchen.

"Do you ever do your software development from home?" I ask, pulling a few things from the fridge to make a smoothie.

He looks at me curiously. "You know about my job?"

"I do." I've heard him talk to Niko about it.

"Well, no, it's rare for me to work remotely," he says, poking through one of his boxes. "In fact, I don't do the coding side of things much anymore. I mostly deal with clients and coordinate projects amongst the staff."

"So you're in charge," I note, popping some berries into the blender.

Kipp chuckles. "I mean, no. I'm not the boss. That's Carly."

"But it sounds like you keep everyone organized. I don't think you're nearly as much of a mess as you think you are, Kipp."

He looks at me with a crinkled sort of smile. "Heh. Not sure about that."

I shrug, powering on the blender. The yogurt and fruit mixes, the sound of it temporarily blocking out conversation. Once done, I dump the contents into two glasses, setting a reusable straw in one. I offer it to Kipp. "Here."

"Oh. Thanks," he says, accepting the drink. He takes a sip as I start cleaning out the blender. "Holy shit. Teddy. That's *good*."

I chuckle, although the sound he makes as he sucks down more of the smoothie has me feeling things I'd rather not think about. "Glad you like it."

"Love it," he says, tucking the cup in the crook of his arm as he brings some clothes down the hall.

I shake my head. "*Stop it*. He's not yours."

Kipp saunters back into the room, straw in his mouth. His cheeks hollow as he drinks.

Not. Yours.

"Should we cut the cake?" he asks.

I still. "What?"

Kipp motions to the white mini-monstrosity on the counter. "Our cake."

I clear my throat and grab a knife, handing it over. "Have at it."

"*No*. Teddy, you have to do it with me," he pleads, apparently not caring that he's systemically chipping away at every single wall I've so carefully erected. Hell, I'm pretty sure he knocked his way clean through the other night.

"Do I, though?" I ask weakly.

"Yes," he says, tone firm. "I mean, *shit*, this might be the only time I ever get married. I want to do it right, you know?"

This man... He's dangerous.

Blowing out a breath, I concede with a nod. "Fine. Let's cut the cake."

Kipp grins.

When I step up beside him, I curl my hand over his own on the handle of the knife. I dutifully ignore the rapid thudding of my heart.

"Okay, so how do we do this?" Kipp asks. "Do we cut through all layers at once or only the top?"

"I vote top."

He nods, and with more care than the occasion warrants, we cut a line through the center of the top tier of cake. Then we make a second cut, creating a small wedge. I let go, and Kipp uses the knife to pry the piece free. He plucks off a crumbling corner with his fingers and turns to me.

"Here. Open up," he says before his eyes light. "Hey, it's like Friday night!"

I huff a breath, shaking my head. Against my better judgment, I open my mouth.

Kipp's fingers drag lightly across my bottom lip as he sets the bite of cake on my tongue. His gaze is focused, serious, even, as he watches me chew. Then, with a glimmer of mischievousness, he rubs the rest of the piece down my nose and chin.

We both freeze at the exact same time, and Kipp blinks at me, his face drawn in shock. "I, uh," he stammers. And then he takes off, running out of the room before I can stop him.

"Kipp!"

"I'm sorry!" he yells from down the hall. "Shit, I didn't mean to."

I wipe the cake off my face, huffing a laugh. "Kipling! Get your ass back here."

"Or what?" he calls back, sounding very far away. "You'll spank me?"

Oh, if only he knew...

"I'm not ready to die, Teddy!" he shouts. "I haven't even been divorced yet."

My laughter falls from me like dominoes, one leading to another and another, until I'm all but toppled. Despite being supposedly terrified, I can hear Kipp laughing from down the hall, too.

Fucking hell.

No good can come from having feelings for my husband.

Chapter 6
Kipp

"Kipp."

"Huh?" I mumble, still half-asleep.

"*Kipp*. You're humping my leg again."

I go still, and Teddy lets out a quiet chuckle.

"Sorry," I groan, detaching from my much-too-tempting bedmate and rolling onto my back. The room is still dark, the tiniest bit of light filtering in through the window from the nearby streetlights. This isn't the first time this week I've tried helping myself to some midnight Teddy. It's becoming a problem. "Maybe I'll find someone to hook up with tonight," I muse aloud. "Take the edge off."

Teddy is quiet. I can't even hear him breathing.

"Is that...okay?" I feel the need to ask.

"Of course," he says quickly.

"I wouldn't bring them back here," I assure him, in case that's what he's thinking.

I see him nod in my periphery, but he stays silent.

"Right, then, I'll just..." Reaching over, I check the time on my phone. It's five in the morning. "I'm gonna get up. Sorry for waking you early."

"It's fine," Teddy says softly.

I slip out of bed and change into running shorts. Then I head out the door.

I follow the same path Teddy and I ran earlier this week, my breaths puffing out in even intervals as my leg muscles churn. I try to outpace my thoughts, but it doesn't work. They stay with me, the same way the guilt of avoiding my family does. I have yet to call them back, although most of the missed calls and texts have come from Vaughn, not my parents. My brother always did enjoy needling me given the chance. I guess that hasn't changed in the time we've been apart.

I know I need to buck up already and give them a call, but I'm afraid of what they're going to say. I'm used to the passive-aggressive—sometimes plain aggressive—barbs from my family when it comes to me and my sexuality, but what if they want to talk to Teddy? What if they want to yell at him, too? He doesn't deserve to go through that.

So why the hell don't you get the annulment already?

I don't have an answer for my conscience.

When I get back to the apartment, body sweatier but mind no less quiet, Teddy is up. I pause in the doorway of the bedroom for a moment, simply watching him. He's a big guy, not only muscled and thick, but tall, too. And yet there's something graceful about the way he moves, each shift of his body calm just like his temperament. I have no doubt Teddy could toss me around if he wanted—and *whoa*, isn't that a thought—but there's an energy about the guy that screams *safety*. He's measured. Careful.

I wasn't lying when I said I trust him.

Teddy stills when he sees me in the doorway, a small smile flitting to his face.

"Hey," I say, clearing my throat. "Couldn't get back to sleep?"

"No, but it's fine," he says, pulling a shirt out of his dresser and tugging it on.

Still, I feel bad for disrupting his schedule. "Regretting this yet?"

The look he gives me is both soft and stern. "Not one bit, Kipp. So get that idea out of your head."

"Okay," I breathe out, relieved. The idea of disappointing Teddy doesn't sit well with me. "I'm gonna hop in the shower."

Teddy's eyes slip down my body at that, and I don't miss the appreciation in his gaze or the way he lingers, specifically, at my crotch.

Well, well...

"You like these shorts?" I ask, grinning as I step into the room.

The look he gives me feels a lot like a warning. So, of course, I spin so Teddy can see the backside.

"Kipp," he says, a growl.

Slowly, I pull the band down below my ass. "Oops."

Teddy is behind me in a flash, the backs of his fingers skimming my skin as he tugs the band back up. He leans into my space as my heart thunders, his lips close to my ear. "You do that again, and I'm reddening your ass."

My cock jumps as Teddy backs away. "Promise?" I ask a little shakily.

"Go take your shower, Kipp," Teddy says, disappearing into the en suite.

Fucking hell.

I guess that's what I get for poking the bear.

With a groan, I head into the bathroom. It's going to be a long damn day.

"How's married life?"

I huff a laugh, dropping into a seat across from Niko. We decided to meet for lunch today, a welcome distraction after the way my morning started. I can still feel the heat of Teddy's fingers brushing against my ass. *Ungh.*

Work is a distraction in its own right—a good one, at that—but I could use someone to talk to about all of this. And who better than my best bro-friend, Niko?

"There's a lot less fucking in this marriage than I thought there'd be," I joke. Although it's the absolute—*unfortunate*—truth.

Niko tilts his head, his expression making it clear he sees through my bullshit. He can tell I'm struggling. "Have you two filed for the annulment yet?"

"Yeah," I say slowly. "About that..."

"Spit it out, Kipp."

"We're *maybe* going to stay married? For now?" I give him a reassuring smile for good measure.

"Like a test run?" he asks, nodding.

I pause. "Wait, what?"

Niko pops his straw out of the wrapper, putting it in his drink and taking a sip. "You two are giving it a go," he says. "Trying the whole *together* thing. Most people date before getting married, but hey, you do you."

I sputter. "We're not...*together.*"

His eyes pinch. "No?"

"Uh, no."

"Huh," he says, shrugging.

"What's that supposed to mean?" I all but whine.

Niko huffs a laugh. "I don't know. I just thought... Well, I could have sworn he liked you. And I know you like him." He shrugs again, digging into his sandwich.

My mouth opens and closes, my own lunch sitting untouched in front of me. "He doesn't *like* me," I finally reply. He might be attracted to me, sure. The way I've caught him staring at me these past few days is proof enough. But that doesn't mean he *likes* me.

"If you say so," Niko says.

"*Nik*," I groan. "He won't even *fuck* me."

His eyebrows pop up at that, a muffled laugh leaving his lips as the woman at the table next to us whips her head our way. *Whoops*.

Lowering my voice, I say, "He won't. And I've asked. Which, you know, *fine*. Whatever. It's not like my feelings are hurt."

Not *much*, at least. The man works in porn, but he still has standards for who he sleeps with. And he should. He's a total catch. Any guy would be lucky to have him.

I guess that guy just isn't me.

"Kipp," Niko says, touching my arm to get my attention. "I think there's more there."

"What do you mean?" I ask, perking up a little.

He takes another sip of his drink before answering me. "He hasn't talked about it, but I get the sense there's a reason he doesn't date."

"I didn't ask to date him," I point out, finally unwrapping my sandwich. At a mumble, I add, "I just want him to dick me so hard into his mattress that there's a permanent divot left behind."

Niko chuckles. "Well, what'd he say? When you asked for the dicking?"

"Something about it being too messy for us to have sex since we're married and all that, *blah, blah, blah*," I say, waving my hand.

"Sure," Niko says slowly. "I mean, I get that. But damn, does that explanation seem flawed."

My laugh is slightly pained. "Right?"

"Let me ask you this," he says, leaning forward. "*Do* you like him? Like, *date him* like him, not just *sex him up* like him? I mean, there has to be a reason the two of you got married, drunk or not."

"It doesn't matter, Nik," I say, my chest pulling tight. "He's made it clear his answer is no to anything I have to offer, and I have to respect that. I will."

"Fair enough," he says, although I can tell he doesn't quite believe me. "So if you're not *together*, then why are you staying married?"

I bite into my sandwich, chewing for a *very* long time. I'm not avoiding. I'm just *hungry*. "How's Mal doing?" I ask.

Niko shakes his head, but there's a smile on his face. "Mal is great. He and Henrik adopted another cat."

Mal was a performer at Elite 8 Studios not that long ago, nicknamed Malibu on set. He ended up falling for an escort client who happens to be blind. Last I heard, they were living together and happy.

Good for them.

"And your sisters?" I ask.

"You're very bad at this," Niko says, crumpling up his trash. "They're fine, which you would know if you returned any of their texts. I haven't heard the end of it this past week. I can't stall them forever, you know."

"Yeah, sorry," I mutter. Niko's sisters are like sisters to me, too, the same as Niko is my brother, in a way. I *have* been avoiding their messages, along with everyone else's. I don't know what to tell people. "I've been…"

"Hiding," Niko fills in. "Like you're doing now."

I let out a breath. "My family," I say, answering Niko's original question about *why* Teddy and I are staying married. "My parents found out."

Niko's expression turns dark, a far cry from my usually laid-back friend. "You're allowed to cut ties with them, Kipp."

"Am I, though?"

"Yes," he answers immediately. "All they do is tear you down. That's not what family is supposed to be."

"I know," I say, reaching across the table and squeezing his arm. "Because you've shown me what it means to be family. But they're still my blood."

He shakes his head, but he doesn't push it. We've had this conversation many times before.

I let his arm go with a sigh. "Anyways, you know how weird they are about the sanctity of marriage. They don't believe in divorce—*or* being gay—so I thought it'd be better if they were only mad at me for one of the two, you know? But they're still going to be upset, and they'll probably yell at me, and—*fuck*." I scrub a hand through my hair. "Why am I dragging Teddy into this?"

"Tell them it's none of their business," Niko says, as if it's that simple.

"I don't know how to do that."

"Kipp, I say this with love." *Uh-oh*. "You have the sweetest heart of anyone I know. But you need to grow some thorns."

"I'm very horny," I shoot back.

Niko looks as if he wants to bang his head on the table, or bang *my* head on the table, but then he laughs. "Fuck, I love you."

"Love you, too, bro-friend," I reply, making a heart with my hands. "You're my number one."

"Yeah, yeah," Niko says, grinning. "Just do me a favor, will you?"

"The last time a favor was mentioned, I moved in with my husband."

"Your life, Kipp," he says, shaking his head.

"I *know*. I'm a natural disaster."

"More like a national treasure," Niko says.

"D'aww."

"Just... Don't beat yourself up over this, all right? It's not your fault."

"It's not my fault that I got your coworker wasted, asked him to marry me, moved myself into his apartment, told him I didn't want a divorce, and then proceeded to hump him most every night because the man is built like a tree?"

He doesn't seem to know what to do with that. "Are you calling yourself a dog?"

My face scrunches. "That'd be pissing, not humping, wouldn't it?"

Niko waves his hand in the air. "You know what, I don't need to know."

"What? No, I'm not saying I *want* to mark the man with my urine," I say indignantly, cringing when the woman next to us gets quickly out of her seat and leaves.

Niko barely holds in his laugh. "What I'm *getting* at," he says forcefully enough to get us back on track, "is that these things happen. If Teddy is on board with this whole continued marriage thing, then stop taking all the blame onto yourself. Maybe, when all is said and done, the two of you will end up being good friends."

"*Wesleepinthesamebed*," I mumble.

"Come again?"

"We sleep in the same bed, Nik. Is that friendly?"

He laughs, hand over his face as he shakes his head. "You're so screwed, bud."

Maybe so, but if Teddy isn't willing to be the one doing the screwing, then I'll just have to find someone who is.

Chapter 7

TEDDY

I'm not doing a very good job of keeping myself distracted. Kipp has been gone all evening, and I *know* what he's trying to accomplish. After getting home from work, he got dressed in a pair of pants that should be illegal considering what they showed off, added a tight white shirt that displayed his gorgeous body far too well, and then sauntered out the door with a cheeky, "See ya later, honey."

I nearly cracked a molar.

It's my own damn fault. I know that. Doesn't mean I have to *like* what my husband is out doing.

Damn it, this whole situation is messed up.

I'm just about to admit defeat and force myself into bed when Kipp bursts through the front door in a cloud of chaotic energy and frustration. My pulse skips as he shoves the door shut and comes to a stop, holding up his hand.

"I was wearing my ring," he huffs.

"What?" I ask, twisting from my spot on the couch to see him better.

He waves his hand, gold band flashing. "My *ring*, Teddy." The man storms over, falling onto the couch and rolling to his back, his head near my hip, shoes still on his feet. "I tried to pull at the club, but the guy saw my ring and freaked. I told him you gave me permission, but he said *hell no* and that he didn't want any part in my weird cuckolding marriage. What the fuck?"

I press my lips together, fighting a laugh despite this predicament being less than amusing. I can't say I'm disappointed Kipp struck out, but I do feel bad, considering how downtrodden the poor guy is.

I sift my fingers through his hair.

"You want to know the *other* fucked up thing?" Kipp asks.

"Tell me."

"I can't get it off."

Now that *definitely* shouldn't make me happy.

"I tried in the bathroom at the club," he goes on. "And it's stuck. See?" He proceeds to tug at the band to no avail before his hands flop onto the couch. "I'm going to die of neglected dick because I'm in a sexless marriage and can't even *lie* about it by taking off my damn ring." A beat of silence passes before he adds, "I can honestly say I never thought that sentence would come out of my mouth."

"Did you wash your hands before you left the club?" I ask.

He tilts his head back to look at me, brows pulling together. "Yeah. I came home right after the bathroom fiasco. Why?"

I grab Kipp's hand. His mouth falls open when I suck his ring finger between my lips, getting it good and wet before I try to wiggle the band over his knuckle with my teeth. He swallows heavily, body twisting slightly so he can watch me.

I know I'm playing with fire, but I can't seem to help myself. Can't deny Kipp at least some measure of comfort, even though I'm well aware this goes beyond *comforting*. But most of all, I can't stop myself from *wanting* him.

I knew the moment I first met Kipp that he and I were kindred spirits in opposing forms. Call it intuition. Call it a hunter's instinct. Whatever the reason, I could sense the side of him that so desperately longed to *let go*. That little rabbit heart, beating fast, waiting to surrender. And *God*, how I want to be the one he'd show his belly to.

But I *can't*. Can't ask that of him. Can't demand it.

The thing that really gets me is that I don't think he knows it. As far as I can tell, Kipp has no clue he has a submissive streak a mile wide, and that fact, more than anything, makes it nearly impossible for me to resist this man who's currently looking up at me with wonder in his eyes.

The things I could show him.

It takes maybe half a minute before the ring slides over Kipp's knuckle. I pull his finger from my mouth and set the gold band gently onto the coffee table. Kipp's chest rises and falls, his pupils nearly blown as he stares up at me, waiting. Seeing what I'll do.

"There," I say softly. "You're all set."

"Um, thanks," he mutters, expression shifting to confusion. "So, uh, you really want me to get laid, huh?"

He chuckles, a nervous sound, and I internally curse, frustrated with this situation, the question I can't truthfully answer, and the fact that I want Kipp to be *mine*, no matter how much I try to convince myself otherwise.

"I just didn't want you to hurt your finger getting it off," I say, brushing his hair off his forehead. It's not exactly a lie.

Kipp's voice halts me as I stand. "Teddy."

I close my eyes for a long second before turning. Kipp sits up, looking so lost that it tugs at me again.

"What's going on here?" he asks.

My heart thumps, a near painful thing.

"You said something that night," he goes on. "Before we got married, I remember you saying you wanted to *own* me. What does that mean?"

"Kipp..."

"I always felt like you were ignoring me," he says, driving a nice little knife between my ribs. "If we ran into each other, you were perfectly nice, but it's like you went out of your way to avoid me. Until Friday night. Why?"

Because I couldn't stand watching you pick another man that wasn't me.

I scrub over my eyes.

"Do you want me?" Kipp asks quietly.

Fuck.

"Doesn't matter," I answer. "We're not having sex, Kipp."

He makes a frustrated sound. "Then why do you keep flirting with me and, like, giving me finger blowjobs? I don't get it."

I heave out a breath. "You're right. That's not fair of me to do, and I'll stop."

"No," he says quickly, blue eyes flaring wide. "I don't want you to stop. I just... I don't understand, Teddy. And I'm not trying to push you past your boundaries. I won't do that. But you keep saying 'we're not,' not 'I don't want to' when it comes to us fucking. And I don't really know how to take that."

When I don't speak, unable to come up with a suitable response, Kipp's face scrunches.

"Sometimes it seems like you want me," he says quietly, looking so vulnerable it physically hurts. "But sometimes..." He shakes his head. "If you don't, it's fine. Just say so. I'd rather know, okay? Then I can stop making a fool of myself chasing after someone who clearly has no interest—"

"That's not it," I interject, unable to let him believe for a single second I think him foolish or undesirable. My throat is tight, voice hoarse when I speak, but I can't help it. "Kipp, if I have you, I won't be able to stop."

Silence falls.

"I don't have a problem with that," he says, his voice nearly a whisper.

My hands clench at my sides. "You don't understand what you're asking of me."

"I'm not asking for commitment, Teddy. You might be my husband, but I don't need a boyfriend. I just need..."

He doesn't finish his thought, but he doesn't have to. He just needs someone to take care of him, whether or not he realizes it.

I watch Kipp look down at his lap as my head wars with my heart. He's not asking for a romantic partnership, maybe because he doesn't think he deserves one. But for me, I'm not sure I'm capable of keeping feelings out of the equation. I already care for this man. If he puts himself in my hands, will I ever be able to let go?

"If we do this," I say slowly, "it's on my terms."

His head snaps up.

"You'll come to me," I say, hardly able to believe the words coming out of my mouth. "You won't pick up guys at the club or the bar. There won't *be* other men. Not while we're together."

He nods quickly, cheeks flushed.

"And when we get a divorce, that'll be it. No more fucking around."

"Yeah, okay," he says immediately, pulse feathering visibly in his neck. "Whatever you want."

Jesus. This man. Does he even realize how perfect he is?

"Lie back," I tell him hoarsely, feeling that cage around myself crack wide open.

"What?" he asks. When I raise a brow, he moves quickly, spilling onto his back on top of the couch. His feet hang off the end, and he quickly kicks off his shoes.

I watch him for a moment, my pulse coursing hot and heavy through my veins, like liquid fire. His chest rises and falls as he waits, trying his best to be patient. His twitching fingers give him away. He's so goddamn *beautiful.* The dark hair over fair skin, the bright blue eyes, the height and breadth of him. He's solid, not small, but to me, he's precious. And I'm going to treat him as such.

"Teddy..."

"Here's how this is going to go," I say, stalking forward. Kipp's breath stutters when I climb over his legs, settling with my knees on either side of his body. I tug his obscenely tight pants open and drag them far enough down to have full, unfettered access to his dick. It bounces up proudly as soon as it's free, flushed pink like its owner's cheeks. I wrap my hand around the base of it before meeting Kipp's gaze. "You're going to lie there and be good for me. And then you can come."

"Oh, fuck," he breathes, eyes rolling up as I stroke him once. "Teddy, *fuck.*"

I stop the motion of my hand when Kipp moves with me, hiking up his hips. "What did I say?"

"What?" he asks, blue gaze pinging between me and his cock.

"What did I tell you to do?" I repeat.

He wets his lips, stilling. "Uh...lie here?"

"And?"

His tongue runs along his lips again, his words coming slower this time. "Be good for you?"

The heat in my chest boils over. "That's right," I say, giving him another slow stroke. "Can you do that?"

"Yeah, *fuck*. Anything you want."

Good answer.

He groans when I stroke him again. I increase the pressure, my hand milking his cock, but when his hips chase the motion, I stop. His head falls back, and I go again, stroking, watching his eyes shutter, tracking the pulse in his neck. He stays still until my thumb rolls over his crown, and then he's thrusting up again.

"Fuck," he says when I pull away. "*Teddy.*"

I ease up over his body, our chests not quite touching, our faces close. I turn his chin to the side, and he doesn't fight it, but his breathing picks up.

"Do you want me to continue?" I ask, lips near his ear.

"Yes," he hisses out, groaning when I snag his earlobe between my teeth.

"Yes what?"

Five seconds pass. "Yes, please?"

"So polite," I say, dragging my tongue over the pulse point at his neck before I sit back, my weight on his thighs. Kipp's gaze meets mine when I let his chin go. I grab his cock, stroking with one hand as I roll my palm over his crown. The muscles in his abdomen quiver, evidence of his battle to keep still. He manages a pretty decent job of it, too, fighting off his impulses for a good minute or two. But as soon as I tighten my grip with the intention of getting him off, he chases the pressure. I release him.

"*Fuuuck*," he says, covering his face with his hands.

"You can do this, sweetheart," I say gently, giving him a slow stroke. "Just let me take care of you."

His eyes meet mine again, uncertainty there but also a steely sort of determination. Kipp is a pleaser; it's something I've noticed in his interactions. He's charming and forthcoming, and

I'd bet my life savings that he often leads his sexual encounters as a way to make sure his partners are getting what they want. Yet now, I'm asking him to hand that power off to me. He wants to—*craves* it—I can tell. But he's scared.

He doesn't need to be.

"Let me be the one to take care of you," I repeat.

His swallow is heavy, but he lays his arms above his head, his own attempt to release control, at least physically. That's good. The mental will follow if he allows it. His hands flex a few times before he closes his eyes, letting out a breath.

My chest swells with pride.

"There you go," I say softly. "Beautiful."

His mouth opens, a sigh leaving his lips. I pick up my pace again, stroking him, spitting on his cock—once, twice—before jerking him harder. He moans, thrusting up, and I stop, waiting a beat as he settles. I start again, my fist gliding smoothly over his flesh. His breathy little moans have my heart trying to claw its way out of my throat, but I lock myself down tight, sliding my free hand under Kipp's shirt, finding his nipple and flicking it with my thumb. His back bows, hips moving. I stop.

"Fuck," he groans, a blush over his cheeks and neck. "Teddy, please."

"What's your job?" I ask.

"Lie here," he says around a panting breath, "and be good."

"That's right," I reply, easing my hand out of his shirt and running my fingers through his hair. He leans into the touch. "You don't have to think, Kipp. You don't have to *do*. Trust me to get you there."

He nods, tongue sliding over his bottom lip. "Okay."

I lean forward again, turning Kipp's face so I can bring my lips to his jaw. I feather kisses along the sensitive curve of his neck as I resume stroking him, slowly at first, and then a little faster. His breathing picks up, pulse skittering against my lips.

"Look at you," I breathe into his skin, wanting to imprint my words there. "You're gorgeous, Kipling."

He stutters out a breath, chest brushing mine before it falls. I can feel the exact moment he truly lets go. When his body melts and he gives himself over. His neck muscles relax, his head sinks against the cushions, and every line in his body goes from tensed to lax, like a marionette that's had its strings cut. It's a beautiful thing, and I mutter my praise against his skin as I jack him off in earnest.

He lets out a few quiet sounds, his body starting to tremble beneath me. There's, "*Oh, oh,*" and then, "*Teddy.*" I stroke him quickly, and when Kipp's cock starts to swell in my fist, the man himself remaining at my mercy, I press my lips near his ear.

"Good boy. You can come now."

The sound he lets out is surprised, tortured, and he spills between our bodies in an instant. His moans float into my ears like the sweetest melody, and I close my eyes, tucking my face against his neck as I work him through his release, my entire being singing in tune to this man who has me wrapped around his pinkie finger, whether or not he knows it.

I thought I could keep my distance. I thought, maybe, we wouldn't end up here.

I thought wrong.

As Kipp's moans change in pitch, I gentle my ministrations, holding his cock in a loose grip. I squeeze once before letting go.

"Fuck," he mutters between panting breaths.

I ease back, watching Kipp's face, registering the still hazy expression in his gaze. He's not questioning it. *Yet*. But it will come.

"Here," I say, using the hem of my shirt to give him a perfunctory wipe. I grab his next, rolling it carefully upwards to keep his cum contained. Kipp lets me, watching with blissful blue eyes as I tug the garment over his head and off his arms. I do the same with my own. "Stay here a second?"

He nods, a lazy motion, and I get up, standing beside the couch for just a beat—making sure he's okay—before I head swiftly down the hall. I drop both of our shirts in my hamper and grab a cloth from the bathroom.

Kipp hasn't moved an inch when I return, and I use the damp cloth to clean his cock. "Thanks," he mumbles, finally starting to stir.

I offer my hand, which he accepts with a soft chuckle.

"Take it slow," I tell him.

"I'm fine," he replies, running his fingers through his hair as he sits upright. "I, um..." He seems to shake himself loose. "Here, let me return the favor."

"I'm good," I assure him before he can reach for me.

His forehead creases with his frown. "You don't want me to?"

"You were perfect, Kipp," I tell him honestly. "That was everything I wanted."

He still looks unsure, but I hold out my hand again.

"Come on," I encourage. "Let's get to bed."

"Yeah, okay," he agrees, letting himself be pulled to his feet.

We make our way down the hall, both of us brushing our teeth before we change. Kipp looks a little nervous as he climbs under the sheets, like maybe his mind is just now kicking into overdrive, so I climb in quickly after, tugging him close to me and maneuvering him onto his side. Chest to his back, I wrap my arm around him.

His huff sounds like a laugh. "Are we cuddle buddies now?"

"I like to cuddle after sex. Is that okay?"

He lets out a tiny hum, but I don't miss the way he relaxes. "Yeah, I suppose that's fine. I mean, we *are* married. A little cuddling between husbands is no big deal."

"Exactly," I say, pressing a kiss to his neck. "Glad you see it my way. Sleep well, Kipp."

"Night, Teddy."

The last thing I remember is Kipp's arm curling gently over my own.

Chapter 8
Kipp

Niko doesn't answer the first time I call, so I try again, keeping a casual eye on the door as my phone rings. Teddy wasn't in bed when I woke, nor inside the apartment, but there was a note on the nightstand—a literal *note*—saying he'd be back shortly.

Niko picks up right before the call can go to voicemail. "Kipp?" he says sleepily.

From the background, I hear, "The fuck is he calling this early for? It's not even ten on a goddamn Saturday."

"Tell Dixon sorry," I say quickly. "I just, uh..."

Niko must hear something in my tone because he says soothing words to Dixon before a door shuts. "What's up?" he asks.

I tug at my hair a little, eyeing the door again. "I had sex with Teddy," I whisper. "Sort of."

I can practically hear Niko's slow blink. "Start at the beginning."

"Okay, so I came home last night, and Teddy sucked my finger. Which, hello, what? But then he tried to act like it didn't mean anything, and I was like, *dude, no way.* And he was like, *fine, maybe I want you for all time*. Which, rad. So Teddy sat on me and told me to lie there and take it, but in a super respectful way, and then he edged me for, like, half an hour with a *handy*, Nik. The *best* fucking handy. And then…"

My voice peters out, lost.

"And then?" Niko encourages.

I tuck my hand over my mouth. "And then he called me a *good boy*."

Niko doesn't laugh like I half-expect him to. He hums thoughtfully. "How'd you feel about all that?"

"I mean, it was really fucking fantastic," I admit, my body flushing just remembering it. How nice it was to let Teddy take care of me. To just go with the flow and not think. I shiver a little at the memory of his hand on my cock, his other in my hair. "The orgasm was—holy shit, Nik. But… The 'boy' thing threw me."

"Because of your dad?" Niko asks.

"Yes," I say, relieved he got it. My dad has a distinct way of calling me *boy* that makes it feel like I've failed at life. It didn't sound like that coming from Teddy's lips, but still. It was a strange-as-fuck choice of endearment. I'm far from a boy.

"I assume you told Teddy you didn't like it?" Niko asks.

"Um…"

"Kipp," he says, huffing a laugh. "Is it going to happen again? You and him?"

"Yeah, I think so. He made it sound like it was on the table."

Which *thank fuck*. Sex with my hot-as-hell hubby? Yes, please. This whole marriage thing is already looking up.

"Okay, then you need to tell him," Niko says, being much too reasonable.

"Yeah, maybe," I mumble.

He chuckles. "But otherwise, you enjoyed it?"

"A lot," I say. "I just wish…"

Again, I trail out, and Niko gives me a verbal nudge. "You wish what?"

"We didn't even kiss," I tell him. Which, yeah, maybe I'm a little disappointed about that. I like kissing, and Teddy has great lips. I bet his beard would be soft with the right amount of bristle. I sigh just imagining it.

"If not kissing is a limit for you, tell him," Niko says. "You have to communicate these things."

"A limit," I say slowly, wondering at the weird way in which he worded that.

There's a brief pause, and then Niko says, "Uh, you realize Teddy is a Daddy Dom, right?"

I can feel my mouth drop open. "*Whaaat?*"

"Oh my God, Kipp!"

"How the hell was I supposed to know that?" I defend, standing up and pacing the living room.

"Well, for starters, how about the fact that he called you *good boy?*"

"Yeah, I suppose there's that," I admit, my mind cycling back through every moment of last night. The way Teddy took over. How he wouldn't let me come until he was entirely satisfied I was going to lie there like he asked and be good for him. How utterly commanding he was in a calm, controlled way that made it incredibly easy for me to follow his demands. How he was happy to take care of me without reciprocation. "*Oh.*"

"There it is," Niko says.

I swallow roughly, whispering into the phone. "Does that mean he wants me to call him…*Daddy?*"

I swear Niko chuckles, but it's a quiet thing. "You'll have to ask him."

I groan, walking over to the window. "I can't ask him that with *words*. And what does that make me in this scenario?" The door unlocks, and I hiss urgently, "*Shit*, he's here. Gotta go."

I slip my phone in my pocket as Teddy comes through the door, a couple grocery bags in hand. He notices me immediately, a small smile on his face as he looks me over.

"Hey, you're up," he says, all calm and handsome and stuff.

I'm pretty proud of my response, all things considered. "Hi."

Teddy tilts his head a little, pausing. "You okay?"

"Sure."

His smile shifts, crooking up at one end. "I can hear you thinking from here. Just a second. Let me put these away real quick."

Teddy heads into the kitchen, still fully visible but facing away from me, and my eyes catch on the coffee table where my ring is sitting. It's odd how quickly I got used to wearing it and how...*bereft* my hand feels now that it's gone. Would it be weird to put it back on? Teddy is still wearing his.

Before he can turn around, I snatch the ring off the table and stick it on my finger, having to give it a little wiggle to get it over my knuckle.

"All right, come on," he says, waving me toward the door.

"Wait, what? Where are we going?"

"I figured we could walk and talk," Teddy says. "You'll be more comfortable if we're moving."

Jesus, it's like this guy knows me.

"Yeah, okay," I agree.

Teddy waits as I slip into shoes, and then the two of us head down to the sidewalk, Teddy leading me in a direction that looks more residential. We're quiet for a few minutes until the sound of traffic dies down. The houses in this area are pretty, many of them with landscaped front lawns suited to the desert climate.

Teddy is the first to speak. "You're wondering about last night."

I puff out a breath. "Yeah."

He nods, as if he expected as much. "Were you at all uncomfortable?"

My instinct is to say no because, with the exception of that one short *b* word, I wasn't uncomfortable in the least. Frustrated at first, sure. I considered taking myself in hand a time or two when Teddy decided he was going to stop playing nice with my dick. But then...then I just let him lead, and it was nice. A *relief.*

In the end, I answer truthfully. "For the most part, no, I wasn't uncomfortable."

Niko would be so proud.

"Which parts weren't you comfortable with?" Teddy asks.

Shit, I have to say it?

Teddy reaches over and gives my hand a squeeze, like he knows I'm having trouble. He looks down, seemingly surprised to find the ring back on my finger, something I refuse to feel guilty about. It's my ring; I'll wear it if I want. Even if it *is* maybe a size too small.

Teddy lets my hand go before long, but the squeeze helped.

"Are you really a Daddy?" I ask, amazed by how even my voice comes out.

Teddy hums. "I have been."

"But you aren't now?"

"I didn't say that," he responds. "I'm not sure that ever truly goes away, but... It's not something I've acted on in a long time."

"But, with me last night..." I let the question hang.

"I couldn't quite help myself," Teddy answers, a little smirk on his face.

"I'm the same age as you," I point out, confused about that. "Well, shit, that's not true, is it? I'm, what, seven years younger? But that's not a *huge* gap. I'm not *young*. You're not old."

He chuckles. "It doesn't always work like that, Kipp. The dynamic has nothing to do with age."

"You called me boy."

There, I said it.

Teddy hums again, watching the side of my face. I find a very nice tree to look at. "Is that the part that bothered you?" he asks evenly.

"Yes," I admit, finally catching his gaze. There's nothing but kindness there.

"I won't say it again."

I nearly stutter a step. "That easily?"

"That easily," he says. "All I want is to make you feel good, Kipp, and if that didn't make you feel good, I won't do it again."

"Well, shit," I mutter.

His chuckle is warm. "Was the *sweetheart* okay?"

"Christ, Teddy. You realize I'm five foot eleven and three-quarters, fill a shirt pretty nicely if I do say so myself, and shave on the daily, right? I'm not the small *sweetheart* type to most guys."

"I'm well aware of what you look like, Kipp," he says, lips quirking. "And that didn't answer my question."

"It was fine," I mutter, most definitely *not* blushing.

Teddy makes a pleased sound that drops my shoulders, like he has a direct line to some sort of *relax Kipp* button. It's effective, that's for sure.

"Teddy," I say, stopping for a moment. He stops with me. "I'm all for this." I point between us. "And I'm not opposed to meeting some of your less intimidating dildos. I just... I don't know what this means. I don't know if I can be the sort of partner you want."

"Kipp," he says, the one word soft. "You're already exactly what I want."

The way that lights me up should scare me. It really, really should. But all I want is to bask in the glow.

"Come on," Teddy says gently, steering me in the opposite direction. "Let's go home, make a late breakfast, and we'll talk."

"More talking," I deadpan. "*Yay.*"

Teddy snorts. "It'll be painless, I promise."

"Good. Because I have to tell you, I don't think I'm a masochist. If you're into flogging, you might be outta luck. I nearly fainted the last time I got my blood drawn. That shit *hurt.*"

My sexy-as-fuck husband chuckles, a smile on his face as the two of us head home. I can't quite help but smile, too.

"So...you'd basically boss me around," I sum up after Teddy finishes explaining the whole *Daddy Dom* thing. I stuff a bite of pancake in my mouth as his lips twitch.

"Only in the bedroom," he clarifies.

"Okay, but yesterday was in the living room," I point out just to be contrary.

"Stand up," he says.

"What? Why?"

"So I can swat your ass."

The expression on Teddy's face lets me know he's teasing, but *damn*. That doesn't sound like the worst thing.

Setting that aside for now...

"You really think I'm submissive, though?" I ask, still not quite getting that part, even though I *did* really like what happened last night. "I mean, I'm pretty assertive when it comes to sex, Teddy. I've never been one to let the other guy do all the work."

It sounds selfish even considering it, and yet... Teddy sure didn't seem to mind running the show last night.

"It's not about work, Kipp. I don't want you to think of it in those terms." Teddy pauses for a moment, thinking over what he wants to say. His plate is empty now, as is mine, but neither of us moves from the island. "In a power exchange, each person should benefit equally. The dominant partner enjoys having control, and the sub enjoys giving it. That's not to say the submissive partner is powerless. Not in the least. And to answer your question, yes, I think letting go of control is something you'd enjoy given the chance."

"How do you know that?" I ask quietly.

Teddy's gaze turns sharp. It's a look that has me taking immediate notice and sitting taller in my seat.

"Because," he says, voice low, "if I told you to hop up on this counter and let me have you for dessert, you'd do it without hesitation."

"I mean," I cough, adjusting myself, "who would say no to that?"

His smirk has me pondering the answer to that question.

"Let me ask you this," he says, turning his body my way. "In your past relationships, were you happy? Were you getting what you needed?"

His question nearly pulls the air from my lungs. Because *no*, I haven't ever found a guy that gave me everything I needed. Who made me feel settled and secure. I've never met someone I wanted to spend my life with. Never been in love.

There *has* been something missing all these years. Some intangible piece of the puzzle I've been searching for. I started to wonder if maybe I just wasn't made for relationships. If I'd be the perennial bachelor who had to make do with friendships in lieu of true partnership.

But I do want partnership. No matter how much I've tried to prepare myself for the possibility that I'd never find my person, I want to fall in love and create a family of my own and have that knowledge that me and him—we'll be forever. And love, well, doesn't it start with lust? Or even like?

I sure as hell like Teddy. And I more than liked how he made me feel last night. I still don't understand it—why Teddy seems to think I have some sort of untapped submissive potential. But maybe I don't need to understand it. I trust him. And I'm curious enough to explore what it is he's offering. After all...

If I'm lucky, maybe my husband could be the one.

Chapter 9

TEDDY

Since it looks like Kipp's head is about to explode, I suggest we take a breather. He nods wordlessly before bringing his plate to the dishwasher and loading it inside. I follow, giving his neck a squeeze before he can run off. He shoots me a smile, his shoulders lowering, and then he leaves the room.

I settle on the couch, letting him have the privacy of the bedroom. He only stays in there for five minutes.

"I want to kiss," he declares, storming back into the room.

"Right now?" I ask, my pulse jumping.

"In general," he says, waving his hand through the air. "We're supposed to negotiate terms, right? That's a thing?"

My lips twitch. Has he been Googling? "We can do that."

"So, kissing," he repeats, sitting next to me on the couch. He stays that way for all of three seconds before he flops sideways, his head landing in my lap. "Is this okay?"

"More than," I assure him, sifting my fingers through his hair.

"Okay, so I like kissing," he goes on. "And I'm vers, but I do prefer to bottom."

His eyes meet mine, checking in, and I give him a nod.

"And, um..." He falters. "I don't know. You go."

I give his hair a gentle tug until he relaxes against me. "I want to hold you after sex, Kipp."

Blue eyes flash to mine in surprise.

"Aftercare is just as important to me," I explain. "I need to be close, to know you're safe and not having an emotional drop."

"That can happen?" he asks.

I nod. "Anyone can feel down after a physical connection, but submissives in particular are putting themselves in a very vulnerable position. Sub drop can happen after you experience an endorphin high, and if you feel yourself crashing, emotionally or physically, I want to know. I don't want you to hide that from me."

"Okay," he says, swallowing.

"Thank you," I reply, toying with his hair again. "Beyond that, my tastes are quite simple."

"Bossing me around."

My lips twitch again. "I only want to make you feel good, Kipp. That's what I enjoy."

"So, like...no contracts or punishments?"

"No."

"And no whips and chains and stuff?"

"None of that," I assure him.

"That's not so scary," he says, which makes me laugh.

"No, it shouldn't be."

"And, uh..."

I tug his head back, waiting until he meets my eye. "What is it?"

He swallows roughly. "Do I need to call you Daddy?" he asks, voice shaking slightly.

Ah.

"Only if you want to. If it makes you uncomfortable, then no, simple as that. If you want to, well..." I shrug. "I do like it."

"Because...you want to take care of me," he says, not quite a question. More like he's puzzling it out for himself.

I give him a warm smile, running my hand down his chest and anchoring there. "Yes."

He blows out a breath. "Sounds kinda nice."

It's almost unbearable, the fondness I feel at those words. It's a tight, hot thing in my chest, the steam of it rising up and making my eyes sting. I've shied away from this for so long. *Years.* But I can't turn away from Kipp. Can't deny him anything. This man...he's brash and excitable, a bit reckless at times, and most definitely scattered. But he's also sweet and sincere, and I don't think he's ever had someone there to take care of him. Someone to tell him it's okay and that he doesn't have to keep it together all the time. That he can be messy and bright and beautiful and imperfect. That he can fall down, and someone will be there to pick him back up.

I want to be that person, however inadvisable. I want to be the one he trusts, even if our time is limited. Even if, when all is said and done, Kipp and I get divorced and go our separate ways. It's going to hurt no matter how much further I fall.

I might as well enjoy the plummet.

"What are you doing today?" I ask, sensing our conversation is over for now.

"Oh, um... Not sure, actually," he says, stretching his legs. "Usually on the weekends, I just catch up with friends and do laundry and stuff."

"Well, if you want, you could join me. Some of the guys from the studio are helping Emil move his things to his new place."

Kipp tilts his head, catching my eye. "Manual labor? Sign me up!" he says, hopping up and bouncing on his toes. He claps his hands together once. "Well? We doing this or what?"

Chuckling, I follow Kipp off the couch. He smiles widely, and for a brief moment, my gaze drops to his lips, gut swooping as his one and only demand rings in my ears. *"I like kissing."*

No, I'm not sure I will survive this. But fucking hell, I've already made my choice.

"Let me text Emil," I tell Kipp. "And then we'll get going."

"Whoa," Kipp breathes, stepping through the open front door into Emil's apartment. "That's a lot of books."

He's not wrong. On the floor are boxes and boxes of books, mostly paperbacks and hardcovers in neat stacks. But there are textbooks, too. Dozens of them.

"Emil is a psych major," I explain.

Kipp knows Emil—who goes by Felix on set—just as he knows all of my coworkers. But considering Emil tends to keep to himself and Kipp generally joins us to party, I'm guessing the topic might not have come up.

"So the smarty-pants glasses aren't only for show," Kipp jokes.

"No, I'm incredibly farsighted and have astigmatism," Emil says, appearing from down the hall. "Can't see a thing without them." He gives us a shy smile as he comes to a stop a few feet away. "Thanks for coming. I appreciate the help."

"Of course," I tell him. "Are the other guys on the way?"

Emil nods, glasses slipping down his nose. "Yeah, they should be here any—"

"Bro-friend!" Kipp yells in excitement, dragging Niko in for a hug as the curly-haired man clears the door. Niko chuckles, slapping Kipp's back. Kipp holds out his fist to Dixon next. Dixon, rather reluctantly, taps their knuckles together.

"Oh, me, too!" Alex cries, launching himself onto Dixon's back.

"For fuck's sake, where did you come from?" Dixon grumbles, even as he grabs on to Alex's legs, making sure the smaller man doesn't fall.

Alex holds his fist Kipp's way. "Bring it in, Kipper."

With a massive grin, Kipp pounds Alex's fist. They make dual explosion sounds afterwards.

And that about sums up the next ten minutes. Alex's boyfriends come in the door behind him, more of our coworkers arrive, and pretty soon, we're all hauling boxes and furniture down the stairs. At least there's only one flight.

"This is fun," Kipp says, wiping his forehead as we stand beside the moving truck. I shake my head as he tugs up his t-shirt, clearing nonexistent sweat from his brow. He gives me a swift grin, well aware of what he's doing.

"We've been at it for five minutes," I point out. "You might be singing a different tune later tonight when you're too sore to climb into bed."

"You could draw me a bath," he suggests, batting his eyelashes. "Maybe rub my sore muscles a bit?"

I bite my tongue. He's definitely been Googling. "You're going to test me, aren't you?"

Not that I thought for one second Kipp would stop being his flirty, confident self just because he agreed I could boss him around in bed.

Kipp feigns shock. "Me? *No.* I'll be good." He walks a step past me before whispering, "*Daddy.*"

The slap to his ass should not have been a surprise, but Kipp yelps and runs off, laughing as he disappears inside the building.

Fuck, this man *is* going to test me. I have no doubt I'll enjoy every minute of it.

When I get back up to Emil's apartment, Dixon and Niko are maneuvering a couch through the room. I step out of the way, noticing Kipp off near what looks to be a small terrarium.

"Who's this?" Kipp asks Emil.

"Oh," Emil huffs, stepping closer. "That's my hermit crab."

"*Emil*," Alex says sternly from across the room. He has his hands on his hips. "We talked about this."

"Alex," Emil groans.

Alex raises an eyebrow.

Emil sighs, turning back to Kipp. "That's Sir Arthurpod, His Royal Cuteness, Burrower of Sand and Creator of Dreams."

Alex looks mightily pleased, whereas Emil seems ready to disappear into the floorboards.

Kipp beams, bending down and waving at the hermit crab. "Hi, Sir Arthur." Noticing me nearby, he points at the tank. "Teddy! A hermit crab. Can we get one? Please? They can have playdates."

"Crab daddies!" Alex shouts.

"No crabs," I tell Kipp.

My five foot eleven and three-quarters, twenty-nine-year-old, *I-shave-my-face-every-day* husband pouts. *Pouts*.

"Put that away," I say sternly, aiming a finger at his face.

He does, but not before grabbing another box off the floor and blowing me a kiss.

"Oooh," Alex sings once Kipp is out of sight, his hazel eyes turning my way. "Teddy and Kipper, sitting in a tree.

K-I-S-S-I-N-G. First comes dancing, and then comes marriage. Then comes a baby in a—*hey*." Alex bats my hand off his mouth. "*Rude*."

"You're trouble," I point out, wiping my palm before grabbing an upholstered armchair.

"And proud of it," he retorts.

Yeah, yeah.

I head down the stairs with the armchair in tow. Kipp stops when I walk past him at the bottom landing. "Uh," he says, turning to watch me. "Can I be next?"

I set the furniture in the truck, pushing it against the side before facing Kipp. He's waiting with a grin.

"Sure," I reply, striding his way.

His eyes go wide. "Wait, what?"

Kipp grunts when I haul him over my shoulder. I secure my arm above his ass and head for the stairs.

"Holy shit," he breathes.

I get a strong sense of satisfaction as Kipp goes silent for the rest of the short climb up to the second floor. When I set him down, his face is flushed and his hair is disheveled, giving him a decidedly sexy bedhead look that would only look better earned naturally.

"Fuck, Teddy," he whispers, recovering quickly and fanning his face. "Is tossing me around on the table? Because I've never been with a guy who could pick me up before, and that was hot as hell."

"Yeah, sweetheart," I say in a low voice, tugging his shirt back into place, fingers lingering. "I think that could be arranged."

His blush darkens.

My ringing phone interrupts the moment, and I pull it from my pocket, the smug smile I'd been harboring slipping away. I'm tempted to dismiss the call, but I have a feeling I know why my brother is trying to get in touch, and it'd be better to head him off now before he gets any big ideas.

"Excuse me," I mumble to Kipp, walking down the hall. His forehead pinches in clear worry, but he heads back inside as I answer my phone. "I'm not selling my shares, no matter what Antoni implied."

Cameron is quiet for a beat. "Is it true? You got married?"

I sigh, stepping out of the way as Alex and his boyfriends pass with boxes in their hands. "None of your business."

"It is my business if it becomes *our* business. Did you get a prenup?"

Jesus Christ. "Let me repeat myself, Cam. My life is none of your business. It stopped being your business the moment you fucked me over. With my *boyfriend.*"

"Theo," he chides. "Are you really hung up on that? It was five years ago."

I clench my jaw tight. I haven't been *Theo* for a long time. Cameron and Antoni are the only ones who still call me that, and the nickname chafes like an ill-fitted boot.

"If you're asking if I'm ready to forgive you, the answer is no," I say.

"Why won't you sell the shares? You don't even work here anymore."

"And whose fault is that?" I grit out.

He doesn't deign to answer me. "You're not acting on behalf of the firm. You don't care about running the business. You're just holding onto those shares to spite Antoni and me."

"You never understood," I say, shaking my head.

"Understood what?" he asks, sounding put out.

"What it meant to me. Starting that business with you, Cam. Building something from the ground up. You didn't care that it was my dream. You didn't care that it was never about profits to me. You were greedy, and you stomped all over me on your pursuit to the top. You made my staying impossible, and you never looked back. And now, what? You want me to sell?" I let out a frustrated sound. "I don't care about the money. I never did. And believe it or not, I don't sit around plotting ways to get my revenge. Those shares are mine. I earned them with my own goddamn sweat and tears. They *mean* something to me. And you can't ever take that away. I'm not selling."

I hang up before my brother can respond, and then I block his number like I should have done years ago. Family doesn't betray you. Family doesn't stab you in the back. I thought, once, that Cameron loved me. And maybe he did. Maybe he even does. But not all love is healthy, and I've come too far to let myself be dragged back into that twisted mess.

With a sigh, I stick my phone in my pocket and head down the hall to Emil's. My costars are hard at work, nearly having cleared the entire space. Kipp catches my eye from the kitchen, a small box of utensils in his hands.

"Hey," he says, walking over. "Everything all right?"

As I look at Kipp's gentle smile and the way his eyes are creased in concern, I think that *yeah*, maybe everything will be.

"Yep," I tell him. "Feeling sore yet?"

"Why?" he asks a little cautiously.

"Just wondering what temperature you prefer for your baths."

He looks surprised for all of a second before he laughs, loudly and without restraint. "Do I get salts, too?"

"Anything you want, Kipp."

Anything you want.

Chapter 10
Kipp

We get Emil set up in his new apartment without issue. He thanks us profusely, buying pizza for the entire porn star fam, which I guess includes me now. I've officially become part of the HABs—*husbands and boyfriends* club—even if, technically, my whole marriage with Teddy is a sham. Doesn't matter. I've leveled up.

By the time Teddy and I get home, the sun has set, and I'm a strange combination of sore and horny. I know the bath thing was a joke—one I started—but damn does that sound good right about now. Although, anything with Teddy's hands and my body sounds pretty damn good, if I'm being honest. Watching the man haul furniture all day was a lesson in patience. And I've never been a patient guy.

I'm debating the merits of whining about my muscles just to see what would happen when Teddy tugs off his shirt. "Come on," he says, heading toward the en suite. "Hop in the shower."

"Seriously?" I ask, gaping after him. He wants to shower together?

"If you want," he replies, his smirk telling me he knows *exactly* what I want. I don't think I've ever moved so fast.

Teddy chuckles as I race past him and tug off my clothes. He starts the shower, and I simply stare at him. His broad, furry chest. The ridiculously strong arms. His dark beard and *holy shit*, there go his pants. My eyes skim downwards, taking in the curve of his ass, his thick, hairy thighs, and his beautiful, fat cock. *Fuuuck*.

"Have I told you how hot you are?" I ask. "It's unfair, really."

Teddy's lips twitch as he checks the shower temp. "Get in."

"I mean," I go on, stepping inside the stall, "you look like *that*, but you're also a nice person. Like, genuinely kind. Do you know how rare that is?"

Teddy backs me into the wall, and my breath leaves me on a gasp. His thigh slides between my legs, forcing me to widen my stance, and his hand trails up my chest until he's gripping the side of my neck, his thumb beneath my chin. I swallow against the digit.

"I don't always play nice," he says, his voice deceptively soft. "Can I touch you?"

I refrain from blurting *you already are*. Instead, I nod vigorously. "Yes. Anytime. Blanket permission."

He smiles, his hand circling my erection. My eyes roll up as the back of my head hits the tile.

"I want to be clear about something," he says, stroking me slowly. "A couple somethings, actually. First, when we're like this, I'm in charge."

I nod again. Yes. Yep. Got that message loud and clear.

"Good," he says, thumb rolling over my slit. I buck into his hand, unable not to. Unlike last time, he doesn't tell me to keep still. He rolls his thumb over my crown again and again until I'm moaning, writhing, and then he stops.

I pant a breath as his hand squeezes my neck gently.

"But outside of sex," he goes on, waiting until I meet his eye, "you're not under my control. I'm not going to tell you how to act or give you rules to follow. I'm not going to dictate your life, and I don't think you want me to."

I shake my head. No, I don't. I can see why the concept would appeal to some—the loss of choice, the enforcement of routine. But I've been treated like a wayward child by my family all my life, and I don't want the same treatment from my partner.

Teddy starts stroking me again, the shower forgotten. "That brings me to number two," he says, thumb skimming the front of my throat as his other hand works my cock so slowly I feel like I might combust. "I'm not your guardian, but that doesn't mean I don't want to take care of you."

My breath catches.

"So if you want a bath," Teddy says softly, "I will run you one. I will cook for you sometimes, as I suspect you might for me. If you're cold, I will get you a blanket. It has nothing to do with control. It's about looking after what's mine. Got it?"

I nod, even as my heart pounds. It sounds a hell of a lot like Teddy is talking about what people do in a real relationship, but we don't have that, do we? We're just two husbands having sex, which, *fuck*... That doesn't sound better.

"Good," Teddy says again, letting my neck go. "Now that that's settled, we can have some fun."

I don't have time to ponder those words before Teddy is removing his thigh from between my legs and spinning me toward the wall. I catch myself, palms flat on the tile, as Teddy grabs my leg, hoisting it up until my foot is on the ledge at the side of the shower stall.

"Jesus," I breathe out, pulse racing at the quick and easy manhandling. "You make me feel like a damn ragdoll, Teddy."

He steps in close, the heat of him at my back. His fingers trail over my ass, between my cheeks, down to my balls.

"Would you like that?" he says in that calm, low tone. He toys with my sac, his other hand landing flat beside mine on the wall. "Do you want to be my doll, Kipp?"

My breath leaves me in a rush.

"Mine to toss around and care for," he says, lips near my ear. His hand journeys along my perineum before he taps my bent leg. "Mine to maneuver however I want, *fuck* however I want."

Holy shit. Yeah, yes, please.

Teddy's hand returns to my ass, fingers pressing against my hole. "Mine to use and cherish and play with. Is that what you want, Kipp? To be treated like the precious babydoll you are?"

Fucking hell. I drop my head to the wall, panting into the steamy air.

"Words, sweetheart."

"Yes," I whisper, licking my lips. "Yes. *Please.*"

He rumbles, his touch leaving me. I nearly whimper, but then I hear the click of a bottle. I try to turn my head, but Teddy grabs my neck, stilling me.

"Don't fucking move, babydoll. Stay where I put you."

Fu-u-uck.

My cock throbs, dribbling precum. Teddy doesn't remove his hand until I plant my forehead against the tile. His fingers sink into my hair.

"Good doll."

My knee gives out, but Teddy is quick to grab me, his arm around my waist.

"So fucking pretty," he says, his hand sinking between my ass cheeks again. He rubs over my hole, his fingers wet. "Just look at you. Ready and willing for me."

So goddamn willing.

He sinks a finger inside my ass, and it takes everything in me to stay upright, even with Teddy's firm hold around my middle. I groan into the tiles, every nerve ending in my body sensitized as if Teddy has been working me over for hours, not mere seconds. His finger strokes in and out before he presses in with two, the stretch burning in the best way. The ache boils over into pleasure as Teddy rubs my prostate.

"You should see yourself," he says, fucking me with his fingers, the angle intent on driving me mindless. "You should see the way you look, cheeks flushed and body opened up for me. My perfect porcelain doll."

I let out an unintelligible response, my legs shaking, my arms feeling like jelly.

Teddy tightens his hold. "Easy. I've got you, babydoll."

And *fuck*, I believe him. I do.

I rest my cheek on the tile, giving myself over, letting Teddy do with me as he pleases. He hums, an immensely satisfied sound, as he rubs and rubs and *rubs* right where I need him.

"That's right," he all but coos, his lips brushing my cheek. "Beautiful. Pliant. *Mine.*"

My orgasm hits me before I even register I'm about to come. One second, there's Teddy's fingers in my ass, his arm around my waist, and the feel of his beard bristling my jaw as he says that word—*mine*. And then I'm shooting, my cock bucking against air, my cum hitting the shower wall as everything around me blanks. I'm so boneless I barely register the loss of Teddy's fingers. But then I'm being spun back around, and strong arms are supporting me, one of Teddy's hands behind my head, cushioning me from the wall. He stares at me for the longest singular second of my life, and then he kisses me.

I swear I come again, just a little. It's like an electric spark, a jolt through my system. And then...*bliss*. His lips are soft yet incessant. Warm. They're the promise of something too wonderfully scary to name. He kisses me like he wants to, not because I asked him to. He kisses like sweet summer rain.

When he hikes my leg up over his hip, I don't think; I just hold it there.

"Gorgeous," he says, lips meeting mine again as he strokes himself.

Yes, yes. Fuck. Come on me.

I can't get my mouth to work, but Teddy seems to have the same idea. The sound of his fist working his cock rises above that of the shower, the *slick, slick* of it making me groan. Teddy draws back, dark eyes meeting mine. "Do you have any idea how much I want you?" he rasps.

I don't answer. Can't.

The hand behind my head tightens in my hair, lifting my chin. My eyes slip shut, and Teddy growls, his nose against my exposed neck before his teeth fit to my skin. The sensation is brutal, perfect, as he blooms a bruise to the surface of my neck. I don't move a muscle, letting him mark me and loving every second of it. His mouth is back on mine the next instant, just as hard, just as demanding.

"No one touches you but me," he says, the words not the threat they should be. "Say it, doll."

"No one," I whisper.

His seed hits my stomach and hip as he starts to come. It's hot, same as the reminder of his lips on my neck, and I can't do a thing other than smile. His deep groan fills my ears, and I *do* feel gorgeous, like he said. I feel wanted. I feel *good.*

Teddy's hand leaves the back of my head, his fingers on my chin. "Look at me, sweetheart."

Fuck, were my eyes closed?

He smiles when I meet his gaze, something so very warm lingering in the depths of his eyes. "There you are," he says gently. "You were perfect. Stunning. Let's get cleaned up now, okay?"

I think I nod.

Teddy helps maneuver me under the shower spray, his arm staying around me. The water is still hot, much to my surprise. He must pay a small fortune for utilities. I don't think much about the fact that Teddy is washing me. It feels nice, and he said he wanted to take care of me, right? Who am I to argue?

When we step out of the shower, Teddy wraps a towel around my waist. He grabs another, drying my hair. I think my eyes slip closed again.

His chuckle is warm in my ear. "Do you need me to carry you?"

"What?" I mutter.

He chuckles again, swooping me up over his shoulder like he did earlier. "Come on, doll. Let's get you to bed."

Mmm.

Teddy drops me onto a soft surface. A few seconds or years later, warm arms wrap around me from behind. With the last of my strength, I roll toward the source of that heat, burrowing against a firm yet comfortable pillow. No, not a pillow. A chest. Arms tighten around me.

The last thing I remember is fingers in my hair and the feeling of utter peace.

Consciousness is slow to come. Everything feels fluffy and white, like I'm floating amongst clouds. There's the nicest-smelling *something* beneath my face—vanilla and cloves, if I had to guess—and warmth is all around.

My eyes snap open when I remember last night. I glance upwards, finding Teddy still asleep on his pillow. My pulse settles almost instantly, but my cheeks heat when I remember Teddy's new nickname for me. *Doll.*

Fuck, why is that so hot? I shouldn't want to be compared to something pretty and delicate and oftentimes feminine, should I?

Then why did you like it so much?

Fuck if I know. Nor do I know why it was so much easier this time to let Teddy have his way with me. There was barely a fight inside my mind. I *wanted* him to take over, to show me what he claimed I'd enjoy. And damn if I didn't enjoy the ever-loving heck out of it.

I've never dabbled in BDSM. Don't know much about it apart from what I've recently learned via Google and Teddy himself. But I always thought it sounded mean. That it was about pain and tying people up and flogging them into sub-mission. Obviously, my preconceived notions weren't entirely correct. Not to say some people don't enjoy those things, but the way Teddy treats me is nothing like that. He's soft and sweet, and only the right amount of hard. If that's what I have to look forward to with him as my...*Dom*, sign me the fuck up. It felt natural. Intimate, even.

And holy smokes, do I need to slow my roll. I shouldn't be thinking *intimate* and *Teddy* in the same breath. Because he told me—as soon as we're divorced, this is done. It's not long-term. It's just about getting off.

Right?

"Morning," Teddy says, startling me.

"Oh. Hey."

He rubs my arm, and I tilt my head back, meeting his eye. He taps the point between my brow. "Thinking hard?"

"Yeah," I mumble, chewing my words for only a second. "I think I might be submissive."

Teddy snorts, but it's a gentle sound. "Yeah, I think so, too."

"Well, I didn't know, mister, but just you wait," I say, stretching out my limbs. "Now that I do, I'm going to be the best goddamn sub you've ever had."

"That so?" Teddy asks, eyes crinkling with his smile.

"Uh-huh." I groan as my back pops. "I'm not a 90-percent-effort sort of guy, Teddy. If I'm doing something, I go all in."

"In that case," he says, hand trailing down my back and coming to a stop at the top of my ass. He holds there possessively. "If you still want *me* to go all in, I'll need your test results."

He taps between my cheeks for emphasis, as if his meaning wasn't abundantly clear.

"Yeah," I cough out, the idea of Teddy's cock in my ass making my dick perk. "I'll go to the clinic tomorrow."

Teddy leans down, smudging a kiss against my forehead. "It's not that I don't trust you, Kipp. I just need to be careful with my job. And, on that note, you need to decide how comfortable you are with the risks involved in partnering with a sex worker. We test frequently at the studio, but you and I can use condoms for oral if you want. I have no problem with that."

I take a second to truly consider it, knowing Teddy would want me to. "How long have you worked at Elite 8?"

He hums. "Five years."

"Have you ever contracted anything?"

"No," he admits.

"Then no condoms for oral," I answer. I'm tempted to tack on *or anal*, but Teddy didn't offer that as an option. Maybe he doesn't want to go there with me. After all, bareback screams commitment, and Teddy and I are... Well, not quite committed.

The ring on my finger flashes in the light, calling me a liar.

"So, anyways," I say, whipping out a smile. "You said something last night about cooking for me?"

Teddy's rumbling laugh has me grinning from ear to ear.

Chapter 11

TEDDY

"Hey. Phillip, is it?"

The teen across from me nods, fiddling with his work shirt. There's a badge for a gas station on his breast pocket. Scott, the head of the LGBTQ+ community center where we're meeting, told me Phillip is eighteen, but the kid looks a good couple years younger than that.

I extend my hand. "It's nice to meet you, Phillip. I'm Teddy."

He shakes my hand quickly before resuming his nervous fidgeting.

"Scott said you could use some help," I say, hoping to lead him into discussing why he's here. Or, rather, why *I'm* here.

"Um, yeah," he says. "But I don't know what you can do."

"Well," I say, opening my palms. "Why don't you explain what's going on, and we'll figure it out?"

"Okay, so..." More nervous shirt tugging. "I moved into a place earlier this year when I turned eighteen."

I nod, encouraging him to go on.

"Um, and my landlord keeps raising my rent. He says it's normal, but I don't know anyone in the building well enough to ask. And, uh, he keeps making comments. About me being gay."

"You think he's discriminating against you because of your sexual orientation," I say gently.

The kid nods before shaking his head a little and shrugging. "I don't know."

"Well, in Nevada, a landlord needs to give their tenants notice before implementing a rent increase. At the very least, that would be fifteen days, depending on your lease agreement. Is he giving you any notice?"

Phillip shakes his head. "No. He just tells me the price when the rent is due."

Yeah, that's certainly not legal.

I give Phillip a gentle smile. "First, let me assure you I *can* help with this, okay?"

He nods, and I open my notebook.

"All right, then. Let's start at the beginning."

Phillip and I chat for a good thirty minutes before he needs to leave for work. After our brief preliminary meeting, I have a list of rent payments Phillip made to his landlord, price hikes included, an emailed copy of his original lease agreement, and as many details as the kid could remember of his landlord's bigoted comments. It's enough.

Scott catches me as I'm packing up my things in the small sitting room Phillip and I were using. "Hey," he says, tapping the doorframe. "Everything go okay?"

"Yeah," I tell him. "I'll take his case."

Scott exhales in relief. "Thanks, Teddy. I honestly don't know what we'd do without you."

I give him a smirk. "You'd find some other lawyer to do pro bono work for you."

"Maybe," he agrees. "But you're the best."

"Flattery will get you everywhere."

He laughs at that, and we walk down the hall. "Coffee before you go?"

"Sure. Thanks."

Scott and I detour into the community center's small café. It's set up like a real coffee shop, with espresso machines and a couple employees who serve drinks and a limited selection of bakery items. It's free for the kids and young adults who come here. At the moment, there are a few college-age students on a couch in the corner, working on homework. Another sits at a table, scrolling through their phone.

Scott grabs me a black coffee and orders a latte for himself, and we take a seat. "How've you been since the last time I saw you?" he asks.

"A whole month ago?"

He chuckles. "Plenty can change in a month."

That's true.

"Actually," I say, holding up my left hand, "I got married."

Scott's eyes shoot comically wide as he sees my ring. "Holy shit." The nearby kids snicker, and Scott says, voice louder, "Sorry, all. Swearing is bad. Stay in school."

They go back to their work, and Scott shakes his head, grimacing. There's a smile in his eyes, though. Scott has a good rapport with the kids here at the community center. I noticed it the first time I visited over three years ago. They trust him, and I guarantee he could name every single person in this café and those walking through the halls. This place and these people are Scott's life, his passion. And ever since he enlisted my help, it's become a bit of a passion project for me, too.

"So, who's the lucky guy?" Scott asks. "I didn't even know you were dating."

"Would you believe me if I told you it was a drunk Vegas wedding?"

Scott eyes me before snorting. "Not a chance. What's the real story?"

I keep my laughter to myself. Mostly. "I've known him for a while, but nothing happened until recently."

"Why's that?" he asks, taking a sip of his drink.

Because I was scared? Because I got burned so badly by my last relationship that I can still feel the scorch marks?

"I guess the timing wasn't right," I answer.

I probably shouldn't be discussing this with Scott in the first place, but he would have noticed my ring eventually. Besides, I count him as a friend, and it feels nice to speak freely about Kipp. To talk about him as my husband, not the guy I'm accidentally married to. My coworkers at Elite 8 Studios know what happened between Kipp and me wasn't real, and yet...that doesn't mean my feelings are fake. Is it so bad to want to share that with someone?

Of course, the wise choice would be to take my ring off and pretend the whole thing never happened. But *fuck*. I can't do that. I just can't.

"I guess the important question is—does he make you happy?" Scott asks.

Easy. "Yeah. He really does."

After my visit to the community center, I stop by the gym for a workout. It feels good, putting my body through the paces. I try to exercise daily, a habit that keeps my mind centered and my body in shape.

By the time I get home, it's early evening, and Kipp is back from work, stretched out on the couch like a cat. He perks up when I walk through the door, a grin lighting his face. I try to ignore the way my insides warm at seeing him.

"Hey, where've you been?" he asks before wincing. "Yeesh, I swear I didn't mean for that to sound so suspicious or, like, needy. I'm smashing this whole husband thing, aren't I?"

I huff a laugh, toeing off my shoes and setting down my gym bag. "You're doing just fine."

"Were you at the studio?" he asks, sitting up.

I don't for one second consider lying to Kipp. "No, I wasn't. I was at the gym, and before that, I was working a case."

Kipp's head tilts to the side. "A case..."

Here goes. "I guess this is the part where I tell you I'm a lawyer."

His mouth falls open. "Are you freakin' kidding me?"

"No," I say with a chuckle, heading into the kitchen.

Kipp pops off the couch and walks my way, stopping on the other side of the island with his hands braced against the countertop. "Are you telling me my husband is a lawyer by day and a porn star by night? Do you, like, wear sexy singlets under your suits in the courtroom?"

My laugh is louder this time. "When have you ever seen me wearing a singlet?"

"Never," he says. "Which is a damn shame. Are you serious? About the lawyer thing? Not that I'm doubting you, but *fuck*. That's..."

"It's what?" I ask, pulling some pasta from the cupboard.

"I mean, impressive as shit. And hot. Can you debrief me?"

I bark a laugh, and Kipp grins.

"I *am* serious," I tell him, filling a pot with water. "I do practice law, just not as part of a firm any longer. I do pro bono work for a LGBTQ+ community center downtown, mostly."

Kipp blinks at me.

"What?" I ask.

"Can I suck your cock?"

"*Kipp.*"

"I'm not kidding!" he says, laughing once. "Holy shit, Teddy. You deserve a goddamn cock suck for that."

I shake my head, fighting my ridiculous smile. "Maybe after dinner."

Kipp groans.

"Actually, no oral yet, remember?" I point out.

He groans again, slumping against the counter. "*Yeah.* I went and got tested during my lunch break today. Should have results within a few days."

I pull out my phone, scrolling to my most recent results. I aim the screen Kipp's way. "All negative on my end."

He barely glances at the screen before nodding. "If I can't suck your dick, is there anything I can do to help with dinner?"

My lips twitch. "Want to make a salad?"

"Lettuce?" he says with a shiver, coming around the island. "I've never understood the point."

"It's good for you."

"Yes, Daddy," he mumbles.

He yelps when I whip him with a towel. And then he cracks up.

When we sit down to dinner a short while later, my phone rings. "Mind if I pick this up?" I ask. "It's my grandparents."

"Of course," Kipp says, waving me on.

I accept the call, putting it on speaker. "Allô."

"Salut, mon chéri. Ça va?"

"Hi, Maman. I'm good," I respond. "Could we talk in English, please? I have a friend here."

"Oh!" she says. "Oui. Of course. Who's your friend?"

"His name is Kipp. Kipp, my grandmother, Elodie."

"Hi, Grandma El," Kipp says easily.

Her soft chuckle comes over the line. "Hello, Kipp." In the background, she calls for my grandpa, telling him she's on the phone with me and my *friend*. I don't miss the way she says the word with meaning. "Are you having dinner?" she asks, her accent curling around the letters in a way that's familiar. It reminds me of warm, blanketed hugs and garlic cooking in the kitchen.

"We are," I answer. "Chicken parmesan."

"I made the salad," Kipp puts in.

My grandma chuckles again. "That's good, mon chéri. Vegetables are important."

Kipp rolls his eyes when I give him a victorious smirk.

"Théodore?" my grandpa says.

"Hi, Papa. I'm here with my friend, Kipp. Kipp, my grandfather, Luca."

"Hello, Kipp," my grandpa says. "It is very nice to meet you."

His English is a little more stilted and formal than my grandma's. He speaks the language well, but he grew up in a community of almost entirely French speakers. My grandma, on the other hand, was bilingual from the time she was young. Same as me and Cameron.

"Nice to meet you, too," Kipp says, smiling at my phone in between bites of his pasta. "I have to ask, was Teddy as adorable as a baby as he is now?"

My grandpa laughs, pleased, as my grandma answers. "Oui. You should have seen his cheeks. So pinchable."

Kipp's eyes trail down my body, landing on the side of my ass. "I don't doubt it," he says, bouncing his eyebrows.

"Behave," I mouth.

He draws what I believe is supposed to be a halo above his head.

"Mon chéri," my grandma says, "you should show him your photo album."

"Oh, yes. Teddy, you should," Kipp agrees.

"Maybe another time," I say, shaking my head as Kipp pouts. "Papa, how's the garden this year?"

My grandpa launches into a rundown of their vegetable garden as Kipp and I finish our meal. It doesn't surprise me how at ease Kipp is while talking to my grandparents, but it does make me wonder about his own family.

After my grandma grills Kipp about his job in software development, to which he happily answers her questions, our conversation wraps up.

"It was so nice to meet you, Kipp," my grandma says. "We'll have to talk again soon."

"Yeah, I'd like that," Kipp says, his cheeks turning an adorable shade of pink.

My grandpa gives his love in French, I return the sentiment, and then it's my grandma's turn.

"Bisous," she says.

"Kisses," I reply.

When I end the call, Kipp gives me a smile. "Bisous means kisses?" he asks.

I nod. "It's how we say goodbye. It includes a kiss on the cheek if we're together."

"That's really nice," Kipp says, expression soft and yet almost sad. I'm guessing, based on what he's said of his parents, they don't have something similar. "So, your name is Theodore."

I hum, collecting our dishes. "It is."

Kipp grabs our glasses, following me around the island and into the kitchen. "And chéri? What's that?"

"It's an endearment, like darling or beloved. Or," I add, clearing my throat, "sweetheart."

Kipp is quiet for a moment before saying, "Your grandma called me that, too."

"Yeah. She's always been like that," I explain. "Warm and maternal."

He helps me load the dishwasher before leaning against the counter. "You call them Mom and Dad, right? Maman and..."

"Papa," I fill in, nodding. "Yeah, I do. Because they basically are. They raised me and my brother from the time I was one and a half." When Kipp's face falls in sympathy, I explain, as succinctly as possible, "My parents died in an accident. No one's fault, really. But my grandparents on my dad's side took us in. I never knew my mom's family. She met my dad in Canada while on a study permit. Her parents didn't approve of the marriage."

"I'm sorry to hear that," Kipp says. "All of it, really. But...I'm glad you have your grandparents."

"Yeah," I say with a small smile. "I am, too."

"You didn't mention about us being, well, you know," he says, his words almost tentative.

"Does that bother you?" I ask.

"No," he's quick to say. "I mean, it's not like our marriage is real. It's no big deal. I was just wondering."

There's a twinge in my chest that I do my best to brush off. "I'll tell them eventually. Maybe the next time I visit." *Once I figure out what to say.*

"Yeah, I get it," Kipp says. "Um, wanna watch some TV?"

"Sure. Let's do it."

Kipp walks ahead of me into the living room, practically leaping the last few steps onto the couch like the kid at heart that he is. I chuckle, not minding one bit when he shifts around to set his head in my lap. I sift my fingers through his hair, wondering what the hell I'm doing.

Wondering how I'm possibly supposed to give this up once Kipp decides he's ready to go on his way.

Chapter 12
Kipp

"Having a husband is great," I tell Jacob. "I have someone to eat dinner with and watch TV with. We take showers together, which is just plain good for the planet, you know? All that water conservation. And I have someone to cuddle with anytime I want."

That might be my favorite part. All the cuddling. Or Teddy's chest. Or his thighs. Or, *damn*, am I really supposed to pick a favorite?

Oh! Teddy is my favorite. There. Solved.

Jacob looks at me a little strangely, standing in front of my desk with his project notes in hand. Granted, he didn't *ask* for an update on my life, but hey, he was updating me about his web design. Figured I'd return the favor. "Were you not doing those things before?" he asks.

Oh. Right. "I mean, Teddy and I are closer now since the wedding." *True.* "I feel like I know him better." *Also true.*

"Well, honestly, I'm happy for you, man. Are we going to meet him soon?"

"Yeah, maybe," I mutter, wondering how much longer I can keep putting that off. We're a pretty small company here.

Everyone and their mother has asked about Teddy. "So, uh, you had a question about integrating the preexisting logo into your design?"

"Right," Jacob says, getting back to it. Twenty minutes later, he heads off to his desk, and my phone rings.

Vaughn. My day was going so well, too.

"Hello?" I answer, leaving my office and heading for the exit. It's close enough to lunchtime that I can take my break now, as well as this long-overdue phone call.

"Wow. He lives," my brother says.

"Yeah. Sorry about that. I—"

"We're coming to visit."

My blood runs cold. "What? Why?"

"Why do you think, dumbass? You got married without telling anyone. Mom and Dad are worried."

About me or my choices?

"That doesn't mean you need to come here," I say, well aware of the frantic edge to my voice.

"Too late. You weren't returning our calls. We're coming Friday."

Shit. *Shit.*

"I...I'm not even at my apartment anymore. I'm living with Teddy, and I don't feel comfortable giving you his address, so—"

"Fucking hell, Kipling. What, you need to ask his permission first? I guess that answers *that* question."

"What question?" I ask, my ears ringing.

"About who wears the pants in your relationship." He scoffs. "Tell me, do you bend over every time he snaps his—"

My brother's voice cuts off, and it takes me a second to realize why. Oh shit. *I hung up on him.*

His text comes swiftly.

Vaughn: Friday, princess. You better text your fucking address.

With a groan, I slump against the outside of the building. What a goddamn mess. Why are they even coming? I'm nearly thirty years old. It's not like they can tell me what to do anymore.

I pull up Teddy's number and call before I can second-guess myself. A voice that's definitely not his answers.

"Why, hello, Kipperoo."

"Alex?" I ask, checking my screen.

"In the metaphorical flesh," he says cheerfully. "What can I do for you? Teddy is currently indisp—*hey*." Alex's voice gets quieter. "I was talking. And *damn*, Teddy Bear, that towel is much too small for you."

"Kipp?" Teddy asks, his voice rumbling through my ear. "What's wrong?"

My shoulders drop, and I lean my head back against the building, feeling a little bit like I might cry. *Ridiculous*. "My parents are coming. And my brother."

"Today?"

"Friday. I don't know what to do," I admit.

"Do you want to see them?" he asks softly.

I shake my head. "I have to."

He doesn't ask why, and I'm grateful for it. How do I explain they're my family? I can't just...say no to them, can I?

"Do you want me with you?" Teddy asks, his voice breaking through my thoughts.

"Fuck, Teddy, I do, but...but I don't."

"Why do you?" he asks, his tone gentle and without judgment. I can hear Alex saying something quietly in the background, and Teddy mumbles a response before his voice is in my ear again. "Kipp?"

"Am I interrupting work?" I ask, pushing off from the wall. I walk behind the building, where a small sliver of green space sits.

"No, I'm done filming," Teddy answers. "I'm in the locker room now. So why do you want me there?"

Because... "You make me feel safe."

And *shit*, did I really just say that out loud?

Teddy hums. It sounds like approval, and suddenly, I don't feel so bad about my admission. "And why don't you want me there?" he asks.

"Because I don't want you to meet them. They're not nice people, Teddy. I don't want them to be not-nice to you."

He seems to mull that over. "But it's okay if they're not-nice to you?"

"This sounds like a trap."

He huffs a small sound that might be a laugh. "I'll be there with you."

My body deflates in an instant. "I don't want them at the apartment, though."

"Then you pick a place," he says. "And if we need to leave early, we will."

"Thank you," I whisper.

There's that hum again. "I've got you, sweetheart."

Fuck.

I clear my throat. "You're good at this husband thing, you know. Pretty sure I hit the jackpot when I locked you down."

"Pretty sure you're good at it, too," he counters.

"How do you figure? 'Cause I'm messy, can't cook nearly as well as you, I tend to hump you when you're trying to sleep—although, granted, I'm usually mostly asleep, too...sometimes—and I legit don't even know how to balance a checkbook? Actually, does anyone even own one of those anymore? The point is I'm pretty sure you pulled the short straw, my friend."

"Kipp," he says, warm laughter bleeding through his tone. "You called."

"Yeah," I say slowly. "I know I called..."

"No," he says, definite laughter in his voice now. It tempers, though, when he says, "You called *me* when you were upset. That means a lot."

"Oh," I whisper.

"Don't worry," he says softly. "You're nailing this husband thing, too."

God, this is complicated, isn't it?

"A bit," he says, making me realize I said that aloud. "Don't overthink, Kipp. I'm here if you need it. It doesn't have to mean more than that."

But it does. It means so much more.

"Are you wearing a towel?" I ask, desperate for a change of topic and belatedly remembering Alex's comment.

Teddy hums. "I am."

"A small towel."

"It's a normal-sized towel," he says.

"But you're not a normal-sized man. You're, like, a bear. Which, honestly? Go us queers. That's such a good description."

He huffs a laugh. "Kipp."

"I feel bad for twunks, though. Like, wouldn't minks be better? Muscle twinks? Instead of twink hunks?"

"Kipling..."

"I'm just saying there are better options. And don't even get me started on otters—"

"Sweetheart, are you supposed to be working right now?" Teddy asks, pulling out what I now recognize as his *Daddy voice.*

"*Oh*," I say, my entire body rolling in a shiver. "Right. Uh, lunch, actually. But, yeah, my time is running out."

"Go get something to eat," he says gently.

I snort. "Is this where you tell me to eat my greens or you'll redden my ass? I didn't think we were doing that whole *do what I say or I'll punish you* thing."

The sound Teddy makes can only be described as a purr. "Believe me, Kipp. My hand on your ass would be far from a punishment."

Oh?

I clear my throat and try again. "Oh?"

His chuckle is dark but his words soft. "Thank you for calling me."

"Tell Alex thanks for answering."

I swear he mutters, "Such a brat," but it sounds so fond I can't even be mad about it. "See you tonight, Kipp."

"Later, hubs."

When I end the call, I sigh. I actually freaking sigh.

I'm in such deep shit.

When I get home, my afternoon having been thankfully free of family-related disturbances, a grunt greets my ears. I perk immediately, seeking out Teddy like a homing missile. I find him on the weight bench, my shoes getting left behind me like detritus. My work bag follows.

"Daaamn," I say appreciatively, eyes sweeping over Teddy's form. He's doing bench presses, his tank top decently soaked with sweat. His legs are spread, thick thighs on display as his arm muscles pop. "Honey, I'm horny. *Home.* I'm home."

He snorts.

"Is that safe to do alone?" I ask, grabbing a chair from the island so I can watch.

He sets the barbell in its cradle before sitting upright and giving me his full attention. "I keep the weights low when I'm at home, so yes, it's safe."

I nod. "Uh-huh, uh-huh. So you don't need a spotter?"

His lips twitch. "You want to spot me?"

"I want to do *something* to you," I mutter as my eyes catch on a piece of paper on the countertop. "Hey, what's this?"

Teddy answers as I pick it up. "Marriage license. It just arrived."

Holy shit.

I skim through, reading aloud. "—join in lawful wedlock Theodore Maxwell Lavoie and Kipling Delaney...*Lavoie?*" I clear the squeak from my throat and try again. "Kipling De-laney Lavoie, né Mercer."

We're both quiet for a moment.

"I took your last name?" I finally ask.

"Seems so," Teddy says quietly.

My mouth opens and closes a few times. How drunk was I?

I have the briefest flash of memory. The back of the club. Teddy's hand in mine. The words, *"I will keep you."*

It flits away like smoke.

"I'm sorry," I whisper.

I don't realize Teddy has moved until he's standing right in front of me, smelling like a decadent mix of man and sweet vanilla. "What for?"

"For…all this," I say, waving my hand at the marriage license but meaning *everything*. "For fucking up your life and stealing your name, and just—*fuck*. Dragging you into my mess."

"I thought we covered this already," he says calmly, his fingers in my hair pulling me around to face him. "You didn't drag me into anything. And you aren't fucking up my life."

"I'll get it changed," I whisper, unable to look away from those deep brown eyes. "I'll give you back your name."

"Kipp," he says softly, shaking his head. He opens his mouth but closes it again before letting me go. I try my best not to mourn the loss, but it feels a little like I'm a boat that's just been unmoored. "It's not a legal name change. You'd have to file paperwork with the Social Security Administration. You're okay."

"Oh," I say, wondering why the hell I'm so disappointed by that. "So I'm still a Mercer?"

There's a pause before he says, "Yes, you are."

"Okay. Well, there's that, at least," I mutter, blowing out a breath. "Guess the pictures weren't wrong, though, huh? We really did tie the knot."

"Guess so," Teddy says.

"Who, um…who's John Elvis?" I ask, pointing at our witness.

Teddy snorts. "I'm guessing we got married with an Elvis impersonator."

I groan. "I can't believe my memories of this are gone. If we ever get married again, we're recording the whole thing."

It only takes me a second to realize what I said.

"Not that we'd get married again," I hasten to add. "Or if we did, it wouldn't be at a Vegas chapel. It'd probably be somewhere understated but nice, like near the mountains at sunset. That'd be a pretty backdrop, you know? And holy shit, I swear I'm not planning our second wedding."

Teddy chuckles, which is good because otherwise I'd be very concerned about getting tossed out on my ass. The man is definitely a saint for putting up with me.

"You want an outdoor wedding?" he asks, his fingers tracing over the shell of my ear.

I swallow. "I haven't actually thought much about it." *Lies.*

He hums, his hand falling away. "Maybe next time."

What?

"What, Teddy?" I call after the man who's now halfway down the hall. "Teddy! You can't honestly tell me you'd marry me twice. You've met me. You know my red flags. Every single one of them." I pause to consider. "I think."

He chuckles loudly. A second later, the shower comes on.

Fuck.

Why the hell does my husband have to be so damn charming?

And why the hell don't I want him to stop?

Chapter 13

Teddy

"Daddy."

Silence.

"Daddy. Daddy. *Daddy.*"

I press my lips together tight.

"I can see you smiling," Kipp says. "Just because your eyes are closed, that doesn't mean you're invisible."

I do my best not to laugh, I really do, but a snort sneaks out.

"Aha!" Kipp cries triumphantly. "You're awake."

"What do you want, brat?" I ask, peeling an eye open.

Kipp is sitting on the bed next to me, dressed and ready for work. He gives me a grin. "I made you breakfast."

"You did?" I ask, not having expected that.

He nods, grin widening. He looks so damn proud of himself that my chest swells about two sizes bigger. "You mentioned taking care of each other," he says. "When, uh, we were in the shower."

Oh, I remember. Based on Kipp's sudden blush, so does he.

"And, anyways, I liked that," he goes on. "I want to do nice things for you, too, to show you how much I appreciate you taking me in like a stray dog."

"You're not a stray dog," I say with a chuckle, sitting up.

"Well, no," he agrees. "I don't piss on you. Not that I *want* to piss on you. Christ, I don't know why everyone thinks that."

"Who's everyone?" I ask a little warily.

He waves me off. "Breakfast isn't much, but I make a mean pancake, if I do say so myself. I put blueberries in them because you seem to like being healthy or whatever. Which, solid choice, I guess. Have you seen you? And I ran into the market on the way home from my run to grab syrup. The *good* kind 'cause I swear to God, Teddy, for being Canadian, your choice in maple syrup is deplorable. What?"

I grab Kipp by the back of the neck and haul him in for a kiss. He makes a surprised noise but melts instantly, tasting of maple syrup and something uniquely *him*.

"What was that for?" he asks when I let him go.

For making me pancakes? For calling this *home*? For being so damn sweet it's impossible to keep my walls up?

"Do I need a reason to kiss you?" I ask instead.

His smile is decadent. "No. Kiss me anytime. Very pro kissing."

As if I could forget.

Kipp stands as I swing out of bed, his eyes dropping to my crotch. A groan follows. "*Dude.*"

I snort. "Not your dude."

"Your dick is just *right there*, goddamn happy to see me, by the looks of it."

I tug on a pair of briefs, and Kipp makes an unhappy sound.

"That's oppression," he says. "And suffocation. Can the poor guy even breathe?"

"You want to give him mouth-to-mouth resuscitation?" I ask, lips twitching. I pull on jeans next.

"Uh, yes," Kipp says. "Obviously. But *someone* won't let me. My husband is a cruel man."

"Your husband wants to try your pancakes."

"Oh, right!" he says, heading for the door. He pauses as I start to follow him. "You're not going to put on a shirt? You know what? Never mind. Stupid question. In fact, I've heard eating in the nude is a really great—"

"*Kipp.*"

"Yep."

I shake my head, smiling as Kipp walks ahead of me into the kitchen. He pulls out my chair, looking damn giddy as he does so. There's one plate set out on the counter, a couple pancakes on top. They're perfectly golden and dotted with blueberries having turned purple around the edges as they cooked.

"You're not joining me?" I ask.

"Can't," Kipp says, checking the time on his phone. "I have to get going, like, now."

"Okay," I say, pouring the syrup over my pancakes. Kipp doesn't make a single move to leave, only stands less than a foot away, staring at me as I cut into my meal. I bring a bite to my mouth and give an approving moan. Kipp wasn't kidding. He makes a mean pancake.

"Good?" he asks quietly, eyes on my lips.

"Mhm. Perfect. Thank you."

"Yeah," he breathes, eyes still on my mouth.

I make a show of my next bite, groaning low as I pull the fork tines from between my lips. Kipp's mouth pops open. "So. Good," I say slowly.

He exhales. "Yeah."

"You okay?" I ask, licking some syrup off my thumb.

Kipp whimpers.

"Don't you have to go?" I remind him, enjoying this *far* too much.

"Do I, though?" he whines.

I hum. "I think so."

He groans. "Then you've gotta stop making porn noises, Teddy. I mean, *Christ*, how am I supposed to walk away when, at any moment, you're bound to invite your lonely neighbor in who needs a cup of sugar, you'll say *sorry, no sugar, sugar, but I've got syrup*, he'll say *swell*, and then you'll rail him against the counter while he jerks himself off with the *good* dark amber syrup that you should have had stocked in your fridge in the first place? You really expect me to miss that?"

It takes me a moment to respond, so many different thoughts cycling through my head. One stands out the most. "Why wouldn't it be you?"

"Pardon?" Kipp asks, looking dazed.

"Why wouldn't I be railing *you* in this fantasy?"

"Because it's porn," he says, like it's obvious. "Porn isn't real life. It's fiction. And you would never treat me with anything but honesty."

The way my breath punches from my lungs.

"You're right, though," he says, grabbing his keys off the counter. "I do need to go. I'm probably already going to be a few minutes late, which, not a big deal, but still." He leans in and smacks a kiss against my cheek. "Enjoy your orgasm pancakes, honey. Later."

And then he's out the door.

I sit there for a long minute, reeling. *"And you would never treat me with anything but honesty."*

When I finish my thoughtfully made breakfast, I clean up and pull out my notes for Phillip's case. I'm hoping his landlord will agree to a settlement, but whether or not we take him to court, Phillip shouldn't have to remain in that building. It takes most of the morning to find a suitable alternative: an apartment with similar cost of rent in an area that would be safe enough for an eighteen-year-old kid. I make an appointment with the realtor to check it out this afternoon.

When I call Scott to make sure I'm not overstepping, he insists I'm not and that it's a good idea. He also says he'll join me for the viewing.

"You don't have to," I tell him.

"I know that, but if the idea comes from me, Phillip might be more agreeable to moving. This way, I can say I checked out the place and approved," he says, which I can't really argue.

And that's how I find myself inside a shoebox apartment a few hours later with Scott and the realtor, Allison.

"It's small," Scott points out.

"So was his last place," I note. I looked up the building online.

He nods, walking around the tiny living space and peeking out the window. "Decent neighborhood."

"It is," Allison puts in, a collection of information about the apartment on a clipboard in her hands. "Low crime rate, lots of older couples nearby or families starting out. Are you shopping for your son?"

"Not quite," Scott says, leaving it at that. "Would you be able to hold the place for twenty-four hours while we make a decision?"

"I can do that," Allison agrees before handing off a pile of papers.

We thank her, the three of us heading out of the building. Allison gets in her car with a wave and drives off.

"You'll check with Phillip?" I ask.

Scott nods, rubbing his hand over his mouth. "Yeah, as long as you don't mind. It's not that I want to steal your thunder, but he knows me. I think he'll listen if I suggest he get out of his current place."

"It might not be safe for him there," I say. The landlord hasn't threatened Phillip directly, but his words and actions are not congruent with a kindhearted man. There's no telling what he might do when we serve him papers.

Scott nods quickly. "No, I know. Which is why I'm glad you thought of this. I'll let you know what Phillip says."

I nod, checking the time. "Are you heading back to the community center?"

"Nah, no point. I'd just turn around and go home. Want to grab a bite?"

I consider it. "We could do that, so long as you don't mind me inviting my husband. Or you could come back to my place and I'll cook us something."

"Well, shit, let's do that," he says, clapping me on the shoulder. "I'm not one to turn down a homemade meal. Lead the way?"

I nod, and after texting Scott my address just in case, we get into our respective vehicles. Kipp isn't home yet when we arrive, and I show Scott around, giving him a brief tour of the apartment. He walks the living area with an appraising eye.

"This is nice," he says. "Love the black-and-white artwork."

"Thanks. Most are pictures from Quebec."

He hums.

"Want a drink?" I ask.

"Sure," he says. "Anything's fine. I'm not fussy."

I grab a couple beers and hand one over before looking through the pantry. "How do you feel about pork chops and sweet potatoes?"

He doesn't have a chance to answer before Kipp walks through the door, a wide grin on his face. "Honey, I'm—" He cuts off when he sees Scott. "Oh. I'm not interrupting a sugar exchange, am I? Hi, I'm Kipp."

I huff a laugh as Scott walks forward, accepting Kipp's hand with a quizzical expression.

"Kipp, this is Scott from the community center I told you about," I say, offering introductions. "He's here for dinner. Not sugar. Scott, my husband, Kipling Lavoie."

Yeah, I have no clue why I added that last part, and by Kipp's widening eyes, neither does he. But fuck it. I like the sound of my name attached to his.

"Well, damn," Scott says, letting go of Kipp's hand. "Teddy, you didn't tell me your husband is a damn *GQ* model."

Kipp's grin widens. "Oh, I like him. And just Kipp is fine. Tell me, Scott, have you ever spotted Teddy in a singlet?"

Oh Lord.

Scott's amused face turns my way. "There's a story here."

"There's really not," I assure him, grabbing a beer for Kipp. I twist the cap before handing it his way.

"Thanks," he says, planting a kiss on my cheek before taking a seat at the island with his drink. He pats the chair next to him for Scott, who accepts the invitation. "Here's the thing. I'm half-convinced my husband is a superhero. But I don't know where he stores the spandex."

Scott barks a laugh. I just shake my head, grabbing the pork chops from the fridge.

"I've never seen him in spandex," Scott says. "But there was Halloween a few years back."

Kipp perks up. "Tell me."

"He came to the party at the community center dressed as Aquaman. *Momoa* Aquaman."

Kipp nearly spits out his beer. "Holy fuck," he breathes.

Scott laughs again. "Totally rocked the vibe, minus the long hair. Did you never show him pictures?" he asks me.

Kipp's eyes meet mine, wide and unblinking blue. "Teddy. Teddy, are there pictures?"

"Christ," I mutter, lips twitching as I pull out my phone. I find my one and only picture from the event and flip the screen Kipp's way.

"Sweet baby Jesus," he mutters. "Why do you look *wet?*"

"Broke a couple hearts that night," Scott says, an almost wistful tone to his voice.

"Probably broke a couple dicks, too," Kipp puts in rather inappropriately, to which Scott laughs. "You realize you likely have a standing role in many guys' spank banks, right? I mean, especially considering..."

Kipp trails off, eyes flaring wide as he realizes what he almost let slip—my job at Elite 8 Studios. Although, in truth, I wouldn't mind Scott knowing.

Scott simply makes a *pft* sound. "I'm well aware Teddy works in porn."

"You are?" both Kipp and I ask at once.

Kipp looks relieved. "Thank fuck. Not my fault," he says, hands raised.

Scott huffs a laugh.

"You never said anything," I say to Scott.

He shrugs. "Neither did you, which is why I didn't bring it up. But c'mon, Teddy. I run a queer community center. Someone recognized you the second time you stopped by. I had to explain that yes, that meeting in my office was strictly professional."

Kipp snorts before covering his mouth. "Sorry," he mumbles.

"I hope that hasn't caused issues for you," I say seriously.

Scott gives me a look. "You know we're a 'no judgment' zone. You're a good person, and that's all that matters."

"The best," Kipp puts in.

Well, shit. I shake my head, cutting up the sweet potatoes for dinner.

"So, Kipp," Scott says, moving on from that minor bombshell. "Teddy tells me you guys knew each other for a while before you got together. What precipitated the change?"

Oh boy.

Kipp's smile spreads slowly across his face, his eyes meeting mine for a drawn-out moment. "Well, you see," he says theatrically, "like any good story, it began with a crown of dicks."

Chapter 14
Kipp

"I like him," I tell Teddy, turning the lock on the door now that Scott has left. "Seems like a good guy."

Teddy shakes his head, although there's a smile on his face. "You just had to tell him about us getting blackout drunk, didn't you?"

"Hey, I didn't say it was our wedding night," I defend, sure that has to count for something. "Move over. I'm doing dishes."

Teddy steps aside without complaint, wiping his hands before crossing his arms across his rather nice chest.

"What?" I ask, sensing his gaze on the side of my head.

"You're quite enchanting, you know."

I nearly drop the plate I'm holding. "What? *Enchanting*?"

"You are," he says around a chuckle, taking a step closer. My blood pressure shoots up. "You had Scott wrapped around your finger practically from the moment you met. Same as me."

"I don't..." Teddy isn't wrapped around my finger, is he? That's preposterous. He barely *acknowledged* me for over a year.

"And I've seen the way you charm others. *Men*," he says, his words a touch on the hard side, even though I can tell he didn't mean for them to be.

"You've been watching me?" I ask quietly, staring at the soap bubbles on my hands.

"Would that bother you?" he asks, another step closer.

It feels like a hot stone has been dropped into my gut, the sensation not at all unpleasant. "No," I whisper.

He hums, so close I can feel the vibration. "Good thing none of them can have you. Isn't that right, sweetheart?"

Ungh.

"Words," he whispers, lips brushing my ear.

"None of them," I reply, my voice hoarse.

Teddy squeezes my neck. And then he walks away.

I spin my head to follow his departure. "Where are you going?" I ask, trying not to sound indignant.

"Bed," he answers. "It's late."

"It's not *that*—oh."

Teddy chuckles from down the hall, and I wash dishes faster than I've ever washed dishes before.

When I get to the threshold of the bedroom, only *slightly* out of breath, Teddy is in the en suite. I run across the hall, freshening up in the other bathroom at superhuman speeds, and then I shuck out of my clothes, nearly tripping on my way to the bed. By the time I'm half-under the sheets, my heart is pounding.

Teddy comes out from the bathroom and spots me immediately, his eyebrow twitching up the tiniest bit. I try to play it cool.

"Hey," I say, up-nodding.

He stifles a laugh, grabbing my shirt off the floor and walking slowly to the closet. He drops it in his hamper, followed by his own shirt. His pants come off next and get carefully hung up. His briefs stay on.

I'm pretty sure I'm about to find out if spontaneous human combustion is real.

Teddy takes his time as he comes over to the bed, an effortless swagger to his step. When he slides under the sheet and pulls out a book from the shelving on the headboard, I gape.

"Teddy?"

"Mm?"

Is he seriously *reading* right now?

"Um," I say slowly. "What'cha doing?"

And why isn't the answer me*?*

"This is a good book," he says, opening his arm in invitation. "I'm just going to finish this chapter before bed."

What. The. *Fuck.*

"Come on," he says, waving me in, as if *cuddles* are what I want right now. Which, okay, maybe they wouldn't be *bad*. But still. This is not what I thought was happening, and my dick hasn't gotten the memo to cool the fuck down.

Deciding that *okay*, if Teddy wants to cuddle, he can feel exactly how *excited* I am to cuddle, I roll into him, head in the crook of his arm, my leg thrown over his and my dick poking his hip. I make sure to give a little wiggle, so there's no way he can miss my bare, hard-as-hell *excitement* on his body.

He smirks. *Smirks.*

Well, *fine*. If he's going to be like that...

The moment my hand slides toward my dick, Teddy's arm tightens around me. "Don't you dare," he says in that low, calm voice, never once looking away from his book.

"Teddy, what—"

My follow-up dies on my tongue as Teddy's gaze turns my way. "Did I say you could touch, doll?"

Oh shit. *Shit.* Teddy is in *Daddy mode.*

I feel momentarily faint as all of my blood rushes south. I manage to shake my head the tiniest bit. "No."

"That's right," he says, eyes back on his book. "I take care of you, remember?"

My *yes* is a garbled moan.

"So be a good doll and keep me warm while I finish this," he says, turning the page with his thumb.

My heart pounds heavily as I try to decode his meaning. "Um, what, uh..."

Teddy switches his book to the hand near my shoulder, keeping a hold of it as he grabs my hand that's resting on his chest. He moves it slowly down his abdomen—happy trail bristling my palm—and under the band of his briefs. When we reach the base of his cock, I grip instinctually, and Teddy hums, letting go.

"Good doll."

Holy fucking hell.

I swear I almost come. I've never—*never*—had anyone talk to me the way Teddy does. So *sure.* So in control. So confident I'll do whatever he asks me to, as if he truly does *own* me. That's what he said he wants, isn't it? That's what he meant that night at the club.

"I don't want to fuck you, Kipp. I want to own you."

Well, mission accomplished. Shouldn't that scare me? Because all it feels like is the most amazing hug. Like strong, warm arms wrapped around me, cocooning me from the rest of the world. Protecting me.

The sound of Teddy flipping another page in his book is like a paintbrush caressing my skin. It sends a shiver down my spine, my hand squeezing Teddy's cock reflexively. *Fuck.* I'm holding his cock. Just holding it. Why is that so goddamn hot?

The minutes feel like hours as Teddy makes me wait. Delayed gratification, maybe? I've never been very patient, but I've also never been so damn hard in my life, so maybe there's something to it.

When Teddy's fingers start stroking through my hair, I realize his book is gone, back on the shelf behind him. I must've zoned out. I meet his gaze, that molten brown, seeing nothing but approval there. It's like static settling over my skin, a pleasant buzz. Teddy nudges me onto my back, rolling over my body. My hand never leaves his cock.

"None of them get to have you," he repeats, fingers tightening in my hair like he's holding a leash. "Tell me again, doll."

"None of them," I answer, my heart flitting, my mind calm. "I only want you."

Teddy grins, and then he's kissing me. He plucks my hand off his cock, putting it above my head. He collects the other, too, holding both of my wrists tight in his grip as he rubs against me, dick on dick.

As Teddy gets us off—whispering sweet words all the while about how I'm his precious babydoll, how I'm so perfectly good for him, how I'm beautiful and *his*—I float off into space.

"It'll be okay," Teddy assures me for the billionth time, his gaze finding mine in the mirror.

We're meeting my parents in an hour.

I finger brush some product into my hair, trying to tame the strands. "My hair is getting too long."

Teddy steps up behind me, dipping his lips to the back of my neck. I close my eyes, heat and comfort following his touch.

"I like your hair," he murmurs.

"Like holding it," I shoot back.

I open my eyes to find him smirking at me. Smug bastard.

"You look hot," I tell him because he does. He's wearing smart gray slacks and a salmon-colored button-down that I'm fairly sure is a statement for my family. A *yes, I'm a man who likes men and wears pink—got a problem with that?* I approve wholeheartedly.

"You look good, too," he says, eyes raking over me in a way that has my dick perking.

"Yeah?" I say with a grin. "Wanna show me how much? We could stay here and—"

Teddy smacks my ass, the sound a sharp echo in the bathroom as he leans close. "Behave."

And then he walks out the door.

Ungh.

"Ted-dy," I moan, adjusting my dick. "That was *mean.*"

"But are you still thinking about your hair?" he calls.

"No," I grumble, wriggling my hips. "I'm thinking about my husband's big-as-fuck hands."

My phone pings on the counter. A text.

Nik: Doing okay?

I let out a breath, heading into the bedroom as I compile a response.

Me: Think so. Ask me again in a couple hours.

Nik: I wish you'd let them go.

I don't know how.

Nik: Text me if you need to bail.

Me: Thanks, but Teddy will be there to defend me. Have you seen the man? Pretty sure he could carry me away like a football.

Nik: I'm shaking my head. Good luck.

I pocket my phone, searching for a tie before I decide *fuck it*, I'm not wearing a tie. It's just dinner with my ultra-conservative parents and outwardly homophobic brother. No big deal.

Christ.

"Kipp?" Teddy says softly, standing in the doorway.

"Yeah, I'm ready," I tell him, trying to believe it.

Teddy and I load into his car, him driving. The restaurant I asked my family to meet us at is all the way across town. I wanted the distance.

"Would you tell me a little about them?" Teddy asks.

I groan but nod. It's only fair. "Yeah, so I came out when I was sixteen. It just wasn't really an option for me not to. I knew they weren't going to react well, but you've seen me. I'm a *what you see is what you get* kind of guy."

Teddy huffs quietly.

"I ended up blurting it over dinner one night," I tell him. "My brother, Vaughn, is two years older than me. He looked about ready to kick me in my face. My parents were calmer, but they were just *oozing* disapproval. That was the first time they told me I had to make better choices."

"Better choices," Teddy parrots, shaking his head. He doesn't sound happy.

"Yeah, I know," I mutter. "They *do* think it's a choice, being gay. Or queer. Or anything remotely non-heteronormative. My dad told me to lock it down tight, and my mom enrolled me in a youth group at our church."

"And Vaughn?" he asks.

"Yeah. He basically just started being a dick to me. All the time. Hasn't stopped, really."

Teddy takes a turn, his movements calm even as his eyes look flintier than usual. "When did you move out?"

"They moved, actually. We came to Nevada when I was fifteen for my dad's job. He's a pilot for a private jet company, and they wanted him here. That's how I met Niko. I was the new kid at school, and he took one look at me and ushered me under his wing. I think he could tell I was part of the alphabet mafia, you know? We stick together."

"Yeah, we do," Teddy says with a small smile.

"Anyways, my family, Vaughn included, moved back to Indiana while I was in college. *That* was an argument, let me tell you."

"They wanted you to go?" he asks, braking at a red light and giving me his focus.

"Well, yeah," I say with a shrug. "I think they just wanted to keep an eye on me. Make sure I wasn't *straying too far from the path*. But..." I shake my head. "There was no way I was going back. I made a life here. Had friends here and was *open* here, even if my family never knew about that part of my life. Maybe it was cowardly, but at that point, I just... I stopped talking to them about anything real. I played nice, and then once they left, I avoided seeing them whenever I could."

It was easier. I could pretend we were still a normal, happy family when I didn't have to see the hateful looks in their eyes.

"But now they're here," Teddy says.

"Now they're here," I agree.

"Well," he says, reaching over and snagging my hand, twining his fingers with mine. "Whatever happens, I'll be in your corner."

I blink a few times, looking out the window and willing my voice to come out even. "Thanks, Teddy."

He hums softly.

We pull up to the restaurant with five minutes to spare, and I start sweating immediately. "They've never seen me like this," I mumble.

"Like what?" Teddy asks.

"*Gay*. Outwardly gay."

He squeezes my hand, waiting for me to meet his eyes. "You've always been *you*, Kipp. If they couldn't see that, it's their loss."

Fuck.

"How do you want to play this?" he asks gently, never looking away. "Do you want me to keep some distance? Treat you like a friend? Because I can do that if you want. Or I can be the most adoring, loving husband a man could ever ask for."

It only takes me a moment to find my voice. "Be my husband, Teddy. I'm done hiding."

A smile curves his lips. "There you are. Let's do this, sweetheart."

"Yeah," I breathe out. "Let's go."

Chapter 15

TEDDY

Kipp walks into the restaurant with his head held high, but I can see the moment he catches sight of his family. He jolts slightly, his hand tightening in mine, and he tries to mask his emotions.

His worry still rings out loud and clear, though.

Kipp tells the hostess he sees our party, and I follow his lead as we walk their way. Their gazes find us one at a time. First, his mother, her eyes widening and flitting down to our clasped hands. Next, his father, his head turning and an immediate glower jumping onto his face. Last is Vaughn, Kipp's older brother. He looks *excited*, as if he gets off on making Kipp hurt. Maybe he does.

"Kipling," his mother says in a hushed tone the moment we reach the table. "Mind yourself. Anyone could see."

I assume she's referring to our scandalous hand-holding.

"I don't care if they see," Kipp says, his grip bruising as he takes a seat. I sit beside him, making sure my chair is close.

"Told you," Vaughn says with an air of haughty nonchalance unbecoming of a thirty-one-year-old. "He's not even trying to hide his indecencies anymore."

"*Boy*," Kipp's dad says sternly, seemingly unbothered by his other son's comment. "You will cease this nonsense at once."

"What nonsense?" Kipp says with a near-manic laugh. "Holding my husband's hand?"

He raises our joined hands above the table for emphasis, and his mom turns a little pale.

"We raised you better than this," she says quietly, her finger-tips against the necklace on her chest. "How could you...*defame* the holy bond of matrimony?"

"There's nothing unholy about being queer," I put in, figuring, at this stage, we're past the point of polite introductions. And honestly, Kipp's family is pissing me off.

Vaughn snorts as his father looks right through me.

"This was such a mistake," Kipp mutters under his breath.

"Are we ready to order?" a waitress asks.

"Another minute, please," I tell her, since everyone else at the table appears to be in a silent standoff.

She nods before quickly hustling away.

"Kipling," his mother says again, not even acknowledging me. "Were you coerced?"

"Coerced?" he asks in surprise.

She fidgets uncomfortably before holding her hand to her mouth, like maybe she thinks I won't hear her. "We want to help," she whispers. "If you were coerced, we can help you."

"Help me," Kipp repeats, his tone flat. He grabs his water off the table, downing it in three neat gulps.

"Yes," his mother says. "You can get an annulment if you were...*forced*."

"Oh my God," Kipp mutters, setting down his glass and dropping his head into his palm. "Holy shit."

"*Language*, boy," his father grits out. "You will not take the Lord's name in vain."

"Like he cares," Vaughn says, waving a hand dismissively. "The little fruit is obviously going to hell. What's blasphemy on top of it?"

I do my best to breathe through my sudden, overwhelming anger. *This* is Kipp's family. These are the people who are supposed to love and support him. They're the ones who should have his back, who should be accepting of the whole of him. Instead, they're only here to condemn him.

Kipp warned me. I just didn't expect...*this*.

But I suppose if anyone understands what it feels like for family to fail you when you need them most, it's me.

I squeeze Kipp's hand, trying to get his attention. He looks over at me, blue eyes devastated. Much to the audible horror of his family, I pluck his chin up from its downcast position and bring my lips to his. It's short, just a press of mouths. But Kipp's sigh makes it oh so worth it.

"Can I?" I ask, lips skimming his.

His eyes ping between my own for a brief second before he nods. Letting go of his chin, I turn to his family.

"Kipp is gay. That's part of who he is, not a choice. But even if it was, I'd be proud of him for choosing it. For loving a person who makes him happy, even in the face of those who'd disapprove. Do you know how hard it is being out? How much strength that takes, even in today's society?"

"Because it's unnatural," Vaughn says.

"It's not, actually," I reply. "There are plenty of species that exhibit homoerotic behavior."

His mom gasps.

"Your son is remarkable," I go on. "He's kind and sweet and wholly himself, and I couldn't be more happy to call him my husband. If you can't support that, maybe we should go.

No offense, but I already don't see family Christmases in our future."

I chance a glance Kipp's way. He's smiling at me, his eyes wet.

"You have no right being here," his dad cuts in, his voice low but undeniably laced with a threat. "You're not a part of this family."

"He's a part of mine," Kipp says, blowing out a breath. "And Teddy is right. We shouldn't have come."

Kipp slides his chair back, and his mom makes an aborted noise. His dad sets a hand on the table near Kipp, the *thump* of it stalling his departure.

"We never threw you out," he says, his blue eyes nothing like Kipp's. They're cold and harsh and uncaring. "We didn't abandon you because of your proclivities."

Kipp sighs tiredly. "That's not the ringing endorsement you seem to think it is, Dad."

"We tried to help you," he goes on. "You should be grateful that we care."

Kipp takes a second to look at his family, one at a time. Finally, he says, "Caring shouldn't hurt so much."

I don't hesitate to stand the moment Kipp does, and together, we walk out of the restaurant. Vaughn lobs an insult at our backs, but I ignore it, my chest bursting with pride. Kipp makes it all the way into the car, strong and solid and sure, before he finally cracks. The moment the doors shut, his hands land on the dash in front of him, and he takes in a shuddering breath. "*Fuck.*"

"All right?" I ask, gripping the back of his neck.

He shakes his head, even as he says, "Yeah. I don't... I don't know what I was expecting. Part of me thought, just maybe, they were going to be happy for me? That they wanted to come meet you because you were someone important to me? Or so they would have thought," he says quickly.

I give his neck a squeeze. "I know what you mean," I say, not wanting to linger on the tenuous validity of our marriage.

"But...they only wanted to make sure you hadn't, like, brainwashed and kidnapped me. Which—sorry about that. *Fuck*." He lets out a shaky sigh. "They're never going to be proud of me, are they?" he asks, meeting my gaze. "No matter what I do, they won't support me. They won't approve of me being gay."

"I don't think so," I tell him truthfully, slipping my hand up into his hair. He closes his eyes, hanging his head between his arms. "But you don't need their approval."

"I know," he whispers. "I just wanted it."

"I know, sweetheart."

He huffs a small sound, leaning into my touch as I lightly scratch his scalp. "Fuck, that feels good. You always make me feel good, Teddy."

My heart tries to take flight. "How about you let me take you home, then," I say. "I can make you feel real good."

"Yeah?" he says, turning his head. A smile settles on his lips. "That was cheesy, I hope you know. But hell yeah. Let's do that."

A slap on the window has the both of us turning. "I hope it's worth it," Vaughn says through the glass, his face an ugly, twisted facsimile of the man beside me. "I hope you enjoy spreading your legs for this asshole, you ball-less bitch."

"Dude," Kipp calls back. "I'm not spreading my legs for an asshole. I'm spreading them for a dick. Get your goddamn facts straight."

Vaughn slaps the window again before backing up and making a lewd gesture at his crotch.

"And you bet your ass it's worth it!" Kipp yells.

Vaughn flips him off as he walks away.

"Jesus," I mutter. "He's a charmer, isn't he?"

Kipp's laugh is devoid of humor. He plunks his head back against his seat, turning to face me. "He doesn't get it. He thinks one of us has to be the 'woman' in the relationship. Guess he decided it's me."

"You know that's bullshit, right?" I can't help but say.

Kipp rolls his eyes. "Of course I do, Teddy. Not only is his implication that women are lesser downright archaic and misogynistic, but being a man or a woman or any combination or absence of the two has nothing to do with what someone chooses to do in the bedroom. Gender isn't a status, a box to check, or a certain standard to live up to. It's whatever it means to each individual person. I'm proud to be a man who takes it up the ass. There's no goddamn shame in that."

"You," I say slowly, "are quite possibly the most magnificent creature I have ever met."

His smile is instantaneous, lighting up his whole face. It dims quickly, however. "Teddy, I'm sorry. After all that... I guess there wasn't really a reason for us to stay married, was there? We should've just gotten the annulment in the first place. Not because I was *coerced*, obviously, but..." He shakes his head. "We can get divorced now if you want. This whole idea was stupid."

I bite back my instinctual response that I don't *want* a divorce. That none of this is stupid. That it feels terrifyingly, utterly real. Because how could I admit that? We've been pseudo-together for mere weeks, and I'm the one who implied this needed to stay casual. That sex between us would be only that, and when we *did* get a divorce, we'd be done. I had to. I had to try to keep up some semblance of a wall between me and Kipp.

But this isn't casual. Not for me. And I can't try to convince myself otherwise anymore. So, no. I don't want a divorce. I want more time. But that might not be what Kipp wants.

"If you want me to get the paperwork started, I can do that," I tell him softly. "But there's no rush. You should probably at *least* wait until you're thirty to get divorced, don't you think?"

Kipp huffs a laugh, his smile back. "Yeah, I think you're right. I'm way too young to be a divorcé. I should get over the hill first."

"I think that's forty."

"Well, shit," he says. "I think you're stuck with me for a while, then."

I bark a laugh, but damn if that doesn't sound perfect.

Kipp lets out a small sigh. "Take me home, Teddy?"

There's only one answer to that. "Happy to."

Letting Kipp go, I start the car and get us on the road. When we arrive back at the apartment, I divert to the kitchen with the intent of starting something for dinner, considering we walked out on our meal. Kipp heads straight into the living room, sprawling onto the couch. He lays his head on his arm, and my chest aches. He looks so dejected.

"Okay?" I ask.

He nods, but there's a frown on his face. "I'm just..." He doesn't finish his sentence.

"It's okay to be upset, Kipp. They're your family. That had to have hurt."

"Yeah," he says, voice small.

I abandon dinner plans and head his way, sitting near his feet and removing his shoes.

"Sorry," he mumbles. "Forgot."

"It's fine," I assure him, setting his shoes on the area rug before climbing over his body. I settle myself at his back, hand on his chest. "What do you need?"

Not all that surprisingly, Kipp presses his ass back against my crotch. "You made promises."

I huff a laugh. "That I did. Need me to take care of you, doll?"

"Yeah. Yes. *Please*. Can you..."

"What is it?" I ask, sliding my hand downward, toying with the buttons on Kipp's shirt.

He blows out a breath. "I sent you my STI results at lunch."

I hold back my groan, but just barely. "Yes, you did."

"Can you fuck me?"

My eyes slip closed, my nose resting against Kipp's hair.

"Please don't say no," he whispers.

That hook in my chest pulls unbearably tight as I glide my hand up to Kipp's neck, grabbing his chin and turning his face toward me. "I'm not going to say no, babydoll. Not ever. I told you I'd take care of you, and I will. But we're not doing it here."

He nods in my grip, and I let him go.

"Bedroom," I say. "C'mon."

Kipp slides off the couch, and taking his hand, I lead him to our room. He looks so lost, his usual pluck absent. Despite his request, I know it's not just sex he needs tonight. So when he reaches for the buttons on his shirt, I make a sound to stall him. He stills, eyes catching mine.

"Sit down," I tell him.

He does, waiting at the edge of the bed with his legs apart and his hair in a floppy brown mess around his head. I walk over, raking my fingers through the strands until Kipp is looking up at me.

"Who do you belong to?" I ask.

His mouth pops open. "You."

"That's right," I coo. "You're *my* doll. So whose job is it to undress you?"

His chest rises and falls. "Yours?"

"You're catching on, sweetheart."

Kipp's eyelids feather closed for a moment before those bright blue eyes latch back onto mine. He looks dazed, gorgeous, *perfect*. I understand why Kipp tended toward being the dominant partner in his past relationships. It's all he knew.

But at his core, Kipp longs to let go. He wants to be the one being taken care of and being taken apart. He wants to be praised and loved and doted on.

And he won't find anyone better suited to that job than me.

I let my fingers fall from Kipp's hair, reaching for his shirt and freeing his buttons one at a time. "I need you to pick a safeword tonight, doll."

His breath hiccups. "What? Why?"

The backs of my fingers brush his chest as I open his shirt. I can feel his rabbit heart racing.

"Because..." I say slowly. "Before I fuck you, I'm going to spank you."

Chapter 16

Kipp

It takes a moment for my brain to reboot. I can practically hear the whir of it coming back online, and then Teddy's words register.

"But..." I say slowly. "I thought..."

"It's not a punishment, sweetheart," Teddy says, seemingly understanding my confusion. "Not in the least. Why would I punish you? You're perfect. My perfect, beautiful doll."

My chest warms, a bright pulse of light, even as my brain struggles to catch up.

Teddy pulls my shirt from my pants and opens the last button. "It's to help you relax. If you don't like it, we'll stop. I promise."

I have no doubt of that. The idea of Teddy forcing me to do anything I don't want is laughable. "But you think I'll like it," I say.

Teddy nods, sliding my shirt down my arms, his fingertips leaving goosebumps in their wake. "You will," he says, utterly confident.

"Why, um... Why do I need a safeword? We haven't done that before."

Teddy nods once before crouching. He unbuttons and unzips my pants, tapping my hip until I rise up enough for him to tug the material down. "If you ever say no or stop, I will stop. I need you to trust that."

"I do." Not even a question.

He slips off my socks one at a time, the act far more sensual than it has any right to be. "But sometimes," he says, kissing the inside of my knee, "it might be difficult for you to vocalize if you're feeling too overwhelmed to continue. You might not want to disappoint me. And Kipp, you won't ever disappoint me. Okay? Not ever. Even if you tell me no."

I swallow, nodding, the use of my real name making me feel like Teddy means outside of sex, too. Like, somehow, he's saying I could *never* disappoint him.

He watches me for a moment, and then he kisses my other knee. "But a safeword might be easier for you to say. It doesn't sound like stop, but it means the same thing. Could you pick one for me?"

"Bananas."

He huffs a laugh, his breath ghosting over my thigh.

I chuckle with him. "I hate them," I explain, stomach tightening when Teddy drags his fingers to the band of my briefs. "You won't hear me uttering that word unless it means *no goddamn thank you.*"

"Bananas it is," he says. "Lift, doll."

I lift my hips, and Teddy pulls off my briefs. He hums as his eyes take me in, and a wicked smirk graces his lips. He stands and steps away, and I watch, stomach doing flips as he goes to the nightstand. He drops a condom, lube, and...a butt plug on the bed.

"First," he says calmly, walking back around to where I'm sitting, "I'm going to play with you. Because you're mine. Mine to play with. Mine to pleasure. Isn't that right?"

Fuck yes.

I clear my throat. "Yes."

"That's right, babydoll," he says, tugging my head to the side, the wide grip in my hair not hurting in the least. My pulse thunders. "You are *mine.* Mine to take care of. Mine to enjoy. Which means all you need to do is listen and be good for me. Think you can do that?"

Fuck. "Yes. I can do that."

"Good." Teddy guides my head back around, and, without hesitation, he crashes his lips into mine. The kiss is con-suming—*hungry*—and I whimper into it, my mind already spiraling away. *"I want to own you."* That's what he said.

I want that, too. I want to be *his.*

When Teddy lets me go, I nearly protest. But then his hand is landing flat on my chest, and he's shoving me onto my back. I haven't finished bouncing when Teddy drops to the floor between my legs. He tugs me forward until my ass is at the edge of the mattress, my knees spread wide to accommodate his bulk. I swallow heavily as his brown eyes meet mine.

"Now," he says coolly, "be a good doll for me and lie still. And once I'm done tasting you, I'll let you wear my handprint on your ass."

Oh... "*Fuck*," I shout as Teddy's tongue drags over my rim. He spreads my cheeks wide, that wet heat coming back in for another round. My back bows up, an unintelligible sound leaving my lips.

Rimming. Fucking rimming. It's my damn kryptonite.

Teddy grips me harder. "Still, doll."

Christ, I'm trying, but holy fuck. That tongue, soothing and prodding. That beard against my skin. It's too good. *Way* too good.

Teddy circles my dick, his hand squeezing tight. "Do you want my cock?"

"*Yes*," I groan out. Fuck, yes. *Please*. God.

"Then be still, babydoll, and let me get you ready with my tongue."

Fu-u-uck.

Teddy lets go of my cock, his thumbs pressing the insides of my thighs wider. He buries his face in my ass, licking me relentlessly, and *holy hell*, I try to be still, I really do, but my cock is twitching, my hips have a mind of their own, and I can't stop wriggling. Thank *fuck* he doesn't stop, but he does give my thigh a stinging slap that has my mind blanking with an *oh*. I go boneless a second later.

"There you go," he soothes, his hands trailing over my skin, his tongue lapping at me broadly. "Fucking gorgeous. Look at you spread out like the good doll you are."

Oh God.

Teddy kisses my asshole—*kisses* it with closed lips in a way that has me blushing and fighting the urge to writhe. And then wet fingers press against me.

"*Fuck*," I breathe. When did he even open the lube? The man's a master multi— "*Ahhh*."

Blunt fingers slide in, opening me up with an effortless glide. He curls them upwards. "Do you know why I'm going to plug you?" he asks.

I'd forgotten about that. I shake my head. Lick my lips. "No."

"Because..." He fucks his fingers in and out slowly as my legs tremble. "When my hand is hitting your ass, that plug will be kissing your prostate."

Oh, shit.

"It'll feel *good*, sweetheart. I promise. It'll sting until it doesn't, and you won't be able to think about anything else. But *that*," he says, removing his fingers, "is why you're going to love it."

I don't understand, not entirely, but I trust him. If it's too much, he'll stop. I know he will.

Teddy asked me once if I was getting what I needed from my past relationships. And the answer was no. I wasn't.

I want to know what's been missing.

"Show me?" I breathe.

"Oh, babydoll." The tip of the plug presses against me, and Teddy pushes. "It would be my genuine pleasure."

I breathe out as the plug settles inside my ass. It's no bigger than his fingers, but it's big enough to feel. The base is flared, keeping it in position as Teddy rises up off the floor. The look in his eyes has my entire body flushing hot, my cock throbbing.

This Teddy... This is the one who hides under the surface. It's the one with whip-sharp eyes and a cocky presence that makes it impossible to look away. It's the one who makes me feel as if I'm being hunted.

Is it too much to hope I'm his only prey?

Teddy climbs onto the bed and leans in to kiss me again, his hands in my hair, his presence big and safe and warm as he blankets me. When he pulls back, he catches my gaze. "Remember what I told you I like? What it is I want?"

It takes me a moment to figure out what he means. "You want to make me feel good."

"That's right, sweetheart. And I'm going to do that, okay?"

I nod, and with one final press of his lips to mine, Teddy tugs me upright. He maneuvers me without a word, his hands on me soft even as he flips me around as if I'm weightless. He settles me over his lap, and I have only a second to wonder why the fuck I like that so much when Teddy's palm smooths over my ass.

"You're beautiful, doll. Gorgeous, through and through. Your smile, your eyes, this silky soft hair."

His fingers thread into my hair as if to make his point. It's like a goddamn tension release button, and my muscles go lax as he tugs at the strands in a soothing manner.

"Utter perfection. You can come anytime. Okay?"

Come? While he's *spanking* me?

I don't have a chance to think on it before a loud *thwack* echoes throughout the air. It's like lightning before the thunder. Sharp and shocking and—

Oh, fuck. Holy fuck.

"Teddy?" I question. He wasn't kidding. That stings like a *motherfucker*, the ache of it spreading out like brushfire.

"I know, babydoll," he soothes. "Just try to relax."

Yeah, like those words ever work.

He slaps me again.

"Fuck, fuck, fuck," I mutter, my hips hitching up in the aftermath, my cock rubbing against his leg. "Jesus."

"Give it a minute, sweetheart," Teddy says, his hand caressing my ass cheek. "I promise it'll get better. I'm going to ease up now, but I won't stop this time. You remember your safeword?"

Fucking bananas. "Yep," I grit out. What did I tell Teddy? That I'd be the best sub he ever had? I'm starting to wonder at my commitment.

But then Teddy's fingers in my hair tug, a reminder that he's here, that he's got me, and I drop my cheek to the bed, closing my eyes and choosing to trust. It's just a little spanking, right? I can take that like a goddamn man.

As soon as I'm relaxed, there's another *thwack* against my ass. Teddy doesn't slow this time. He does another. And another, almost too fast for me to keep track of. It *is* gentler, but that doesn't seem to matter because the sting is *everywhere*. On my ass, my thighs, my cock, my balls, even. Without being aware of what I'm doing, I find myself grinding against Teddy's lap, trying to relieve the ache or ease the pressure or—I don't even *know*. When the next slap jostles the plug, I cry out, only to...

"*Fuuuck*," I groan, rubbing harder against Teddy's leg.

"There you go," Teddy coos. "Let yourself fall into it. My beautiful doll. Look at you."

"I..." *Words*.

Teddy smacks me again, and I moan. I *moan*. The ache blooms outward from the point of impact, radiating over my ass, *inside* my ass, to my stomach and cock like a wave of pleasured pain. I think... *Fuck*, I think I like it.

He slaps my ass again and again, all the while telling me how perfect I am. Praising me. Calling me beautiful. Telling me how gorgeous his handprint is on my skin. My fingers tangle in the bedsheets near my head, my entire body on fire, my soul caught in the flames. I start *craving* the hits. The way the plug jostles. That *burn* that licks over my skin. The way my cock throbs every time Teddy's palm greets my ass, as if the sensation is being shot up through my shaft. It's messed up, isn't it? Why the hell does it feel so *good*?

I don't know, don't even care. I lose track of everything except Teddy's hand. I stop flinching. Stop bracing. Every single hit is euphoric. A shot of pure bliss in my veins. I feel like I'm climbing. Like I'm reaching for some precipice, but I don't move a muscle to get there. I can't.

Is this what it's like to put every ounce of your trust into another person? To know they'll be there to take care of you no matter what?

I never want it to stop.

"Gorgeous, babydoll. You're *gorgeous*."

I think I moan as Teddy's palm runs over my skin. He smacks the top of my thigh, a *thwack* of beautiful, flashing sparks.

How long have we been doing this? Minutes? Days?

"You realize I'm never going to be able to let you go?" he says hoarsely, as if that's a bad thing. "You're mine, Kipling. You're fucking *mine*."

And when his palm connects with my ass again, I *fly*. It's an explosion so sweet it feels like I'm a million tiny butterflies, rocketing into the air, wings taking flight. It's a blasting apart of atoms, of my very composition. It's soaring and tumbling and cascading back together in a gentle, spiraling flow. It's knowing I'm not the same person as I was a short while ago. And being utterly okay with that fact.

I don't realize I'm crying until Teddy's thumb ghosts over my cheek. Don't even realize I came against his leg until he shifts me slightly and I feel the sticky evidence. I'm still dancing in the clouds, my tears like rain down my cheeks, cleansing and quiet. Teddy kisses my nose, and I smile. I fucking *smile*.

He shifts me onto my side, curling behind me, pulling a blanket up over our legs. He holds me and rubs my arm, the brush of his pants a reminder of my aching ass. I don't care. I cry, and it feels fucking *good*. Cathartic. I let out the pain of this shitty day. The hurt over my family's betrayal, time and time again. I let out the joy of knowing I'm safe here with Teddy. Safe and loved. *God*, I feel loved. I let the tears flow, and I don't feel an ounce of embarrassment. Not when Teddy is telling me I'm gorgeous. His perfect porcelain doll. *His*.

Did he know? Did he know I needed to cry like I needed air?

"It's their loss," he says quietly.

I nod, grabbing his hand and pressing it against my chest. It doesn't feel like a loss. Not right now.

"Are you feeling okay?" he asks before kissing the shell of my ear.

I nod again, having to clear my throat before speaking. "Thank you."

"Of course, sweetheart," he rasps, his arm tightening around me.

I wipe my cheek, feeling a little more like I'm on solid ground again. I kind of miss the clouds. "You, um...you didn't fuck me."

"Next time," he says gently.

"I can take it," I say a little indignantly, wiggling back against him and hissing when the material of his pants rubs my ass.

"Next time," he says again, kissing my neck. "This one hit you hard. And that's okay. It's really good, Kipp. You..." He blows out a breath, the rush of air tickling my skin. "I wish you could have seen yourself. How absolutely stunning you were. *Are.*"

My heart beats beneath his palm. "I didn't know. I had no clue I was like this. That I could want this."

"I know," he says gently, kissing my shoulder. "Thank you for letting me show you."

Fuck.

"That, um...was that the endorphin high you were talking about?" I ask. "When I felt all floaty?"

Teddy nods against my shoulder. "Yes. It's called subspace. You fell into it beautifully."

I swallow. Every time I'm with Teddy, I feel a little floaty. But this was *more.* "Am I going to crash now?"

"You're already back on Earth," he assures me. "And I'm going to hold you and feed you and look after you tonight to make sure you stay there with me, okay?"

"Yeah," I say, feeling my eyes well again. "Thank you."

"No thanks necessary," he says softly. "That's my job."

It takes me a moment to ask the question on my mind. "And you? You get something out of this?"

He leans his forehead against my neck, lips brushing my skin. "Yeah, sweetheart. I get a hell of a lot out of this."

"Okay," I whisper, so very relieved.

"Do you want me to remove the plug?" he asks, drawing my attention back to that very thing.

I pause, considering that. "Can it stay for a little while?"

He hums, the sound soft and light. "Yeah, it can stay."

I kind of like it. Frankly, I wish it were Teddy's dick instead, but this is nice, too.

"Maybe," Teddy says slowly, lips at my ear, "I could plug you some day before work. Then you could feel me while we're apart."

I suck in a breath.

"Every time it shifts and makes you hard," he says, "you could think about my fingers in your ass, getting you ready. Spreading you open and making you ache. And once you're home, I could bend you over, pull it out, fill you with my cock...because you're *mine*, isn't that right?...and then fuck you to my heart's content. And you'd take it, wouldn't you? You'd take it all like the good doll you are."

I wheeze a little.

"Is that a yes?" he asks, the lovely, smug bastard.

"Mm," I answer, the best I can do.

He chuckles against my ear. "Next time."

"All these *next times*," I croak out, turning my head. "You better make good on your promises, hubby. I know where you sleep at night, and I've been known to get a little randy when I don't get my way."

"Don't you worry," he says, lips brushing my cheek. "I've got you."

And that, I believe.

Chapter 17

TEDDY

"Doing okay?" I ask, lips twitching.

Kipp attempts to shoot me a glare. "*Fine*," he says, squirming a little.

"Mhm. Need more lotion?"

"You're *mean*," he says. "A very mean man who does very nice things to my body."

I chuckle, heading his way.

"What are you doing?" he asks warily, eyeing my hands like he's looking for the lotion I insisted on rubbing over his ass last night and again this morning.

"Let me see," I say.

"What? Teddy, *nooo*," he gripes, not actually objecting when I flip him onto his stomach. "This is humiliating, I'll have you know. I'm a grown man, and you're checking my ass."

"It's a very nice ass," I assure him, drawing his pants down carefully. My blood heats as I see the evidence of last night on his skin, even though the inflammation is minimal. He'll be good as new tomorrow.

Kipp cranes his neck, looking back at me. "Like the new color, do you?"

"Pink suits you."

He stifles a laugh, shoving his face against the couch and muttering, "*I'll suit your face.*"

I give his ass cheek a gentle kiss before pulling his pants back up. "Feeling okay?" I ask seriously, running my fingers up into his hair.

He lets out a sigh, turning his face. "Yeah, Teddy. Honestly? I feel *really good*. Relaxed. Like, I know I should be worried about what happened with my family, but I just can't find it in me to care. I guess I have you to thank for that."

I rub along the shell of his ear. "I'm sorry you've had to deal with their judgment, Kipp. I wish I could erase every mean word they've ever said to you."

He huffs a small laugh, his eyes slipping shut as I toy with his ear and neck. "Pretty sure a few more instances like last night and you'll have smacked every thought of them from my head by way of my ass. Which, you know, sounds weird. But my point stands."

"That can be arranged," I murmur as memories of last night assault me. Kipp laid out over my lap, squirming and flushed. His moans as the sensation shifted from pain to pleasure. How utterly perfect he was in his submission—in his *trust*—and the way he fell into subspace like he was meant to be there.

Kipp swallows, shifting slightly so he can see me. "Can you explain why I liked that? Because it hurt. But then..."

"Then it felt good," I fill in for him.

"Well, yeah," he says quietly.

I nod, running my hand over him. His leg, his side, anywhere I can reach. "Have you ever had a runner's high?"

He cocks his head slightly. "Um, yeah, I have."

"It's kind of like that," I explain. "When you experience prolonged physical or mental stress, your body releases endorphins to counteract the pain. It's a natural defense mechanism that helps you cope. In the case of impact play—like spanking—there's also adrenaline mixed in that heightens your body's stress reaction. You get a dump of those endorphins to balance that, and with enough repetition, it can give you a sort of natural high. Some people find it very therapeutic."

"Um, yeah," he says. "I can understand why."

I give his shoulder a rub. "My goal was never to hurt you," I tell him, wanting to make sure he understands that. "It was to help you past that threshold. You told me you have a low pain tolerance, so I kept the impact light."

"Seriously?" he says, an adorable pout on his lips. "That was light?"

"It was."

"Jesus," he mutters. "So basically, you're telling me I'm a wimp."

"No," I assure him, sliding over his body until he's lying flat underneath me, chest to chest. "You're perfect. *That* was perfect. And it won't be as bad next time because your body will know what to expect."

Kipp blinks up at me, slowly sliding his arms around my shoulders. "I'm not a dainty guy, Teddy. I've never been tossed around, never been handled the way you handle me. I didn't think it would be something I'd like. But you make me feel..."

He closes his eyes for a moment until I nudge his nose gently with my own.

"What?" I ask softly, my heart pounding like a drum.

He lets out the smallest of breaths. "You make me feel fragile in a way I've never allowed before. And I like it. A lot. Please don't break me."

Kipp's phone rings before I have a chance to answer him. It's like a gunshot piercing the air, and we both flinch. I sit up as

Kipp reaches for the device on the coffee table, his expression falling.

"I'm going to answer this," he mutters, bringing his phone to his ear. "Hello?"

I give Kipp's leg a squeeze as I stand up, offering him some privacy. He sighs into the phone as I make my way toward the kitchen.

"I know, Mom," he says quietly. "I *know*. But you have to understand, I can't help how I feel. And asking me to hide who I am and be miserable all my life isn't fair."

He's quiet for a minute, and I keep half an eye on him while I collect ingredients to make smoothies. He sits upright, wincing as he settles on his ass. When he runs his fingers through his hair, he stills and brings his hand out in front of his face. His expression—the way his eyes *soften* when he catches sight of his ring—has my heart pumping wildly.

I turn away, not knowing what my own face might be giving away should Kipp look at me.

"Yeah, I get it," he says, sounding defeated. "If that's how you feel, I can't change that. But I'm a grown man, Mom. I'm not under your roof anymore, and you and Dad don't get to decide how I live my life." There's a hum, and then, "Yeah. Okay. Bye."

Kipp lets out a sigh, the thunk of his phone on the coffee table following.

"All right?" I ask.

He nods slowly. "I guess?"

"What'd she say?"

Kipp leans back against the couch cushions, idly twisting his wedding band on his finger. "She implied it was very rude of me to talk back and then leave yesterday after they came all this way to see me. She said she's extremely disappointed by the choices I'm making. And she reiterated that they only want what's best for me, and *couldn't I try to see that?*" He makes a frustrated sound. "It's...fine. It is what it is. I think this whole thing was a long time coming. I just... I wasn't really expecting to tell them off last night. I don't know where that came from, to be honest."

I hum, dumping some yogurt into the blender. "I think, maybe, you were ready."

"Ready to lose my family?" he asks wryly.

"Ready to put yourself first," I counter.

And, just maybe, having me by his side gave him the bravery to do so. The thought warms me.

"I should call Niko," he says, sounding lost in thought.

"Sure. Want to do that now or after a walk?"

"Is that a thing now?" he asks, standing up and coming into the kitchen. "You taking me on walks? I'm pretty sure that's not my kink."

"No?" I ask, suppressing a smile. "You don't want to be a good pup for me?"

His brow furrows, like he's actually considering it. "I... No, definitely not."

I chuckle, popping the lid on the blender. "I'm glad. I'd much rather play with dolls."

Kipp's face reddens as the blender runs, two spots of rosy color rising on his cheeks. When it's quiet again, Kipp says, "*Dolls?* Plural?"

Oh, did I strike a nerve? I leave our smoothies in the blender as I head his way. He tracks me, bright blue eyes on my person as I come around the counter to stand directly in front of him. I thread my fingers through his hair, tipping his head up half an inch.

"You know what my job is," I say.

He nods. "Yes."

"It's not this."

He shakes his head slowly, and I know he understands what I mean. What I do at the studio is worlds apart from my personal life. I don't have an attachment to my scene partners, emotionally or romantically, and if Kipp held any jealousy over my position at Elite 8 or the fact that I have sex with the men there, I would know. He wouldn't be able to hide it from me.

The same way he can't hide what it is he's feeling now.

"But you," I tell him slowly, "are the *only* one I want. Singular."

He swallows.

"Okay?"

He nods in my grip, tension dropping. "Okay. You, uh...you're really good at this husband thing, you know. Ten out of ten, highly recommend."

"Anyone ever tell you that you use humor as a deflection?" I ask.

He huffs a laugh, his hands coming up to hold my wrists. "Yes. Niko does. All the time. It's a chronic condition, I'm sorry to tell you. You're stuck with it."

"That's okay. I happen to like your humor," I say seriously. "But you don't have to hide in front of me, okay?"

His eyes never shift away. "I know that, Teddy. I really do." His voice drops to a mumble as he adds, "Now are you going to kiss me? 'Cause you're just really fucking close, and you smell like vanilla. *Why* do you always smell like vanilla? No, wait. You told me. Tom Ford. Good choice, by the way, smells great. As do you. And *fuck*, why aren't you kissing me yet?"

Kipp's rambling cuts off when I bring my mouth to his. The sound he makes is one I'm quickly becoming addicted to, soft and pleased as it is, like my lips against his are a surprise every time. His tongue greets mine, his hips press close, and he tugs on my wrists like he's considering using my arms as leverage to climb up my body.

I'm so in trouble when it comes to this man.

When I break away, he mutters, "Fuck."

My thoughts exactly.

"Ready for that walk?" I ask, letting my hands drop.

"Bark," he deadpans.

With a chuckle, I grab two tumblers from the cabinet. Drinks loaded, we head out.

"How long have you lived here?" Kipp asks, his hair flopping over his forehead as we walk. He's dressed casually today, in jeans and a tee, no product in his hair. He looks good. Comfortable.

Relaxed.

"Here as in Nevada or my apartment?" I ask.

He shoots me a smile. "Either?"

"I've been in my apartment for five years and in Nevada since I was eighteen. So… Jesus, eighteen years now."

"Did you come here for college?" he asks.

I nod, taking a sip of my smoothie before answering. "I followed my brother from Canada. Vegas was his dream. Something about the lights and the energy of it. Ever since he was young, he wanted to move here. Got his wish."

"And you?" he asks softly.

I shrug. "I wanted to practice law. And since we were going to do that together, it made sense for me to come here, too."

Kipp is silent for a moment. Not long, but long enough to tell me he's thinking through what I said. "You haven't talked about him much."

"Cam? No, we're not close anymore."

"Why not?"

This time, it's *me* who's silent for an extended beat. "He and my boyfriend got together in an attempt to take control of the business."

Kipp stops walking. When I turn around, he's staring at me with wide eyes. "*What?*"

I huff a humorless laugh. "Yeah, that about sums it up."

Kipp catches up to me quickly. "Holy hell, Teddy. Are you okay?"

"It was a long time ago," I say, which doesn't really answer the question.

"Damn," he says slowly. "I think that might put my family drama to shame."

"Not a competition," I assure him, snagging his hand and giving it a squeeze. "You have every right to be upset over what happened."

He shoots me the tiniest smile. "Yeah, well, so do you. Why would he do that?"

I assume he means Cameron. I've asked myself that a million times in the past five years. *Why?* Was he really that different from me that he cared more about his own success than his brother?

Deep down, I know the answer to that is yes. He's always been determined. A little ruthless. I thought it'd served our firm well, and it did. We had several high-profile clients in our first couple years as newbie lawyers that catapulted Lavoie & Lavoie into the multimillion-dollar company it is now.

I just never thought Cameron would turn his aspirations against *me*.

"I don't have a good answer to that," I tell Kipp. "The way my brother thinks isn't something I want to understand."

He hums. "I get that. For what it's worth, I'm really sorry they did that to you."

"Thanks, sweetheart."

Not for the first time, I get a strong wash of warmth inside my chest as Kipp's gaze catches mine. He's so unlike those from my previous world. It's a very good thing.

The best.

"Did, um..." Kipp looks sheepish. "I'm almost afraid to ask, but did they succeed? In taking over?"

I blow out a breath as we round the curve back onto our street. "They got rid of me. But no. They didn't get the business."

Chapter 18
Kipp

"Did you know Teddy is a lawyer?" I ask Niko.

He's chopping dill for the tzatziki as I dice onions for a stuffed pepper dish. He looks at me in surprise. "Is he?"

"Yeah," I say around a huff that's mostly awe. "Is that not the hottest thing you've ever heard?"

Niko's mother clucks her tongue at me. "Watch your fingers, paidí mou," she scolds lightly, her use of *my child* taking all the heat out of the warning.

"Sorry, Mamá Adamos."

She gives my arm a squeeze, a dish towel over her shoulder as she grinds the lamb for the peppers.

"Who's Teddy?" Elina asks from the other side of the room.

"One of Niko's coworkers," Cassandra answers, helping her young toddler, Calliope, add blocks to her tower on the floor of the kitchen.

"And Kipp's husband," Niko mutters under his breath, giving me a smirk when I shoot a glare his way.

The room falls deathly silent for all of two seconds before Niko's sisters erupt, all four of them talking over one another.

"Oh good, we're allowed to talk about it now?" Ioanna says, abandoning the peppers she'd been hollowing out.

"I never said you *couldn't*," Niko replies. "I just said to be nice."

Ioanna pouts. "I'm always nice."

"You married Niko's costar?" Elina asks. She's the middle of the bunch and by far the scariest.

"I thought you said he's a lawyer," Sofia puts in, Ioanna's twin. They're the youngest.

"People can be more than one thing," Cassandra, the oldest, replies.

"Why the hell didn't we hear about it ahead of time, huh?" Elina asks, hands on her hips.

"He didn't know ahead of time," Niko explains, which isn't as helpful as he thinks.

"And now?" Elina presses. "What do you have to say for yourself, Kipp? Because we've been waiting *weeks* for some sort of explanation as to why one of our favorite people didn't tell us he was *married* of all things, and you've been here over an hour and still haven't said a word!"

My mouth opens and closes uselessly.

"Well?" Elina says.

"Paidiá," Niko's mom cuts in, the Greek word meaning *children*. "Let Kipp breathe."

I shoot her a grateful smile.

"I'm sure there's a very good reason he's been keeping secrets from us," Mamá Adamos adds, which makes my stomach fall somewhere in the vicinity of my feet.

"I was drunk," I blurt inside this blue-tiled kitchen that has held some of my favorite memories over the years. My favorite memories amongst my favorite people.

It's funny how the Adamoses have been more of a family to me than my own blood. From the first time Niko brought me home for a big, traditional Greek meal with his big, Greek family, I felt accepted. And although I knew my own family would disapprove of what happened between me and Teddy, I think I dreaded telling *these* people how badly I fucked up even more. Would I disappoint them, too? I couldn't bear the thought.

But I can't avoid it any longer. Frankly, I'm surprised they didn't pounce the moment I walked through the door.

Sucking in a breath, I prepare myself to air the truth. And accept the consequences. "I was drunk and got married on a whim," I explain to my silent audience. "I don't even remember it. Our relationship isn't real, and Teddy and I are planning on getting a divorce. Soon, I think. I'm sorry."

Cassandra gets up off the floor. "Why are you sorry, Kipp?"

"For disappointing you?" I say, unable to stop the wobble in my voice. "For not telling you the truth? I just... I didn't know what to say."

Cassandra's deep brown eyes, so like Niko's, soften, and she steps forward, wrapping her arms around me without a word. The next second, another pair of arms join. And then another. And pretty soon, I'm enveloped in crushing warmth and the most perfect hug. Everything around me blurs as my eyes fill with tears.

"You could never be a disappointment to us," Mamá Adamos says, her heavily accented voice washing over me like cinnamon and cloves. It reminds me, briefly, of Teddy. Of comfort.

"I'm sorry I yelled," Elina adds.

"We love you, Kipp," Sofia says, her voice softer than the rest. She's always been the quietest of the bunch, which makes her words feel even more profound. "We just want you to be happy."

"Shit," I mutter, immediately wincing as I remember young Calliope. "I mean shoot. I, uh, don't even know what to say. Thank you, all."

A hand lands on the back of my head, and I catch Niko's eye. He doesn't speak a word, but his smile says volumes.

"We're always here for you," Ioanna says as the group hug starts to break up. "But I have a question."

I huff a laugh, wiping my eyes and trying my best not to sniffle. "What's that?"

"You said your relationship isn't real, but...that picture," she says. "The one where you two are smiling. You can't fake a smile like that."

"That's not a question," I point out, although I know where she's going.

Ioanna rolls her eyes. "Do you have feelings for him?"

Fuck. "Yeah. I do," I admit.

Six pairs of eyes soften.

"But I don't know if he could feel the same," I'm quick to add.

Mamá Adamos pats my cheek. "Maybe don't get divorced just yet, hmm?"

I groan as heads nod and knowing looks are passed around.

"*You guys*. Don't encourage me. I don't want to get too attached," I mumble. I'm *already* too attached.

"Hate to break it to you," Elina says, a wicked gleam in her eye. "But you two are married."

"And living together," Niko adds.

Elina's eyes widen. "*And* living together. I don't think it gets much more attached than that."

"*Argh*," I complain. "What am I going to do?"

Cassandra picks up young Calliope, who unintentionally smacks her in the face. "Be yourself. No holds barred. If this guy is worthy of what you have to offer, he won't possibly want to let you go."

My heart thumps painfully in my chest. "And what is it I have to offer?"

Cassandra, my honorary big sister, looks at me with fond exasperation. "Your love, Kipp. If he's worth it, he'll have your love."

Shit.

"I think I need to sit down," I realize.

Ioanna huffs a laugh, pulling out a chair that I unceremoniously plop into. There's still onion residue on my hands, and my heart is running like it's on a racetrack, but all I can think about is the man at home who I maybe, quite possibly have very strong feelings for. Could I love Teddy?

Could he love me?

Sofia sits down next to me. "You said he's a lawyer in addition to working at the studio?" she asks. The whole Adamos clan is well aware Niko works in porn. None of them even batted an eye that Teddy does the same.

"Yeah," I say, a smile creeping onto my face as I imagine Teddy dressed in a suit and tie. With spandex on underneath because, hey, it's my fantasy. I pointedly do *not* think about Teddy's brother. "He does pro bono work for LGBTQ+ youth."

There's a chorus of *awws*.

Yeah, I know exactly how they feel.

"He sounds nice," Sofia says.

"Yeah," I say. "I think it's his superpower."

"Paidiá," Mamá Adamos says, calling her children back to action. She dumps the onions I diced into a pan, and a sizzle cuts through the air. "Someone still needs to roll out that pita."

The kitchen returns to a flurry of activity, and Mamá Adamos gives me a wink. For a few minutes, I let myself breathe, surrounded by the familiar swell of a family I can call my own.

When our midday dinner is done and the kitchen has been cleaned and set back to rights, Niko motions for me to follow him. We head outside and take seats on the back deck, letting the sun warm us.

"Calliope will probably be down for another hour," Niko says. "Do you mind waiting?"

We drove here with Cassandra since it takes about an hour to get to Niko's mom's from Vegas. I don't mind waiting for Calliope to finish her nap before we head out.

"Nah, that's fine," I tell him. "Why didn't Dixon come today?"

Niko kicks his feet up onto the table in front of us. "I thought it would be best for it to be just us. That way, you'd have a little less of an audience."

"For my dressing down?" I mutter.

He huffs. "No, for talking about your feelings."

I pick at the hem of my pants. "You didn't have to do that."

"Kipp." Niko's serious tone has me looking his way. "There will always be room for the both of you here, you know that. But Dixon didn't mind staying home today so you could have our undivided attention. He understands what you're going through."

I nod, throat tight. Dixon isn't close to his family, either. They kicked him out when he was a teen because of his bisexuality. But once he and Niko started dating, the Adamoses swooped Dixon up like he was one of theirs. The same as they did with me.

"Have you heard from any of them since your mom called?" Niko asks. *My family.*

I shake my head. "I think we're probably done."

Niko is quiet for a moment. "That might be a good thing."

"In my head, I know that. But here?" I tap over my heart. "Hurts."

"Yeah," he says quietly. "I get it. How has Teddy been during this whole thing?"

A bark of laughter escapes my mouth, and Niko looks at me curiously.

"What?" he asks, chuckling.

"*Dude.* Teddy is kinky as fuck."

Niko laughs for real, nodding. "Yeah, that's kind of one of those poorly held secrets at the studio. You know, like how Dixon is actually a softie inside, how Jerome and Nathaniel have been in a relationship for years, Teddy is a Daddy Dom, and Emil is an exhibitionist."

"Whoa, whoa, whoa. Hold up. Jerome and Nathaniel?"

Niko shrugs. "I'm like 98 percent sure. Half the time, they're wearing each other's mismatched socks."

"What? What does that have to do with—"

"How do you mix up socks, Kipp?"

I think that over for all of two seconds, the lone hamper in Teddy's room coming to mind. "*Oh.*"

Niko huffs a laugh.

"How'd you even figure that out?" I ask.

"I pay attention," he says with another shrug. "Never heard about Teddy being a lawyer, though."

"Yeah, remember when you said you thought there was a reason he didn't date?"

Niko cocks his head. "Yeah."

"I think it has to do with that."

And the asshole ex who cheated on him with his brother.

Niko hums, but he doesn't pry, and I appreciate it. It's not my story to tell. I don't even *know* the whole thing. But then he opens his mouth and just *has* to ask, "So what kind of kinky shit have you been getting up to, my friend?"

I cough. "Well..." In for a penny, as they say. "The other day, Teddy made me pick a safeword, and then he spanked me until I cried and came."

Niko chokes on absolutely nothing. "Shit," he says, voice strangled. But then he laughs—*loudly*—until I'm laughing right along with him. "Your life, Kipp."

"I know," I sigh out. "Isn't it great?"

As our chuckles die down, Cassandra sticks her head out the door. "Calli is up," she says. "We're ready to leave whenever."

"Thanks, we'll be right in," Niko tells her.

She nods and closes the door, leaving us alone once more.

"Can I tell you something?" I ask Niko.

He nods. "Always."

"I really like it. Being his..." I don't say *boy* because it doesn't feel right. I'm well aware our dynamic is similar to a Daddy-boy relationship. Teddy is dominant. He calls the shots. And he's teaching me, carefully and thoughtfully, how to enjoy submission—something I never even knew I *could* enjoy. Or *crave*.

But our specific relationship is our own. It's unique in a way *any* relationship is. And I'm not Teddy's boy. I'm his doll. For us—for *me*—that's right.

"I like being the one he takes care of," I settle on. "It feels really good to just...trust that what he tells me to do is what he wants. It's no more complicated than that. I trust him, and he takes care of me. And somehow, that makes him happy. It makes me happy, too."

Niko nods slowly, his eyes never leaving mine. "You know, I never thought about it before, but it makes sense."

"What does?" I ask.

"You," he says gently. "You go out of your way to please people. You know you do."

"Maybe," I mumble.

But who doesn't want everyone around them to be happy? If they're happy, they don't have a reason to dislike your actions or you as a person...*aaand* I think I see what Niko is getting at.

"But I assume being submissive means letting go of all that worry, at least for a little while," he goes on. "And with Teddy, you know you're safe to do so. You don't have to *try* with him. Like you said, he tells you how to please him, and you know he won't abuse that trust."

"Yeah," I say a little hoarsely.

"So I can see it," Niko says. "And I'm glad you found someone to help you let go of all that pressure."

"He's not mine, Nik," I nearly whisper.

"Maybe not fully. Not yet. But he could be."

I nod, not speaking for a moment. My throat is burning, and I'm scared to hope. Scared he *could* be the one.

Because what if I'm not *his* one?

"He makes it quiet," I tell Niko.

"What do you mean?"

"It's so loud sometimes. Up here," I say, pointing to my head. "There are opinions and deadlines and second-guessing and... Just a lot of noise, all the time. But Teddy... He makes it quiet."

Niko squeezes my arm. "Sounds nice."

"Yeah," I rasp. "It is."

Niko and I stay outside for a few minutes longer, but eventually, we get up and head home with Cassandra and Calliope. Niko drops me off last, giving me a quick hug from the driver's seat and reminding me it's okay if I like him. That Teddy is one of the good ones.

I tell him I know.

When I get inside after a long afternoon and evening of being gone, I almost expect all of my feelings for Teddy to have been blown out of proportion inside my own head. Like maybe I was remembering him wrong or adding a rosy glow to our kinda-kinky friends-with-benefits pseudo-marriage.

But the moment I see him on the couch, I know that's not the case. He smiles, big and broadly, and my insides light like a supernova.

"Hey," he says warmly.

I head toward him on autopilot, falling onto his lap. He chuckles, his hand going to my hair, and I damn near purr like a cat.

"Have a good time?" he asks.

"Yeah," I answer.

"Glad to be back?"

"*Yeah.*"

His fingers slip under my waistband, just barely touching the top of my ass. "How're the cheeks doing?"

I snort. "You were right. All better."

"See?" he says. "I bet the lotion helped."

"I already said you were right. You don't have to gloat."

He chuckles, fingers drifting along my skin. "I'm glad you're back, too."

My heart beats fast as Teddy's fingers sift through my hair. As his other hand rests above my ass like a gentle claim. As his heat and spicy warm scent envelops me.

Maybe I do have feelings for my husband.

I just don't know how to tell *him* that.

Chapter 19

TEDDY

"All right?" I ask Phillip, who's been staring at the inside of his small kitchen for the better part of two minutes. Scott and I just finished moving him into his new apartment, and although the teen was on board with the switch in location, he seems withdrawn now that we're finished.

"Um, yeah," he says, turning around. "I can't believe you guys did all this."

"It was the least we could do," Scott replies.

Phillip shakes his head, looking around the living room now. He had a couple pieces of cheap art we hung on the walls, but the apartment is still pretty bare.

"Sometimes it feels like no one cares," he says quietly. "But..."

He doesn't finish his sentence, but the look Scott gives me tells me he understands perfectly. It's all too easy for queer kids to fall through the cracks. Sometimes their families turn them away or are apathetic to their struggles. Sometimes they simply need to know they're not alone. That there are people out there who understand what they're going through on a personal level. It's why Scott created the community center in the first place. He wanted to help those kids and young adults any way he could. And he does.

"We're here if you need us," Scott tells him. "And I promise you, there's always someone who cares."

Phillip nods, but he doesn't say a word.

Scott and I leave him to get settled in his new home, having left housewarming gifts in the form of some groceries in his fridge. The kid was living on ramen.

Scott stops me when we get outside the building. "Any response from the landlord?"

"Not yet, but I'll let you know once I hear anything."

Phillip's lease was a month-to-month rental agreement, so it was easy enough to terminate. Usually, it would require a thirty-day notice, but the landlord accepted an early termination when I served him papers for the compensation of illegally obtained rental fees. I've yet to hear whether or not the man is going to fight us on it. All Phillip wants is his money back. Hopefully, we won't have to go to court to get it.

Scott gives me a nod. "Keep me in the loop. And Teddy?"

"Yeah?"

"Bring your husband to the Halloween party this year."

With that, Scott claps my shoulder and heads off. There's no way he could have known how much that innocent comment would sting. Kipp and I might not even *be* husbands once Halloween rolls around. It's not a thought I want to linger on.

I'm halfway to my car when my phone rings. My melancholy lifts as I see the name onscreen.

"Kipp?"

"*Heyyy.*"

I freeze. "What's wrong?"

"Um, so, nothing is *wrong* wrong. Like, not seriously wrong. I just don't feel so hot."

"Are you sick?" I ask, hustling into my car.

"Well, considering I've been kneeling in front of a toilet for the past half hour, yeah, I think I might have come down with a little something. Maybe."

"Shit. I'm sorry, sweetheart. Are you at work?"

There's a faint, "Yeah."

"All right. I'll be right there."

"Teddy, you don't have to—"

"Kipp. I'll be right there."

He sighs, his tone much more light when he mumbles a teasing, "Yes, Daddy."

I shake my head, fighting a smile. "Glad to see your humor is still intact."

"It's the one thing that hasn't vacated my system," Kipp says, deadpan.

I snort, even as my chest pangs in sympathy. "Hold tight. I'm on my way."

Kipp mutters a sincere, "Thanks, Teddy," and then the line goes dead.

I swing by a convenience store first, grabbing some anti-nausea meds, Gatorade, and saltine crackers. It doesn't take long after that to arrive at Kipp's office. What I'm not expecting is the immediate recognition from the stranger at the front desk.

"Oh my gosh!" the woman says, standing up and rushing toward me. "You're Teddy."

"Guilty," I say, offering my hand.

She waves me off, pulling me in for a quick hug before linking her arm with mine. "Kipp's office is just down this way. I'm so glad you're finally here! We've been dying to meet you."

"Is that so?" I ask in some amusement.

"Gosh, yes. Kipp is just the sweetest person—of course, I don't have to tell you that. We're all so happy he met *the one*."

There's that sting again, but I give the woman a smile as we enter what looks like a bullpen of sorts. There are desks scattered around, a few private offices with closed doors, a large copy machine, and a bulletin board that takes up an entire wall. It's plastered in pictures of cats, of all things.

"Everyone," the woman on my arm calls. "Teddy is here."

Heads swivel our way, and before I know what's happening, I'm surrounded by a good dozen people welcoming me and peppering me with questions. It's an absolute whirlwind, and my first and foremost thought is that Kipp must fit in perfectly here.

It takes a couple minutes for the excitement to die down, but as soon as I'm able, I step away with the woman who first welcomed me. "Could you show me where the bathrooms are?" I ask her. "Kipp called me in because he's not feeling well."

"Oh no!" she says, looking around like she's just now realizing he's not with us. "The poor thing. Come on. Restrooms are right this way."

She leads me down another hall, and when we arrive at the bathrooms, I knock on the only closed door. "Kipp?"

A few seconds later, the lock turns, and Kipp appears, looking pale and more disheveled than I've ever seen him. His hair is a mess, his shirt is wrinkled with one corner pulled free from his pants, and if I didn't know better, I'd almost think he was drunk. Whatever he picked up, it clearly hit him hard.

"Sweetheart," I murmur, stepping forward to wrap an arm around his waist.

"I'm kinda sweaty," he says.

I kiss his damp forehead. "Don't care. Come on. Let's get you home."

"Thanks, Teddy," he mutters. When he sees his coworker in the hall, he gives her a weak smile. "Marsha, could you let Carly know I'm heading home early today?"

"Of course," she says, standing aside as we pass. "You just focus on getting better, sweetie."

Marsha heads back into the bullpen as I lead Kipp toward the front door, keeping pace with his slow gait.

"Doing okay?" I ask.

He nods, but it's a measured thing. "I think I'm sick, Teddy."

"Yeah," I say with a huff. "I think it's likely."

"I might get you sick."

"If you do, you do."

He groans as I get him settled in the car.

"There's a bag by your feet if you need it," I let him know.

He groans again, leaning his head back against the seat. "Let's just...not talk about it."

I dutifully keep my mouth shut as I get into the car and drive us home. Inside, I get Kipp set up on the couch, a blanket beneath him that he insisted on because *I'm gross, Teddy*, and another over top of him to keep him warm. I have him take some of the anti-nausea meds and drink some water, but when I pop the top on a Gatorade, he groans again.

"Teddy..."

"Do you need the bathroom?" I ask.

He curses. "Think so."

I whisk him that way, and the moment we reach the doorway, Kipp falls to his knees and hugs the toilet. I rub his back, wincing as he heaves.

"Don't look at me, Teddy. I'm hideous."

"Never," I assure him, brushing his damp hair off his forehead.

He makes a pitiful sound, trying to hide his face. "You're never going to want me again after this."

"Impossible, sweetheart."

His huff is incredulous, and I hand him a wet cloth that he uses to wipe his face. After that, I give him some mouthwash, which he spits into the toilet.

"Want to know a secret that's not really a secret?" I ask, running my thumb along his ear.

He meets my gaze hesitantly.

"I like taking care of you," I say softly.

"But not like this," he says, forehead creased.

"Even like this."

He makes a sound of disbelief, and I know I can't explain it to him without giving myself away. Without telling him how much I care for him. Without saying I want the privilege of looking after him for a very, very long time.

Instead, I help him to his feet and down the hall.

"Let's try this again," I say, giving him some more meds once he's seated.

He downs the small amount, followed by some Gatorade this time. I get him settled between the blankets before sitting down beside him.

"What was with the cats?" I ask, hoping to distract him from how he's feeling.

"Huh?"

"The cats on the bulletin board."

Kipp huffs a laugh. "That was my idea, actually. I figured it'd be a good morale booster. Everyone likes cats, right? So if you're stuck on some code you can't figure out or are having a difficult day, you look over, and *bam*. Cats. Instant mood lift."

"That's a good idea," I tell him, brushing his hair behind his ear.

He shrugs one shoulder. "It's kinda silly, but it works."

"I don't think it's silly at all, Kipp. I think it's smart. From what I could tell, you've cultivated a really good working environment. Everyone seemed genuinely happy in the brief few minutes we talked."

"It's not because of me," he defends.

"But you're part of it. Stop selling yourself short."

He huffs when I give his ear a tiny pinch. "Thanks, Teddy. For...everything."

"My pleasure," I say softly.

"I'm dying," Kipp moans some time later. "That's what this is. I'm sick with death."

"I think it might be food poisoning," I tell him, rubbing his back as he reclines against the outside of the bathtub. We've been at this for several hours, alternating between lying on the couch and rushing Kipp to the bathroom so he can empty the contents of his stomach. I don't think he has any contents left.

"Poisoned," he croaks. "I didn't think that'd be the way I'd go, Teddy."

"You're not *going* anywhere. You'll be just fine."

After Kipp heaves up the tiniest something into the toilet bowl, he looks over at me. "Teddy? What's that?"

I check the bowl, glad, not for the first time, for my steel stomach. There are brown flecks amongst the clear liquid from his Gatorade. "That's dried blood. Okay, up you go."

Kipp groans as I help him to his feet. "Where are we going?"

"The hospital."

"*Nooo*."

"Yes. Sorry, sweetheart. It's likely just irritation from throwing up, but I'm not taking any chances."

Kipp moans as I help him clean up, get dressed in fresh clothes, and head down to the car. But he doesn't once try to stop me. That, in itself, tells me volumes. He leans his head against the window as I drive, the streetlights and other cars brightening the otherwise dark streets. There's a bag at his feet we don't talk about.

When I pull up to the emergency room, Kipp looks over at me. "Niko should get my sex toys."

"What?" I ask, completely mystified.

"If I die. He gets my sex toys. It's what bro-friends do."

"Kipp..."

"And I don't have a huge savings, but what I do have should go toward something nice. Like charity. Oh, the LGBTQ+ center."

"You're not dying," I assure him, getting out of the car and heading around to his side. He leans his weight on me as I help him out.

"If you haven't noticed, I tend to joke around when I'm uncomfortable."

"I've noticed," I say softly.

He nods a little. "I'm just not feeling so good right now."

My chest clenches tight. "I know, sweetheart. That's why we're here. Let's get you better."

"Okay," Kipp says tiredly.

The walk into the hospital takes a minute, and when we arrive, I'm fully prepared to lie about who Kipp is to me so that

I can stay with him once he's admitted. But then I realize... I don't have to lie at all.

He's my husband.

With Kipp's help, I fill in his paperwork, and the receptionist tells us it will only be a minute before we're brought back. Considering he's vomiting blood, I'm not surprised there won't be a long wait.

Kipp leans his head on my shoulder once I reclaim my seat beside him. His emergency bag is in my pocket, just in case.

"Teddy?" he says, eyes closed. He looks exhausted, with dark circles under his eyes and his usually bright complexion waxy and pale.

"Yeah, sweetheart?"

"I'd do it again, you know."

Jesus. He sounds drunk.

"What's that?" I ask, holding his hand between my own.

"Marry you."

I draw in a breath, my heart trying to beat out of my chest.

"I've never wanted to marry someone before," he says. "I never saw someone standing next to me in front of the mountains. But you'd look nice there."

I swallow down the lump in my throat, knowing I can't hold Kipp to those words. He's not himself. He's practically delirious with fluid loss and exhaustion.

But *hell*, how I wish he'd say them for real.

"I'd be proud to stand up there with you," I tell him, meaning it, even if he doesn't remember the words come tomorrow.

He hums happily. "My husband."

I clear my throat. Kiss his temple. Squeeze his neck. "For however long you'll have me."

Chapter 20

KIPP

When I wake up, it's clear I'm in a hospital. The *why* of it takes me a moment to remember.

Right. My inners trying to become outers.

I groan to myself quietly, but when I catch sight of Teddy asleep in a nearby chair, the sound dissipates. The furniture is barely big enough to hold him, and Teddy himself is slumped down, his head hanging back at an awkward angle. But *fuck*. He's here.

And that means a lot.

As if sensing I'm awake, Teddy stirs. He cracks one eye open and then the other. "Hey," he says, stretching and sitting upright. "You're up."

"Yeah, hi. Um... How long have we been here?"

Teddy checks the time on his phone, although the light streaming in through the window tells me it's at least the next morning. "About ten hours. Are you feeling better? You were pretty out of it for a bit."

"Yeah, I'm okay." *I think.* I notice the IV drip and hold up my hand. "I'm guessing this has something to do with that."

Teddy rubs his eyes as he stands and comes over to the bed. "Yeah. They gave you a bunch of fluids and some meds. You don't remember?"

"Only bits and pieces," I admit. "Food poisoning?"

He nods. "Seems so."

I blow out a breath. "Well, considering you didn't get sick, I think we can rule out contamination from the apartment. Must've been my lunch."

"What'd you have?" he asks.

I grimace a little. "Shrimp tacos."

Teddy's lips twitch.

"Never again," I groan. "No more shrimp. *Ever*. Actually, no more crustaceans, period."

"I thought you wanted a hermit crab."

It takes me a minute to remember what he's talking about. I'd almost forgotten my fifteen-second conviction that I wanted a pet crab like Emil's.

"Well, I wouldn't *eat* it," I point out.

Teddy huffs a laugh. "The doctor said you're fine to leave so long as you're feeling well enough. What d'you say? Should I grab a nurse?"

I nod. "Please. Take me home, Teddy. I just want to lie on the couch all day and be a potato."

"You'd be a very cute potato," he says, leaning down and kissing my forehead. My pulse skips, and I'm grateful I'm not hooked up to a heart monitor. "I'll be right back."

As Teddy steps away, I look down at what I'm wearing. "Am I in your sweatpants?"

He shoots me a little grin as he opens the door.

"I have my own sweatpants, you know!"

My call goes unanswered, and Teddy chuckles as he walks away.

Pft. Dressing me in his clothes like I'm... Like I'm his... *Fuuuck*. Like I'm his doll. Because I am. And great. Now I have a boner in a hospital.

Niko is never going to let me live this down.

"Hey, Teddy?" I call.

The man appears from down the hall, his shirtsleeves pushed up past his forearms. It's been twenty-four hours since we got back from the hospital, and although Teddy spent some of that time in his office working, right now he's freshly showered, his hair damp. I drink him in for a moment before remembering my very important question.

"Why do you never talk to me in French?"

He cocks his head. "Do you want me to? You wouldn't understand me."

"Yeah, but isn't it supposed to be sexy?"

His lips twitch. I *hate* that damn twitch. And by hate, I mean love.

Teddy walks into the room slowly, stopping at the end of the sectional where I'm lying and have been for most of the morning. He leans close, his hand on the back of the couch, his arm muscles doing very nice things. "Comment te sens-tu, ma p'tite patate?" he says.

I open my mouth before clearing my throat. *Twice*. "What, um... What does that mean?"

"How are you feeling, my little potato?"

I bark a laugh. "Seriously?"

"Mhm. Did it sound sexier in French?"

"Um, *yes*. Yes, it did. And now I'm very much lamenting the fact that I'm still as tired as a dog because I'd *really* like to hump your leg right now. Which, okay, that doesn't make a whole lot of sense. But you know what I mean."

Teddy leans back and crosses his arms, although his expression is soft. "You sound better."

"I feel better."

Recuperating at home with Teddy probably had a big something to do with that.

Teddy twists his lips a little. It doesn't look like a happy twist.

"What is it?" I ask.

"I'm supposed to head into the studio this afternoon. Would you be okay if I left?"

"Oh," I say, not surprised exactly because it *is* still the work week, and of course Teddy would be scheduled for filming. I'd just gotten so used to having him around while *I* played legitimate hooky, and the idea of him leaving now bums me out.

But I'm an adult. I don't *actually* need a keeper.

"It's fine," I say quickly. "I'll be okay."

"Hm," is all he says.

"What *hm*?"

"Would you want to come with me?"

I perk up immediately. "Come with you to the studio? Where the porn is made?"

There go those twitching lips again. "Mhm."

"Could I *watch*?"

"Would you want to?" he asks, sounding genuinely curious.

"Um. *Yes*. Obviously. Holy fucking fuckballs, can I seriously? Would that be allowed?"

He smiles for real this time, his cheeks dimpling at the sides. "Should be fine. I'll check with Jerome, but as long as you don't interrupt filming, I don't see why not."

"Oh my God, oh my God, oh my *God*." I fling myself off the couch, nearly tripping over my blanket in the process. "Best day ever. Bring Kipp To Work day. Yeah, okay. What do I wear? Leather?"

"How about your normal clothes?" Teddy counters.

"Really?" I ask, frowning. "Not, like, normal *leather* clothes?"

"What leather clothing do you own that would be considered casual wear?"

I ponder that. "The thong?"

Teddy stares at me for a long time. "You own a leather thong?"

"Yeah, the black one with the little bow in front?"

He spins around, walking down the hall. "Tu vas être ma mort, chéri."

"What?" I ask, following after him. "I heard chéri. That's sweetheart, right?"

He doesn't stop until he's in front of his dresser. He opens one drawer, and not finding what he's searching for, he opens another. When he rifles through my underwear selection, locating the piece in question, he hangs his head for the briefest of moments. His eyes, when he turns my way, are lit like *fire*.

"Are you really feeling okay?" he asks, pushing off from the dresser and stepping close, the thong between his fingertips.

I swallow, my voice nearly lost. "Yes."

He nods, looking me over before he undoes the button of my jeans. "I'm going to make you a smoothie before we go. And you'll eat a protein bar, too. And if, at any point, you're not feeling well, you tell me, all right?"

I nod, not breathing a word.

Teddy tugs off my pants, tapping my legs so I step out of them. My briefs follow, leaving me in the nude from the waist down. "You're going to wear this for me," he says, his tone not leaving any room for argument, not that I *would* argue. "And while you watch me fuck my scene partner, you can think about how *I'm* thinking of these."

Fuck.

Teddy eases the leather up my legs, the motion gentle and smooth. He tugs it over my half-hard cock, positioning me just so beneath the unforgiving fabric. His fingers glide over the little bow last, eyes meeting mine.

"Beautiful, babydoll."

I nod, my heart pounding.

Teddy replaces my jeans before standing up. "Ready?"

"Yep," I eke out.

Teddy's grin is a touch feral.

True to his word, my tease of a husband has me eat a protein bar before we leave and drink a smoothie on the way to the studio. Honestly, I don't mind him looking out for me, especially considering I *have* been regaining my strength after the complete upheaval of my intestines.

I've seen the outside of the Elite 8 Studios building before, but I've never been inside it. Today, Teddy leads me right to the nondescript door on the nondescript building, enters a code, and we walk inside.

"Oh my God," I breathe.

Teddy chuckles as I hasten toward the massive neon "Elite 8 Studios" sign on the wall inside the door. It's bright yellow, and I remember it from when Niko started here. He took a picture in front of it and sent it to me.

I hand Teddy my phone. "Please?" I ask excitedly.

He capitulates, taking a picture of me grinning like a fool in front of the sign. I hop on my feet a little when I see it, and then I send it right to my best bro-friend.

"Show me *everything*," I say to Teddy, heading further into the building. His soft laugh follows.

I gasp when we reach the doors leading into the studios themselves. There's three of them, aptly named Studio 1, 2, and 3. Block-letter titles sit beside the door to each, above which rests a light to indicate whether or not filming is in progress. Studio 2 is lit red. The rooms are completely closed off, a necessity from a soundproofing standpoint, and just like I imagined in my most perfect dreams, someone steps out of one of the doors in nothing but a jockstrap.

I grab Teddy's arm, a huge grin on my face as the man walks down the hall. "That was Thor," I hiss. "Did you see? Teddy, did you see?"

He laughs silently as I sprint ahead. Down another hall are what look like offices. Teddy tells me the private rooms are that way, too. There's a glass-walled gym that Teddy uses a few times a week. Next up is a room that, at a peek, is lined in pink orchids. Seeing the table stationed in the middle, I deduce this is where the wax torture happens. I pass quickly by.

Further down the hall, there's a break room filled with comfy couches and chairs, all sorts of snacks and drinks, and nude art on the walls. Past that is a large, open studio space where props are stored, from beds to inflatable pools to a motorcycle. And then... Then, there's the locker room.

I spin to Teddy with wide eyes. "Can I?"

He shakes his head, a small smile on his face. "Afraid not. Performers only."

I groan, although I understand the need for that sort of privacy. Even in porn production, boundaries are important.

"Fiiine," I mutter. And then add, because I can, "My husband is mean."

The playful slap to my ass has my blood pooling south *real* damn fast.

"Fuck," I breathe, my cock pressing against the leather of my thong.

"Behave, sweetheart," Teddy says, grabbing my chin in a light hold and placing a kiss near my ear. He hums before leaning back, and I swear I can feel the rumble of it in my cock. "Come on. You can hang out in the break room while I go talk to Jerome."

"Yeah," I say, clearing my throat. "Sounds good."

As Teddy heads off to clear my visit with the boss, I peruse the art on the walls inside the break room. It looks like stills of the performers, possibly taken during filming. But they're cropped such that they look tasteful, in a way. Like *classy* erotic art.

I wonder if Teddy would let me hang some of him in our apartment. *His* apartment. His. Because I won't be there forever.

Shit. The reminder is sobering.

An excited gasp draws my attention toward the door. "Kipper!" Alex cries.

"Hey, Alex," I say with a grin.

The blonde man comes in for a hug, squeezing surprisingly tight. *My fragile insides*. "Teddy said you were here. How's it going?"

"Good," I say, grateful when the vise-grip hug is finished. "Teddy thinks Jerome might let me watch his scene today."

Alex waggles his eyebrows. "Fun. Excited to see your husband in action?"

"*God*, yes."

His responding smile is bright. "You two are *so* cute. The husbands that share together stay together."

I huff a laugh. "Sure," I hedge. "Except we're not actually together."

Alex's eyes narrow ever so slightly. "Hm."

"What *hm*? Why does everyone keep *hming* me?"

"Just, you know," Alex says, "Teddy has been smiling a whole lot these past few weeks."

"He's always smiley."

"And as soon as his scenes are done, he puts his ring back on. Odd, isn't it? Almost like he doesn't want to be without it."

My heart pounds.

"I notice you're wearing yours, too," he says, hazel eyes sweeping pointedly down to my hand.

"Um. It got stuck."

"Oh. Want some help?"

As soon as Alex reaches for my hand, I yank it away. "I'm good," I say quickly.

His smile is much too knowing. "Mhm. Whatever you say, boo."

Teddy sticks his head into the room, eyes seeking me out. He gives me a warm smile. "Jerome said it's fine. We're ready."

"Have fun, Kipp Kipp," Alex sings, flouncing off toward the snacks while I head out of the room.

Once Teddy and I are walking down the hall, I shake my head. "That one's trouble."

He snorts. "Always."

And that's when I notice what my husband is wearing. "*Oh my good God almighty.*"

"All right?" Teddy asks.

My eyes sweep over his body. From the much-too-tight faded jeans to the toolbelt slung low around his hips to his bare chest and the neon vest hanging off his shoulders.

"You're a slutty construction worker," I breathe.

His smirk is devastating.

"Are you oiled?" I ask in awe, my gaze trailing down his stomach. It takes considerable effort not to touch. "So slippery."

Teddy opens the door to Studio 1 with a flourish. "This is us."

I walk inside, my head on a swivel. In the massive, high-ceilinged room, prep for filming is already underway. There's a pseudo-construction set off along one side, the detail astounding. Crew members are walking about, wheeling cameras into place or connecting wires for lighting. There's someone with a clipboard directing a few assistants. And standing off to the side, looking through a script, is Emil.

"Hey," Teddy says, heading his way.

Emil looks up, giving Teddy a smile. His expression shifts to curiosity when he sees me trailing after my slutty construction worker of a husband.

"Mind if Kipp hangs out in the wings for filming today?" Teddy asks Emil. "Jerome okayed it, but if it'd make you uncomfortable, he can watch from a viewing room."

"Oh, no," Emil says quickly, fidgeting with his glasses. "That's, uh, totally fine. I don't mind. Not at all. Nope."

As Emil blushes, Teddy gives me a grin.

"All right," Jerome booms, entering the room. The door shuts behind him with a click, and he stalks forward, total DILF material in dark jeans and a leather jacket. "We ready to get this show on the fucking road? Felix? Teddy?"

Niko told me how Jerome only refers to his performers by their stage names. And how yelling is his default. Not gonna lie, the dude is a mite bit scary.

"Ready," Emil answers.

Teddy turns to me. "Good?"

"So good," I assure him, giving a thumbs-up.

He huffs a laugh, eyes flicking down to my crotch for a moment. "Remember what I said?"

How could I forget? While I'm watching him, he'll be thinking about *me*. More specifically, the thong he dressed me in.

"Yep," I squeak.

Teddy nods, giving my shoulder a squeeze before following Emil onto the set.

Jerome faces me, lowering his voice but not by much. "No talking. No moaning. No touching yourself. Got it?"

I nod quickly.

He points to a spot behind him where there's a chair. "You're there." Facing the room at large, he shouts, "Let's do this. Places, everyone."

Heart pounding, I take a seat. Teddy finds me, giving me a wink before focusing on his work. I smile so wide I'm pretty sure my cheeks will be aching for the rest of that day.

Worth it.

"Aaand," Jerome shouts, "*action*."

Chapter 21
TEDDY

When I wake before my alarm, it's to a horny Kipp attached to my side. I'm not even sure whether or not he's awake until he looks up at my face, eyes open and hazy.

My smile is immediate, chest warm as I run a hand through his bedhead. "The two orgasms last night didn't wear you out, sweetheart?"

I spent the better part of the evening after we got back from the studio edging Kipp until he was a mumbling, pliant mess on my sheets. I couldn't blame him for being so excited. So was I. Having him at the studio was a rush I didn't anticipate would hit so hard. It was thrilling, knowing he was watching me in that tiny leather thong of his. Knowing he was hard for me and waiting.

Undressing him was satisfying, like unwrapping a gift. So was making him come. The first time was from my hand after a slow, *slow* jerk off that had him spurting as high as his chin. The second round included my tongue up his ass and him spread out, dazed and gorgeous. My beautiful doll.

I came across his ass cheeks right after.

"Teddy, I can't help it," Kipp groans, seeking friction against my hip. "You're fucking hot, okay? Watching you was hot. Sleeping next to you makes me hot. What am I supposed to do?"

I hum, sliding my hand down to Kipp's ass.

He wiggles against me. "Fuck. Yes. *Please.*"

"I have a better idea," I say, rubbing over his hole before I lift my hand away.

"Noo," he whines. "Better ideas don't involve your fingers leaving my ass, Teddy."

"You'll like this, doll. Trust me."

He lets out a slow breath, body relaxing. All it takes now is that single word—*doll*—and it's like a switch flips. Kipp calms, trusting me to take care of him.

It's a heady fucking thing.

"Roll onto your stomach," I tell him.

He does, easing off of me and lying face-down. He watches me as I reach into the nightstand, producing lube and the same plug I used on him before. His mouth pops open a little as I turn back his way.

"Remember what I wanted to do with this plug, babydoll?"

He nods against his arm, eyes tracking me until I'm too far behind him to see. I hoist up his hips, forcing Kipp to his knees. He moans, staying exactly where I put him.

"I'm going to stretch you," I say, palm caressing his ass cheek, "and play with you just a little. And then I'm going to plug you. And all day, you can think about what I'm going to do to you when you get home."

"And what's that?" he asks, voice hoarse.

I kiss one ass cheek and then the other. "You still want my cock?"

His breath leaves him in a rush. "*Please.*"

"Then if you're good," I say, bringing lubed fingers to his ass, "you can have it tonight."

Kipp curses, dropping his forehead against the mattress. He stays perfectly still as I work my finger into his ass, rubbing my other hand over his thigh and the soft hairs there.

"Fucking gorgeous," I murmur, teasing his prostate while I reach beneath him to give his dick a slow stroke. He remains unmoving, even as he trembles. "So good for me, aren't you, doll?"

He groans, letting me work him open, letting me take my time. His legs start to shake in earnest when I fuck him with two of my fingers, my palm rolling over his leaking crown.

"Teddy," he breathes.

I slip my digits free, and he slumps, his breath ragged. "Perfect, babydoll."

The lubed plug slides in easily, settling into place.

"You can take it out if necessary," I tell him, "but it goes right back in."

He nods in understanding.

"And before you come home," I go on, "you're going to go into the bathroom and get yourself ready. But you don't come, got it? No matter how much it aches. When you walk through this door, I want that plug right where I put it, and I want you ready for my cock. Understood?"

He nods again, voice raspy when he says, "*Yes*."

"Good," I say, giving his ass a soft slap. "Time to get ready for work."

It takes Kipp a good long minute to get off the bed. First, he rolls to his back, chest rising and falling, his cock standing upright. After a while, he drops his feet to the ground. I watch as I get dressed and go through my morning routine, a smile on my face I can't quite temper. When Kipp finally pads toward the bathroom, he's still half-hard.

"All right?" I ask.

He disappears into the en suite. "Shut it, Teddy."

I chuckle. "I'll make you some breakfast."

When Kipp comes into the kitchen, he's wearing slacks and a button-down. He looks primped and proper, and it'd be impossible to know he's wearing a butt plug under his workplace attire. Unless, perhaps, he bent over right in front of someone and his slacks pulled tight. But I assume that won't be happening.

Kipp rounds the island gingerly, grabbing himself a glass of apple juice. I slide a plate with toast his way, unable to resist running my hand down his backside until I find the base of the plug. Kipp groans, dropping his head forward.

"You gotta stop, or I won't be able to leave," he says, not actually sounding all that put-out or making a single move to get away.

I rub over the plug lightly, and Kipp lets out a breath.

"I thought you're mine to play with," I say. "Am I wrong?"

He mutters a curse. "Only for...two more minutes. And then I have to go. Wait, no. Make that one minute. I need to eat that toast."

I hum, spinning him until his back is pressed up against the counter. "One minute then."

Kipp moans as my mouth meets his. He tastes sweet, like apples, and he's warm and firm yet yielding as I slot against him, our bodies joining like puzzle pieces. I don't think twice about kissing him. About what it means that I'm doing it when we're not having sex. I don't think about anything other than this man at my fingertips, who feels like all the things I've carefully avoided for so very long.

He feels like *mine*, and it takes every ounce of my willpower to pull back and remind myself that *no*—he's not mine. Not for real.

And I best remember that.

"I'm gonna... have a hard-on... all freaking day," Kipp huffs out, pressing his hand against my chest. I step back, and he turns toward his toast. "All day, Teddy. Do you realize I had to pick out my loosest pants to hide my perma-erection? Thought went into the decision. And here you are just *poof.* Decimating my brain cells. Like, who needs cognitive thought, right? I'll just let my little brain lead the show today. Not like I even have a choice in the matter."

Kipp bites into his toast, shaking his head as he chews.

"When I get home," he says, not even looking at me, "you better fuck me so damn good I pass out. I'm not even kidding. Don't get me wrong, this is hot as fuck. Like, I'm pretty sure it's the hottest thing that's ever happened to me, and I've done my fair share of hot shit. But you better make good on your promise, Teddy, and goddamn make me yours or... I don't know. I'll come up with some sort of threat that isn't humping your leg, and I'll threaten you with it."

My pulse thrums heavily as Kipp finishes his breakfast.

"Now I really have to go," he says, wiping the crumbs off his fingers. "And I'm not going to look at you or my erection will be back. So... See ya later."

Kipp is nearly to the door when I notice his keys sitting on the counter. "Kipp?"

He stops, and I pick up the keys, jangling them. Hand over his eyes, he walks back my way, snagging them without meeting my gaze.

"Have a good day, honey," I tease, my heart still pounding.

He groans, and then he's out the door. In some ten hours, he'll be walking right back through it.

His words cycle around my head like a hurricane.

"And goddamn make me yours."

At noon, I can't quite resist texting Kipp to see how he's doing. I sit at my weight bench, muscles burning pleasantly after my workout, and type out a message.

Me: How's it going?

Kipp's answer comes swiftly.

Babydoll: Today is hard. HARD, Teddy. Everything is hard.

I snort a laugh.

Me: Mhm.

Babydoll: Don't you mhm me. You're the reason I'm in this mess.

Me: Have you been thinking about my fingers inside of you like I asked you to?

Babydoll: Teddddddddy.

God, he's perfect.

Me: Have you thought about what else you'll feel inside of you once that plug is gone?

His call comes through, and I answer with a grin.

"Mean, mean man," is Kipp's greeting. "I'm supposed to be eating lunch right now. Not fighting a boner."

"I think you can multitask."

He sighs. "We're not going to be able to do this all the time, okay? I'm seriously having trouble concentrating today."

My chest rolls with heat at the assumption that we *will* have the opportunity to do this again at some point, followed by worry that maybe this is pushing him too far.

"Do you need to call it quits?" I ask seriously.

He scoffs. "No. Fuck, no. I'm not saying...the *b* word," he practically whispers. "You know which one I mean. This is not a plantain-adjacent situation."

I huff a laugh.

"I *wanted* this," he goes on. "And I'm managing. Sorta. But if I have some big meeting or an important deadline or something—"

"You say no, and it's a no," I remind him.

"Yeah," he answers. "I know. Now distract me while I eat. What are you doing?"

"Well, I just finished working out."

He groans. "Are you sweaty?"

"Little bit, yeah."

Kipp whimpers. "Fucking hell, Teddy. Are you wearing those loose shorts?"

"Mhm."

"God," he mutters. "And that tank top that shows off your nips? Actually, no. Don't answer that. This isn't helping one bit. Be disgusting. Say something horrible. Tell me you secretly hate puppies or children."

"Would you believe me if I did?"

"No," he says immediately. "Because you're perfect. You probably *love* puppies, and kids think you're the coolest because you're like a big teddy bear. They don't know how wicked you really are."

"And you?" I ask. "Do you like puppies?"

"Who the fuck doesn't like puppies?" he says. "I thought about getting one, but I'd feel kinda bad leaving it at home during the day. Besides, I should find my own place to live first."

I hum, not liking the idea of him in his own place. "And kids? Is that something you want?"

"Eh," he hedges. "Not for myself, I don't think? I like kids in a peripheral way. I wouldn't mind being the cool uncle or something, but being a dad? Dunno. I can barely take care of myself."

"You're more competent than you think, sweetheart."

He makes a sound, not really agreeing with me but maybe not disagreeing, either. "It's probably your thing, though, isn't it? Being a dad? You're good at that whole...caretaker thing."

I'm not sure how Kipp and I ended up on the topic of hypothetical children, but I answer honestly. "I never saw myself with kids. I like them, sure, but having my own was never a dream of mine."

"Oh. Well, okay," Kipp says. He chuckles a little. "Um, I should probably get back to work."

"Yeah. Of course. Do me a favor, sweetheart?"

"Okay?" he asks a little hesitantly.

I smile, even though he can't see it. "Next time you go to the bathroom, I want you to fuck yourself with that plug. Three times, in and out."

He curses.

"And text me when you're done," I add.

Kipp blows out a breath. "You're cruel, Teddy."

"You'll be thanking me later."

"No doubt. I'm going now. Bye, husband-mine."

I chuckle. "Bye, Kipp."

Fifteen minutes later, a text comes through.

Babydoll: Done. I hate you so much, you have no idea. You better make good on your promise later—so hard I pass out.

I smirk at my phone. *Deal.*

Chapter 22
Kipp

"Fuck, fuck, fuck," I mutter, each step pure torture. *Torture.*

I've never been so horny in all my life. And that's saying something.

"If he doesn't pounce on me," I mutter to myself, "the moment I'm through the door, I'm going to *die*. And I don't think that's melodramatic. It's the truth."

I breathe a sigh of relief when I step out of the elevator and spot our door.

"So. Close."

I did everything Teddy asked me to today. I thought of him every time the plug shifted inside my ass. I remembered his fingers and the feel of his lips against my skin. I fucked myself *three goddamn times* with the thing after lunch, which was entirely too much and not enough at all. I imagined his cock finally, *finally* sinking inside of me. And, before I left, I cleaned up and relubed myself.

I'm ready. So goddamn ready I'm fairly certain I'm going to come the second he slams inside my body. And he better slam. You bet your ass there better be slamming involved. I have waited a long damn time for this. I've been *good*. I've been patient...somewhat.

I deserve to be railed like a freaking ragdoll, damn it!

My hand shakes as I slip the key into the lock. Every single minute shift of my body has the plug rubbing against me. I've oversensitized, my cock is hard, my *nipples* are hard, and all I want, when I walk through the door, is Teddy.

The door opens without a creak, and silence greets me. I step inside tentatively, my feet shuffling forward. He's not in the kitchen. Not working out. Not in the living room.

I close the door behind me. "Teddy?"

No answer.

I set down my things and toe off my shoes. I consider stripping out of my pants for efficiency's sake but decide against it. I'm Teddy's to undress.

The thought makes me shiver.

I get all the way to the entrance of the hall when Teddy appears, stepping out of the bedroom and into my line of vision. I stop in my tracks, the look in his eye freezing me where I stand.

"Doll," he says simply.

Oh fuck.

"Hi," I whisper.

Teddy takes one small step forward, and I retreat the same. Another step forward. Another step back. There's a smirk on his face as he stalks me backwards. I don't even know why I'm running. No, not running, not really. But I'm making him follow. My body feels charged, hair standing on end, every instinct in me telling me to flee. Because if I do, he'll chase.

And I want him to catch me. I want him to *take* me.

I keep backing up as Teddy walks forward, his steps calm and measured. I've never seen him look quite this intense. I don't think he's going to be gentle with me today.

I don't want him to be.

"How was your afternoon?" he asks from two feet away.

My back hits the island, a chair sliding a few inches out of the way. "Good."

He hums, a foot away now. My body is *vibrating*.

"Did you do what I asked?"

"Yes," I whisper, sucking in a breath when Teddy stops mere inches in front of me. He doesn't touch. Not yet. His gaze runs over me. My face. My neck, where I'm sure my pulse is hammering. My chest. Lower. When his eyes return to mine, his thumb brushes over my bottom lip ever so gently. A small kiss perhaps.

My breath puffs out, and Teddy spins me around.

I *oomph*, hands catching the countertop as he deftly unbuttons and unzips my slacks. He tugs them down, the fabric rubbing over my aching cock and making me hiss. The material falls to the floor, pooling around my feet, and Teddy cups my cock as his other hand slips under the band of my briefs.

I pull in a sharp breath, my heart pounding, anticipation firing like electricity in my veins.

The tips of Teddy's fingers roll over the plug, the tiny movement a spark. "You're not going to come unless I say so," he says, voice utterly calm.

"Um..."

"You won't," he assures me, despite that seeming impossible. He lets my cock go, hands tugging down my underwear. "Because if you're close, you're going to tell me."

Fuuuck.

"Got it?" he asks, letting my underwear join my pants around my feet.

I nod. "'Kay."

"Good doll."

In a quick move, Teddy grabs my hands, stretching my arms across the counter and slapping my palms down flat with a *thwack*. The position has me bent over the surface and entirely at his mercy. There's the brush of his fingertips at my ass again and then the pressure of the plug. My heart hammers as Teddy pulls it out slowly, stopping with the widest portion at my rim.

"Do you know how hard it was thinking of you at work all day wearing this plug?" he asks. "Thinking of you waiting for me to fill you?"

I don't answer. I don't think I can.

He lets the plug go, and I gasp as it settles back inside my body. There's some shuffling behind me, the sound of a zipper, and then his hands are back, one on the base of the plug, the other on my hip.

"Do you know how many times I imagined sinking inside this ass?" He tugs on the plug again. This time, he keeps going, and I breathe a sigh of relief as it slips free. "Are you going to keep my cock nice and warm, doll?"

Fuck. "Yes."

"That's right," he says in that low, even voice. "And why's that?"

"Because..." I swallow, resisting the urge to press back and feel him. "Because I'm yours."

"You. Are. Mine," he says, lifting my leg until my foot rests on the rung of the chair beside me. My breath comes short, fingers curling against the countertop as I feel the head of his cock press against me. I'm entirely exposed, utterly his.

I've never felt anything better.

"*My. Babydoll*," he says fiercely.

And then he slams into me.

Air whooshes from my lungs, my body lurching forward from the impact. My cock *throbs*, but Teddy stills, his hips at my ass, his dick filling me fully and stretching me so perfectly wide I nearly swoon. He doesn't retreat and snap forward again. He only rolls his hips, the gentlest of movements that reminds me exactly of how the plug teased me all day long. I understand why he's doing it. Why he's giving me time to adjust. But *fuck*. I don't want time. Every shift of his cock inside my body only makes me long to feel the full length of him taking me again and again. I want him to obliterate me. I want to be *owned*.

"Teddy," I groan. "*Please*."

The sharp slap to my ass has me going up on my tiptoes. "Who do you belong to, doll?"

"*Fuck*. You."

"Who takes care of you?"

I groan as he circles my cock, jerking me once. "You," I answer.

"That's right. So be good and take what I give you."

I cry out as Teddy slaps the side of my ass again, the burn of it spreading, my entire body tingling, skin tight. He grinds against me, so damn deep inside my body I hiccup a breath. I try to push back on him, try to gain some leverage, but Teddy's hands cover my own, his lips finding my neck as his body drapes over mine, forcing my chest flat against the countertop.

"I will fuck you so damn hard you feel it for days," he promises, still grinding slowly. "I will take you apart and put you back together again. But *first*, I'm going to feel you. Because that is my right. And I've waited a long damn time for it."

My breath punches out of me, and I nod. I nod and nod and nod, and Teddy kisses my neck, a slow press of his mouth, a swipe of tongue, the heat of him at my back, the weight of him holding me down. It's utter perfection, all of it. His fingers interlock with my own, and I'm drowning in him, every sensation on overload. The small flex of his cock in my ass. The brush of his skin on mine. The low grunts coming from his throat and the whisper of his breath.

I feel it all, a hyperawareness, and I sink into it. I sink into the warmth Teddy is promising. Into the spicy vanilla scent surrounding me. Into the slow pace he's fucking me with, knowing, when he's good and goddamn ready, he'll give me everything he knows I need.

I let him have me. All of me.

I surrender.

"Gorgeous, doll," Teddy murmurs, his words spoken like praise.

I feel it; I do. He makes me feel *so fucking good* and gorgeous.

Teddy's teeth skim down to my shoulder, his hips moving a little faster now, the gentle slap against my ass a hint of what's to come. "I could stay like this all day," he says, his hand trailing down to my cock. His fingers roll over my leaking tip, the sensation excruciatingly exquisite. "I'd stay right here with my cock buried in your body. My perfect doll. I'd fuck you for hours just to feel you hug me tight. So goddamn sweet. So eager for it."

I moan my assent, not having the brainpower to produce words.

"And if I needed a break, I'd leave you right here waiting for me, my plug in your ass until I was ready to come back and fill you up again."

Oh God. Why is that so hot?

"You'd be good for me," he all but purrs, picking up his pace a little, his cock retreating a few inches only to slam back in. "Isn't that right, babydoll? Because you're mine. And my doll is *always* good."

I roll my head against the counter. *Yes, yes, anything.*

"That's right, sweetheart. Tell me if you're about to come."

I don't have time to mourn the loss of Teddy's warmth at my back because the moment he's upright, he grabs my hips, slips nearly all the way out of my body, and rams back in again. I suck in a breath, everything in me coiling tight like a spring ready to unload, the anticipation and need and simmering heat that's been eating away at me all day snapping into sharp focus. It's like a wrecking ball, barreling at me with a speed so fast it leaves me dizzy.

"Teddy," I gasp.

He wraps a hand around the base of my cock, squeezing tight as he stills completely. He stays like that for a good thirty seconds before slowly releasing my cock. And then he starts fucking me again.

"Oh God," I breathe, barely having come down at all.

He doesn't slow. He fucks me hard, his hips slapping my ass, his cock ramming home again and again. I *know* he's not aiming for my prostate because the man knows where it is. He's going to make this last, and I can't decide if that sounds like the absolute best thing or the worst.

"Teddy," I groan.

That hand wraps back around my cock. "Good doll," he praises, fucking me in long, languid strokes. His other hand leaves my hip and sifts up into my hair, the touch grounding and familiar, thrilling and comforting all at once. "Beautiful. You take me so well."

I moan. At his words. At his touch. At the way he's denying my orgasm even as he drives into my body. *Fuck*. He's everywhere.

He slows again, grinding shallowly and letting me come down. A good couple minutes pass, and when my breathing has evened out and I don't feel like I'm about to fall over the edge, he lets go of my cock.

"Do you know the first thing I thought when I saw you?" Teddy asks.

I try to shake my head, but everything is weighted. My body, my limbs. Suddenly, I'm grateful for the counter under my chest.

Teddy's fingers comb through my hair, his other hand grabbing a hold of my hip. He thrusts into me hard, nailing my prostate, and I call out, pulling back my orgasm by sheer will alone. He stills again, rocking into me gently.

"I thought, 'That man has the power to bring me to my knees. He's gorgeous, and he *wants*, and I would do anything to keep him. To make him mine.'"

I shake my head. I don't... That doesn't make sense. He didn't want to keep me. He didn't want me at all.

Teddy's fingers tighten in my hair, tugging gently. "Do you understand the power you have over me, chéri?"

I...

Teddy slams into me again, scattering my thoughts. My foot slips off the chair, and he wraps an arm around my waist, supporting my weight and hiking my leg back into place.

"Stay where I put you, doll."

I moan, lying lax against the countertop, trying to keep myself in place as Teddy fucks me with precision strokes. My limbs feel like noodles, and *fuck*, I'm about to come.

"Teddy," I croak out.

He slips entirely from my body, and I nearly fall on my ass.

"Shh," he says, sweeping me up into his arms. My briefs dangle from my foot for a moment before falling to the floor, and Teddy carries me down the hall as I blink my eyes, trying to keep track of where we're going and why even the air on my skin has me ready to blow. I think I say Teddy's name again. He just kisses my forehead before laying me out on the bed.

I watch, the world a little hazy around the edges, as Teddy strips off his jeans. He was fucking me in his jeans? And his shirt? *Holy hell.* He saunters back to the bed, his cock bobbing between his legs with a swagger of its own. He's wearing a condom, and he climbs back over my body, warming me at once. Hands are in my hair. Lips press lightly to my own.

"I'm yours, too," he says, the words barely computing.

"Are you?" I slur.

He nods, his nose brushing mine. He presses back into my body, and I groan, back bowing. Teddy's hips meet my ass, my knees bent up on either side of him. He holds my head in place, his mouth meeting mine, his tender kiss at odds with the way he starts rutting into me.

Oh God. Is there a point *past* coming? Because I feel like I'm there. Like I've floated away from this plane, and somewhere back on Earth, Kipp is coming his brains out, but here, in this place, I'm climbing and climbing and climbing, and the mountain never ends.

Teddy's lips brush over my cheek, my forehead. "You're so beautiful, sweetheart. Every part of you. It hurts. Do you get that? It *hurts* how much I want you."

God. Does he mean it?

"Fuck," he mutters, leaning back. His hand wraps around my cock. "Come now, babydoll. You did so good."

With his permission, I splinter apart. And piece by piece, he gathers me back up, holding me safely in his arms.

Chapter 23

TEDDY

Kipp sleeps well through the night. No dinner. No late-night TV with cuddles on the couch. He passes out before his cock has finished throbbing in my hand, and I clean him up, clean *myself up*, and then wrap him in my arms until morning.

I wake early, before the sun has risen.

As I flip pancakes and bacon, I contemplate my options. I could tell him this has gone far beyond casual for me. I could admit I have feelings and see if he feels the same. I could even suggest we stay married indefinitely because what's the harm? It's worked pretty well for us thus far.

But I'm scared. That's the honest truth. I've been doing my best to convince myself I could walk away when the time comes. That, when Kipp shows up and tells me he's ready for a divorce, I'll sign the papers, shake his hand, and we'll go back to being casual acquaintances or maybe friends or who-the-fuck-knows-what.

But how can I do that? How can I possibly let this man go?

What if he wants me to?

When I hear footsteps padding down the hall, I lower the burner and round the island. Kipp comes into view, looking like an utterly rumpled and perfectly gorgeous mess. He sees me and smiles.

"Hey," he says quietly.

"Hey," I reply, helping him onto a chair. He's wearing sweats but nothing else.

He chuckles a little. "I'm perfectly capable of seating myself."

I don't tell him it's *me* who needs the reassurance that he's okay.

"Hungry?" I ask.

He nods, yawning at the same time. "Fucking famished. Is it seriously morning? You fucked me into oblivion."

I can't quite help the twitch of my lips. I finish plating his bacon before answering. "You *did* tell me to fuck you so hard you passed out."

He snorts. "That I did."

"And?" I ask, a little nervous to hear his answer. Nervous to know whether or not he remembers the words I let slip free.

He plants his elbows on the counter, cheeks in his hands. "Mission accomplished," he says with a huff of pleased laughter.

I smile, trying to catch more from his gaze, but he just blinks sleepily and yawns again.

"Still tired?" I ask.

He shakes his head, like he's trying to knock some thoughts loose. "I mean, I shouldn't be. But damn, I'm exhausted."

"Here," I say, sliding some food his way. "This'll help."

"Thanks," he says, giving me a grateful smile.

He digs in while I grab another plate and take a seat next to him. We're quiet for a minute.

"Did you come?" he asks suddenly, turning to me. "I can't remember, and I just really need to know."

I huff a laugh. "I came."

"Okay, good."

"If you're wondering, it was seconds after you, and I pulled right out after," I tell him. "I didn't fuck you while you were unconscious."

His brow furrows, a strange look crossing his face. "I mean, I wasn't worried about that. Even if you had, I wouldn't have minded. I actually... I mean, I wouldn't mind that."

I freeze, everything in me flushing hot. "You want me to fuck you while you're sleeping?"

He shrugs. "I mean, it wouldn't be the worst way to wake up. If you wanted to try that sometime, I'm on board."

I set my silverware down and scrub my hands over my face.

"What?" Kipp asks, tone worried.

I shake my head. "Nothing. It's just... That involves a level of consensual non-consent we haven't talked about. And you'd really trust me to do that?"

"Why not?" he says, like it's that simple to him. "It sounds hot, and of course I trust you, Teddy. If I wasn't into it, you'd know, and you'd stop. I already told you that you have blanket permission to touch me whenever you want."

I pull in a centering breath.

"Is the idea upsetting to you?" Kipp asks.

I meet his gaze. "No," I say, voice hoarse. "It's just..." *You're fucking perfect and mine, and don't you see that? You were made for me, and I won't ever abuse your trust? If you want me to fuck you awake, I'll make it so good, you won't ever come without my name on your lips again?* "It's just... I don't think you know how rare you are, Kipp. Thank you for having that sort of trust in me."

His huff of laughter is small and light, his cheeks turning a beautiful rosy pink. "You wouldn't hurt me, Teddy."

No, I wouldn't. Not ever.

"We can discuss that sometime," I agree. "But just to be clear, I have no interest in the sort of consensual non-con that would involve you struggling or telling me no and me ignoring it. I don't ever want to feel like I'm harming you, even with a safeword in place."

The smile Kipp gives me is so sweet my heart hammers anew. "That's good, Teddy, because I don't want that, either. You told me you want to make me feel good, remember? I certainly do. You'd never force me, and I don't want to play at that either. I like what we have. I like..." He clears his throat, that color on his cheeks not yet fading. "I like being your doll. I like the way you make me feel safe. And I want *you* to feel safe with me, too. I won't ever ask you to do something you're uncomfortable with, okay?"

"Yeah," I say roughly.

"So we're agreed," he says, going back to his pancakes. "No means no. Stop means stop. And that goes both ways." He hums around his bite of food, holding up a finger. "Plus bananas. That's a big freaking nuh-uh. 'Cause seriously, fuck those fuckers."

I snort. "Any other food aversions I should be aware of?"

Kipp turns to me slowly, expression dead serious when he says, "Shrimp."

I do my best not to laugh. "Right. Can't forget the shrimp."

"Never again," he mutters, snapping off a piece of bacon in his mouth. "Hey, I didn't miss the show, did I?"

"The show?"

He waves toward my workout equipment. "The *show*. You know, the erotic performance art you do each morning."

"You mean exercising?" I ask with a grin.

"Call it what you will," he replies. "But it's fucking erotic, you can't deny that. Did I miss it?"

"No," I assure him, finishing my bacon. "You didn't miss it."

"Thank fuck," he breathes. "Okay, you do that, I'll watch to make sure you don't miss any steps, and then maybe a run? And after that... I don't know. What do you want to do today?"

My smile grows wider, Kipp's assumption that we'll spend our Saturday together warming me through. "Anything, Kipp."

Anything if it's with you.

"Theodore."

I sigh.

I should've known I couldn't outrun this forever. I've been lucky to escape his wrath up until this point. Yet with one word, I know I'm not getting out of it this time. The firing squad awaits, ammo loaded.

Time to face my fate.

Alex clears his throat. Loudly. "*Theodore.*"

"Hey, Alex."

He plunks down onto the bench beside me. I'm already dressed and showered, my scene having finished a while ago. It looks like Alex is just getting here. The locker room is empty except for us.

"You know why I'm here," he says, tone serious.

"I do."

"Before you tell me what I want to know, I'm going to tell *you* something."

Oh boy.

"We've worked together for years," he says.

"Yes," I agree.

"And while I push sometimes, I know when to back off."

"Okay," I say slowly.

"I'm not backing off this time," he says, hazel eyes bright. "And do you know why?"

I'm afraid to ask.

"Teddy Bear, you're always looking after others. You're like a quiet sentinel, watching, checking in, making sure we're all okay. You do that caretaker thing of yours, but you never let anyone look after you."

"I—"

"It's true," Alex barrels on. "And don't try to tell me otherwise. You're like one-way glass. You keep a wall up to protect yourself, and I get it. We all have secrets. But damn it, Teddy, we're here for you. Every single person inside this building wants what's best for you. It's okay to let us in. We're not going to fuck you over like whoever it was that broke your heart."

Silence falls for an extended beat, my hammering pulse the only sound I hear.

"It was a boyfriend," I admit. "And my brother."

Because they *both* broke my heart. For different reasons, yes, but equally painful in the end. And Alex is right. I haven't shared with these people, haven't wanted to let myself be vulnerable to anyone again. But it's too late for that, isn't it? I'm already cracking apart, those tender insides exposed to the air. I let Kipp seep his way in, and now, I'm not sure how to go about shoring myself back up.

I'm not even sure I want to.

"Oh, boo," Alex says softly, rubbing my back. "I'm so sorry."

"I got into porn because I didn't want to risk my feelings again," I tell him, the words spilling free. "I used to be a lawyer. Still am, technically."

"I heard that."

"I'm from Quebec," I go on. "I have dual citizenship."

"That's—"

"And I'm pretty sure I'm head over heels in love with Kipp."

Alex stills. "Teddy."

"I'm terrified," I tell him, meeting his gaze. "Scared shit-less. I fucking love him, and I'm pretty sure I have since before we got married."

It was love from afar, maybe, but I knew the potential was there. I *knew* it. It was all the little things. Like how Kipp's smile made me feel soft, even if it wasn't aimed at me. How, every time he'd dance with someone else, I'd watch him, seeing the cues he left that his partners never picked up. The fact that he was frantically searching for someone to take over. To just *take over* already and let him relax for once. It was how I *knew* I could be that man. I knew I could make him happy if only he'd let me.

I just wouldn't let *myself*.

Until the night when everything changed.

And now... Now I've seen that smile aimed at me. I've tasted his lips, his tears, his cock. I've held him and shared his bed and heard his laugh every single day. I know how utterly right it feels to be the one to take care of him. And I don't think I can give that up. If Kipp left, I think he would take that piece of me with him. Strip it right from my bones. I want to be his husband. For real. For better or for worse and in all the ways that count.

I want to be *his*.

"Teddy Bear," Alex says softly, reaching up to cup my cheek. "That man is gaga over you. You don't have to be scared of him."

"I'm worried I don't think rationally when it comes to him."

Alex's smile goes a little crooked. "Honey. That's love."

I huff a laugh, and Alex's hand drops. "What if I'm only seeing what I want?" I ask. "What if I'm imagining what we are?"

"Well, you see... There's this thing called *talking*."

"Smartass," I grumble.

Alex gives me a wink.

"We talk about a lot," I tell him. "We talk about wants and safewords and limits."

"Oof," Alex says, fanning his face. "To be a fly on the wall."

"But we haven't talked about *us*," I admit. Not since I laid the ground rules the first time I got him off. When I implied we were temporary. That once we got divorced, our game would be done. I cringe. "*Shit.*"

"And there it is, folks," Alex says, standing up and holding his arms wide. He spins in a circle, as if calling to the nonexistent crowd, and then he takes a bow. "My job here is done."

"You are such a little shit."

Alex cackles.

"I need to talk to him," I say.

"Yes," Alex answers, patting my head. "You do." He jumps back when I take a swipe at him. "Let me know how it goes."

As Alex skips off, I blow out a breath, resting my elbows on my knees.

Shit. How the hell do I tell my husband I want to date?

Chapter 24

Kipp

"Uh-huh, uh-huh," I say, nodding along as the client in my ear explains, in excruciating, unnecessary detail, why the color blue we chose isn't consistent with their brand, even going so far as to say it's an *offensive* choice. Yikes. When they finally stop talking long enough to breathe, I cut in. "We can go with a different blue. That's not a problem. How about I have my team draft up a few options for you?"

We finish discussing color choices, and, crisis averted, I end the call and relay the information to Jacob, who's the developer for the project. I'm just sitting back in my chair when my personal phone vibrates with a text.

Teddy: Want to grab dinner tonight?

I squint at the text for an inordinately long time. Don't we usually eat dinner together? He said *grab*. Does that mean he wants to get something from a restaurant? Does he want *me* to get it?

Me: You want me to pick something up on my way home?

Teddy: No, I mean go out. The two of us.

Oh.

Me: Sure!
Teddy: Cool.

Cool? I'm back to squinting. Since when does Teddy say *cool?*

Me: Have you been body-snatched? Quick, what did you say to me this morning before I left for work?

It takes half a minute for his response to come through.

Teddy: I told you if you kept trying to lick the sweat off my thigh, I'd give your tongue a reason to stay perfectly still, babydoll.

I cough, looking around my office. The door is open, but obviously, no one can see Teddy's text. *Sure could see my blush, though.*

Me: I meant your goodbye, but yeah, proof supplied.
Teddy: 7?

Me: ...Inches? I think you're more like 8.5, which you should know. It's in your profile for the studio.

There's a longer pause this time.

Teddy: 7 o'clock for dinner?

Ohh.

Me: Ohh. Yeah, that works.
Teddy: See you soon, sweetheart.

Well that was...sweet. And weird. Since when does Teddy text me ahead of time to confirm dinner plans?

Shaking my head, I get back to work and smash some client calls.

The weirdness continues when I get home.

"Hey," Teddy says the moment I'm through the door. He takes my work bag from my hand, setting it aside and then lingering as I shuck off my shoes, staring at me all the while.

"Hello," I say slowly.

"Good day?" he asks, following me into the kitchen while I grab a glass of water.

"Yes, darling."

If Teddy notices my exaggerated honey-sweet tone, he doesn't comment on it. He watches me as I drink the liquid down, his gaze not that hawk-like one but something much gentler.

"You feeling okay?" I ask.

"Of course."

"Mkay."

Teddy follows me as I head down the hall into the bedroom. I glance back at him once, confused, but he's acting as if him trailing after me is perfectly normal. He takes up position near the dresser, arms crossed casually over his chest as I slip out of my work shirt and into something more comfortable.

"Just gonna stare?" I ask, amused more than anything.

"You like it when I watch you," he comments, that gentle look back on his face. It disarms me somewhat, making this feel less like playful flirting and more like... I don't even know.

"I can give you a show if you want," I say, easing my pants down slowly.

He snorts, lips twitching. "We have dinner plans."

"In like..."—I check the clock—"an hour. Plenty of time for you to...*watch*."

Teddy's arms stay crossed as I kick off my pants, leaving them in a pool on the floor. His gaze lingers on them for a moment, as if he's considering hanging them up, but then I slip my fingers under the waistband of my briefs, and Teddy's gaze snaps back up to me.

"Kipp," he says quietly, almost like an admonishment, except his tone is lacking any sort of sternness to back it up. "You're incorrigible, you know that?"

"I'm well aware," I tell him, palming my half-hard cock. "So are you going to watch or are you going to participate?"

He groans slightly. "I'm trying to be good."

My brows draw together. "Whatever for?"

He laughs. "Kipp."

"*Teddy.*"

He groans again when I slip my hand down to my balls, the motion causing my briefs to uncover the head of my cock. He eases out a breath before stepping forward.

"You," he says, spinning me around and tugging down my briefs before I've even caught my breath, "are impossible to ignore."

"Doesn't sound like a ba—*ah-hah-hah, fuck yes, please.*"

Teddy chuckles against my skin, his palms on my ass and his tongue attempting to bury itself in my body. Yeah. Yep. This is good. *So* very good.

Turns out, we have plenty of time for some pre-dinner entertainment.

"So where are you taking me?" I ask, gazing curiously out the window as Teddy drives us toward the swanky part of town.

"Someplace with shrimp," he says.

I turn my head his way slowly. "Teddy. Don't even joke about that. I'm scarred. For *life.* You should be, too, you know, after having lived through that harrowing experience with me."

I shudder just remembering it. The poor guy saw me at my literal worst. And yet, somehow, he still looks at me like he did earlier tonight, with *want* in his eyes. The thought is weirdly comforting.

"This place actually has great steak," he says. "Sounded good."

"Oh, damn. Yeah. Sounds great."

He hums, looking pleased. Smug Teddy is one of my favorite Teddys.

The restaurant, as it turns out, is nice as hell. The hostess leads us back to our table, where white linen napkins sit draped over small, porcelain plates. Teddy takes a seat across from me, setting his napkin in his lap.

"Teddy," I whisper.

He looks at me.

"I'm wearing jeans."

His lips pull at the corner. "That's fine."

"You didn't tell me we were going somewhere fancy," I mutter, looking around at all the well-dressed people, Teddy included. He's wearing a button-down shirt and stylish black pants, something I didn't pay attention to after he blew my brains out through my cock. "I look like a ragamuffin compared to everyone here."

"A ragamuffin?" he asks, smiling outright now.

"I didn't want to say a hobo 'cause that's rude. Homeless people shouldn't be mocked for a lack of resources most people take for granted. And what? Why are you looking at me like that?"

Teddy reaches across the table, giving my chin a squeeze. "You're lovely, Kipp."

Well, shit. "Um, thanks?"

He nods, pulling his hand back. "And don't worry. No one cares about your pants."

"In that case, you could switch with me?" I semi-joke.

"Sweetheart," he says slowly, the simple word wrapping around me like a caress. "I wouldn't fit in your pants."

"Well, that's rude. Your dick isn't *that* much bigger than mine."

"I meant my waist size," he says calmly, hitching up a brow.

"Oh."

Teddy snorts.

"For what it's worth, I very much like your waist size," I tell him, squirming in my seat. "I like that you're bigger than me. That you can throw me around or hold me down or—oh, hello."

Our waitress gives us a nervous sort of smile. "Hi! I'm Lola, your server for tonight."

"Great," I say as she fills our water glasses. Teddy laughs under his breath when I shoot a wide-eyed wince his way. Lola goes over a few specials, takes our drink orders, and heads off. I hang my head in my hands. "Can't take me anywhere."

"Kipp," Teddy says lightly. "I enjoy your brand of mayhem."

"Is that so?" I ask, raising my head.

He hums. "It's endearing."

"Well, that's new," I say, flipping my menu open as my pulse skitters. "Most guys don't enjoy the effects of Hurricane Kipp."

"Do you think I'm *most guys*?" Teddy asks, using that low, even tone.

My gaze snaps to his, breath catching. "No," I answer quietly. Truthfully.

He holds my eye for a long moment. "Good."

The not-at-all-uncomfortable tension is shattered when someone nearby drops a fork against their plate, the loud clattering making me jolt. I huff a laugh and look through my menu, wondering what it means that Teddy doesn't want me to lump him in with all the rest of the guys I've fucked or dated.

I'm scared to hope.

When our waitress comes back around, Teddy and I order dinner. It's been a long time since I've had steak from a restaurant. I can already feel my mouth pooling with saliva.

"This was such a good idea," I tell Teddy.

"Glad you approve," he says, mouth twisting in that way it does.

"Ugh. Stop it."

"What?" he asks, looking mildly alarmed.

"Stop being so damn attractive. I'm only human, Teddy. If you're expecting me to look at your stupidly gorgeous face all dinner and eat my meat like I'm not thinking about *your* meat, well, I hate to break it to you, but your expectations are set too high."

He huffs a laugh.

"I'm entirely serious. It's a good thing I can't smell you from here."

"Is it?" he asks, tone soft.

"Do you know how hard it is not to bury my face in your neck every time you smell all..." I wave my hand around, looking for the right word. "*You?*"

"It's just my body wash," he says, eyes crinkled.

"No, it's not," I retort with a shake of my head. "It's you *and* the body wash. It's, like, sure, that stuff smells good. But when I use it? It's not the same. When it's on *you*, it's like..." I close my eyes, letting myself sink into the memory. "It's like warmth and sex and comfort all in one. I smell that spicy vanilla *you* scent, and I'm safe and can relax and just *be*. It's contentment, you know?"

When I open my eyes, Teddy's gaze has me pulling in a breath.

"Kipp," he says seriously.

"Yeah?"

He licks his lips. "I wanted to talk to you about something."

"Okay?"

He opens his mouth, but I don't catch a word he says because, at that precise moment, a waitress sets a plate down on the table next to ours. My gaze zeroes in on that plate. On the steak topped with...

"Oh no," I mutter, my stomach rolling. *Shrimp.* "Oh no, oh no."

Teddy freezes mid-sentence, his words about *"wondering if"* coming to an abrupt halt.

"Sorry," I say quickly, pushing out of my seat. "Excuse me."

I hurry toward the back of the restaurant, mortified about my hasty escape and praying I'm not about to lose the contents of my stomach. *Again.* Luckily, the sensation has mostly passed by the time I reach the restrooms. I still lock myself in a stall, breathing deeply for a few minutes to make sure I'm steady. Before I leave, I splash water on my face. It helps cool me down.

When I get back to the table, Teddy is looking down at his folded hands. He eyes me warily as I take a seat.

"I'm so sorry," I tell him, careful to avoid looking at the table next to ours. "I saw a certain horrible crustacean and got a little..."

I wave toward my stomach, and Teddy's eyes widen.

"Are you all right?" he asks.

I wave him off. "Yeah, fine."

"Shit, I thought..." He shakes his head, not finishing his sentence.

"What?"

"Nothing," he says, giving me a smile. I don't have time to pester him further before our meals arrive. Perfectly free of shrimp, thank you.

Two minutes later, with a mouth full of heavenly ribeye, I groan. "My *God*. This is the shit. Best thing I've ever had in my mouth."

Teddy's lips twitch. "The best?"

"Don't go fishing, Teddy. You know there's no comparison when it comes to your cock."

"I hate to point it out," he says quietly, "but you've never actually had my cock in your mouth."

I still, said mouth popping open. "Holy..." I cycle back through every sexual encounter Teddy and I have had, from early morning handies and frot sessions, to him taking me apart methodically and fucking my fist or, more recently and notably, my ass. Which, *Hallelujah and thank you, Jesus.*

He's had my cock in his mouth, but is he right? Have I never given him a blowie? I know I offered, but the man has a tendency to take charge, and all cognitive thought goes *pft*.

"Teddy," I hiss, a mixture of outraged and turned on. "We need to rectify this. Like, *now*."

"You're not blowing me under the table," he retorts calmly.

"I wasn't suggesting that, but damn, now it's in my head."

He chuckles, and I whimper. I shift in my seat as I chew another bite of steak.

"In the car?" I offer.

"No."

"Bathroom?"

Teddy huffs a laugh. "We're not having sex in the bathroom of a steakhouse."

"*But Daddy*," I tease.

The look Teddy gives me has me snapping my mouth shut. "There'll be plenty of time, sweetheart. It can wait until we're home."

And fuck. That kind of warms me through.

"So mean," I mutter affectionately.

Teddy's smile feels a little bit like the smell of his body wash on his skin. Warm and full of contentment.

Plenty of time, huh? I like the sound of that.

Chapter 25

TEDDY

Talking to Kipp at dinner didn't go quite like I had planned. First, he hoofed it away from the table while I was in the middle of explaining to him what these past several weeks have meant to me—a fact that had me thinking the worst until he returned. And then we were talking about blowjobs, of all things, and I couldn't get the moment back.

Now, we're walking side by side toward my car that's parked a couple blocks away, and Kipp is telling me about the *blue incident* he had at work. Hearing him describe his day in such vivid detail, hands flying and eyes bright, has a smile on my face.

When he suddenly stops walking, I nearly trip, having been watching *him* and not where I was going.

"What's that?" Kipp asks, pointing across the street.

I follow his line of sight to a lit-up club. The outside is painted red, the exterior classy but mysterious in a way that leaves you assuming you could be looking at anything from a bar to a brothel. However, I know exactly what's inside, having been there a handful of times before.

"It's a salsa club," I tell Kipp.

He looks at me with wide eyes. "No shit? And how do you know that?"

I shrug. "I know how to salsa."

He stares at me for a solid three seconds before grabbing my hand and tugging me toward the crosswalk.

Oh Lord.

"We're going in," Kipp declares, not asking my opinion on the matter. "I'm gonna see my goddamn husband goddamn salsa, Teddy, and don't you dare think about depriving me of that honor."

I huff a laugh as Kipp smashes the button for the crosswalk. As soon as the light turns green, he tugs me across the street.

"Salsa," he mutters, shaking his head. "Fucking hot. Can you roll up your sleeves?"

"My sleeves?" I ask.

Kipp's eyes trail down my arms for a moment before he focuses on reaching the front of the club. "Everyone knows forearms are prime ogling material, and if I can't see your dick, then I'm going to need you to roll up those sleeves. Preferably slowly and while you're dancing."

"So, basically, you want me to do a forearm striptease for you?"

"Bingo," he says.

I keep my amusement to myself as Kipp drags me inside the building. It looks the same as I remember, even though I haven't been inside in over five years. Red lights aimed at the walls give the club a sensual vibe that's instantly matched by the lively, rhythmic beat of the music. The majority of the space is devoted to the dance floor, but high-top tables sit interspersed around the edges of the room, and a bar occupies one wall. Kipp stares wide-eyed for all of a second before tugging me forward.

Kipp might not know how to salsa, but the man has never had an ounce of shame when it comes to dancing. He stops right in the middle of the dance floor and spins my way, beckoning me closer. With the music pumping through my veins and Kipp's smile lighting me on fire, I step forward, rolling my shirtsleeve as I go. Kipp grabs his chest, feigning a swoon as I reveal my forearm. I do the other, and he fans his face. When I reach out a hand, he takes it without hesitation, and I tug him into my arms.

Kipp's grin is blinding as my hand settles at his waist, my other holding his tight. Partners maintain some space here on the dance floor, unlike at a typical club, so I have room to maneuver Kipp as a Marc Anthony song suffuses the room. His eyes go wide when I roll my hips, guiding him with my hand to do the same. He mouths, "Holy shit," but follows along, picking up the gist of it quickly enough. We move in a circle as we dance, and when I let go of Kipp's waist to spin him out, he laughs loud enough to be heard over the music. I tug him back in, and he collides with my chest, our gazes connecting, both of us stilling. But then Kipp's smile is sweeping back over his face, and he's on the move again, his body flowing effortlessly with the music.

I don't know how long we dance for. Song after song, we stay out on that salsa floor, Kipp picking up more and more steps as we go. He's a natural, and when he copies the woman next to us and shimmies his chest, I can't help but bust out laughing. He winks, the cheeky man.

This time, when I tug him in close, he stays there. With my hand on his lower back and his on my shoulder, we sway together, hips brushing as our feet move. His eyes are bright yet soft as he looks at me, his lips wet when he licks them. Without overthinking it, I duck my head and take his mouth in a kiss. He moans against me, a short vibration I feel more than hear. It sinks inside my veins like the beat, heating my blood and making me feel reckless in that way adrenaline will. I feel alive. Like I'm *living*. Like this, right here, right now, is what I want my life to be.

When I draw back, my heart is pounding. "Are you ready to go?" I ask.

Kipp nods.

I lean close so I don't have to shout. "Just need to use the bathroom."

He points toward the bar, letting me know where he'll be, and we split, the music thrumming through every inch of me like a reminder of Kipp's kiss.

I take a quick moment while I'm in the bathroom to catch my breath. There's a lot on the line tonight, and I don't know how Kipp is going to react when I tell him I have feelings for him. That this casual husbands-with-benefits thing isn't what I want us to be. I don't want there to be an expiration date. I don't want to pretend like this isn't *real*.

But it's entirely possible that Kipp isn't on the same page, and, for all I know, wanting *real* may very well be the end of my marriage.

Christ.

I shake my head before washing up and leaving the bathroom. Kipp is where he said he'd be—near the bar. I head his way, but my pace falters when I catch sight of the man he's talking to. That adrenaline crashes back through me tenfold, and I make my way quickly over, my pulse pounding in time to my footsteps.

The man sees me coming from a handful of feet away. And he fucking *smirks*.

Kipp doesn't jolt in the least when I slide my arm around his waist, tugging him close. He looks at me over his shoulder, the smile on his face quickly falling when he sees my expression. I aim my glare at the man who was talking to my husband.

"What are you doing?" I ask loudly enough to be heard.

Antoni gives me wide eyes, looking for all the world as if he's surprised to see me. "Holy cow. Hi, Theo. It's been a long time."

My teeth grind together.

"You know each other?" Kipp asks, the question directed at me.

I give a short, sharp nod. "We dated."

"For two years," Antoni puts in, a gentle smile on his face that might fool other people, but not me.

"What are you playing at, Antoni?" I ask again, not for one second believing that him talking to Kipp is a coincidence. Him being here, sure. I can buy that. Antoni and I used to come here together. It's how I learned to salsa.

But there's no doubt in my mind he singled out Kipp the moment I was out of sight, and his intentions are not ones I trust.

"I'm not sure what you mean," my ex replies, looking almost hurt. "I just met Kipp here at the bar. I didn't realize the two of you were together."

Bullshit. He saw the pictures of our wedding. He knows exactly who Kipp is to me.

I shake my head the tiniest bit before bringing my lips close to Kipp's ear. "Ready to go?"

He gives me a nod, although he looks confused. I don't blame him.

"Bye, Antoni," I say, turning without another word.

Antoni's only goodbye is to Kipp. "Take care, Kipp."

Cool air washes over my skin the moment we step out the door. I breathe it in as the music gives way to the sounds of traffic. Kipp shoots me a sidelong look as we walk away from the club.

"Okay?" he asks.

I nod before thinking better of it and shaking my head. "What'd he say to you?"

Kipp looks surprised by the question. "Not much. Just said hello. Introduced himself as Annie, I think? It was hard to hear. We talked about salsa for a few minutes and then our favorite cocktails. He seemed nice."

I huff a humorless laugh. "Yeah. He's a good liar."

I can see the gears turning in Kipp's head. He gets into the car before asking, "Was he the one?"

I blow out a breath and turn the ignition. "Yeah."

Kipp reaches over, lacing his fingers with my own in a silent show of support. I appreciate it more than I can say.

Kipp doesn't inundate me with questions on the drive home, but once we get inside the apartment, he halts me, his hand on my waist.

"Will you tell me about it?" he asks.

"It's not a pretty story."

He shrugs. "I know, but it's yours. And I want to know it. I want to know your past."

And *hell*. How can I complain about that?

"Let's wash up first," I suggest. Both of us are sweaty from the club.

Kipp nods, and the two of us make quick work of showering. There are no wandering hands. Not this time. But there *are* heated looks that neither Kipp nor I try to hide.

Dressed in comfy clothes, we sprawl out on the couch, Kipp lying between my legs, his head on my chest. I thread my fingers through his damp hair, one arm tucked behind my head. It takes me a minute to figure out where to start.

"I met Antoni what feels like ages ago. He came on board at our law firm after Cameron and I hit it big. Sometimes it feels like our success was overnight, even though I know that's not the case. We worked hard, and we made a name for ourselves. But with the notoriety came issues."

"What sort of issues?" Kipp asks, his palm resting on my stomach. His fingers toy idly with the material of my shirt, and I focus on that as I talk.

"It was the beginning of the end for Cameron and me. I didn't see it at the time, but he wanted more and more, and all I wanted was to help people. We didn't agree on the clients we were taking. He wanted big names. I wanted good causes. It...it became a problem, even before I started dating Antoni."

Kipp hums, and I blow out another breath.

"I thought I loved him. But looking back, I think I loved what we were. I loved being in a relationship and..."

"And he was your boy," Kipp fills in, making the correct leap.

"Yeah," I breathe out. "He was. But for Antoni, it was never about love. It was manipulation. We were really successful, Kipp. I don't want to downplay that. Cameron and me, we went from making barely any money starting out to making seven figures within a few years. We had lucky breaks, like I said, and we took on some big-name clients. And Antoni, he only ever wanted to be rich. He wanted to be taken care of, and I didn't mind that when it was *us*, but I never knew... I never knew he wanted the security more than he wanted me."

"So why'd he cheat?" Kipp asks gently. "If he already had you, why go after your brother?"

"Because I told him I didn't want to get married."

Kipp looks up at me, his blue eyes wide.

"Yeah," I say with a huff. "Funny, isn't it? I think I knew something wasn't right, even if I couldn't put my finger on it. He asked me to marry him a year in, but I told him I wasn't ready. He *kept* asking when I would be, and I didn't have an answer for him. I think that's when he turned to Cameron, but I don't know for sure."

"And Cameron knew you two were..."

He lets the question hang, but, "Oh, yeah. Cameron was well aware Antoni and I were a couple. The two of them... I don't know who proposed the idea, but they got it in their heads to oust me. Cameron thought I was holding the business back. Being too sentimental about the oaths I took when I became a lawyer. And Antoni, well. Antoni thought I was holding *him* back."

"So what happened?" Kipp asks softly. "How'd you find out about them?"

I blow out a slow breath. "Cameron and Antoni leaked a sex tape at the office. A tape of *them*. They did it from my email, as if I'd ever be careless enough to send a sex tape from my own email address. And then they claimed they'd been dating for months, and I was too petty and jealous to accept it and let them be happy."

"Fuck," Kipp mutters.

"It was *such* a mess. I was blindsided, having just found out my brother and boyfriend were fucking, and yet everyone was looking at me like *I* was the monster. Cameron and Antoni...they just paraded around the office like they were being the bigger men, and what could I possibly do to refute it?"

Kipp is quiet for a moment, his face aimed toward the blank TV screen. His fingers tighten in my shirt, the strain pulling the material tight. "I'm so angry for you, Teddy," he says. "But I know this isn't about me. I just... *Fuck*, I'm so sorry."

I give his hair a gentle tug. "Thanks, sweetheart."

"But I don't get it," he says, turning his face up again. "Wouldn't that tape be horrible for Cameron's career? And Antoni's?"

I shake my head a little. "They were smart," I admit. "They had the network shut down to anything but intra-office communications when the email went out. The tech team had time to scrub everyone's emails, computers, and even check phones before the network went back online. The tape never made it outside those walls."

Kipp makes a disbelieving sound. "But you said they didn't succeed in taking over the business, right? So how'd they force you out?"

"They didn't. Not exactly. I left, but what Cameron and Antoni didn't expect was for Papa to sell me his shares."

"Your grandpa had shares?"

I nod, stroking his hair again. It's as soothing to me as I'm guessing it is to him. "He helped us start the business. Invested. He didn't want anything in return, but he finally accepted three percent of the shares as a thank you. Cameron, being older and having more experience under his belt, took forty-nine percent. I had forty-eight."

"And your grandpa sold you his three," Kipp says. "Giving you fifty-one."

"Yes, he did. When he found out what happened, he didn't for one second think I'd turn on family like that. I didn't expect him to pick sides, but my papa is fierce when he wants to be. He gave me control of the business. I haven't *done* anything with it," I hasten to add. "I'm not looking for revenge. But Cameron wants those shares. Without them, he's vulnerable."

"Are they still together?" Kipp asks. "Your brother and Antoni?"

"Yeah, they are. I don't think they were ever in love, and maybe things have changed, but... I think it's mostly greed and spite that keep them together."

Kipp shakes his head. "I'm really sorry, Teddy. I wouldn't have talked to Antoni if I knew who he was."

"Hey," I say, tugging his hair again so he lifts his face. "It's not your fault. And you talking to him doesn't bother me. It's Antoni I don't trust. I'm sorry I was rude back at the club. I... I don't like who I am around them, Kipp. I don't like being that angry, bitter person I was five years ago. Every time I think I'm past what happened, something like this pops up, and here I am again, turning into the monster they tried to make me."

Kipp huffs a laugh, spinning in my arms and sliding up my body until he's straddling my waist. He leans close, his hands on either side of my head. "Teddy, you are the furthest thing from a monster. It's okay to be angry about what they did. I would be, too. Hell, I'm pissed *for* you. But you are the sweetest man I know, so fuck them, okay? They didn't make you into a monster and they never could. You're a freakin' teddy bear."

My heart beats swiftly as Kipp brushes his lips against my own. Just a press.

"You are good," he whispers. "And you are honorable. And nothing could convince me otherwise. So forget them. They don't deserve space in this gorgeous head of yours."

I open my mouth to respond, but Kipp doesn't give me the chance. His lips fit to mine, and with the sweet taste of him on my tongue, Kipp succeeds in driving every other thought away until all that's left is him.

Chapter 26

Kipp

My feet pound the pavement, the same few certainties circling inside my head over and over again like the *thwap, thwap, thwap* of my shoes.

One. Teddy is sexy as fuck when he dances. *Especially* when said dancing is salsa. Holy hotness, did he have me feeling things. In my cock. In my head. In my *heart*.

Two. Antoni is a bug I want to squash under my heel. The man tried to hurt Teddy, which is inconceivable to me in the first place and unforgivable in the second. Thinking about it makes me want to *rage*, which is why I'm out here running at five in the morning before the sun has even come up.

Three. And maybe most importantly. I don't want to divorce my husband.

It's the thing I keep coming back to. I'm not done with Teddy. At some point, us staying married would be plain weird, and frankly, we may have already passed that point. But how the heck do I suggest holding off on the divorce I promised him so that we could, what—see where things go with each other? We did everything backwards, and now it's a mess I'm not sure how to unravel.

I think Teddy likes me, too. *Really* likes me. But what if that's only part of his whole *Daddy* vibe? The man is obviously an angel.

What if I'm just the mortal blinded by his beauty who doesn't stand a chance?

Christ, maybe I need some help.

Slowing, I pace beside a closed hardware store while I catch my breath. Before I can second-guess myself, I tug my phone out of the pocket of my compression shorts and fire off a group text.

Me: What would be the best way to tell someone you maybe, probably, definitely could see yourself waking up beside them every morning for the foreseeable future until death do you part?

I'm not expecting a quick answer this early, but much to my surprise, one comes through immediately, followed by another.

Cassandra: A simple, romantic date. Like dinner at a classy restaurant. Not fast food.

Elina: And dancing afterwards if you want extra points. Super romantic.

I frown. Teddy and I just did all that, minus the whole date part, of course. My phone pings again.

Nik: Called it.

I roll my eyes.

Me: What are you all doing up this early?

Cassandra: Calliope woke me.

Elina: Haven't gone to sleep yet.

Nik: BJs.

Christ.

Cassandra: Ew.

Elina: EW!

Me: Yeah, ew, Nik. Gross.

Niko sends a middle finger response, and I snort.

Elina: I'm scarred for life. Ack.

Cassandra: You can do this, Kipp. Just be honest with him.

Fuck. Why does that sound so scary?

My phone pings again, another text from Niko coming through. This time, it's in our private chat.

Nik: You okay?

Me: Not sure. I really like him.

Nik: Just tell him. What do you have to lose?

Uh...

Me: A husband. A home. My dignity.

The list could go on.

Nik: I think you two are where you are for a reason. He likes you, too, bro-friend.

I grasp my chest.

Me: You bro-friended me. BUDDY.

Nik: Yeah, yeah. I maybe kind of like you, too. I've gotta go, though. Dixon is grumping at me and about to take matters into his own hands.

It takes me a second to figure out what he means.

Me: You were MID blowjob, and you paused to text me? Dude. That's true friendship.

Niko sends me an eggplant emoji, and I crack up, tucking my phone back in my pocket.

Teddy is still sleeping when I get home, so I slip inside the en suite to shower, leaving the door cracked. When a wash of cold air rushes over my skin, I snap my eyes open to find Teddy in front of the sink, his form blurred through the foggy glass.

I shut off the water and open the shower door.

"Morning," Teddy says around his toothbrush, meeting my gaze in the mirror. His eyes sweep over my naked body, lingering on my crotch. He spits out his toothpaste and turns when I don't answer. "Everything all right?"

Heart racing, I drop slowly to my knees. Teddy inhales a sharp breath, and, emboldened, I slide my palms up his thighs and over the briefs covering his cock. The material dampens under my hands as water drips from me to the floor.

I meet Teddy's gaze. "Please?"

His nostrils flare, the desire in his eyes unmistakable. "Fuck, sweetheart."

"My mouth, preferably, yes."

He huffs a laugh, expression going soft as his hand slips into my hair. My eyes close for a moment as I lean into the touch. But then I open them and ask again.

"Please, Teddy. I want to make you feel good, too."

After only a beat, he lets go of my hair to tug down his briefs. They fall at his feet, his erect cock bobbing in front of my face as Teddy steps out of the material. Standing naked over me, he slides his fingers back into my hair and grabs his cock.

"Open up, doll."

Fuck. Yes.

I open my mouth, tongue flat and waiting as Teddy strokes himself a few times, his hand in my hair keeping me in place. It feels like the easiest thing, kneeling before him. Placing myself at his feet and in his hands. Teddy will show me exactly what he wants, and all I have to do is give it to him. It's a relief.

And it makes me feel powerful. Because what Teddy wants...is *me*.

Anticipation thrums heavily through my veins as the heat of Teddy's thighs warms my palms. My own cock is hard and heavy, and at the first touch of Teddy's dick against my tongue, I groan.

"I missed you this morning," he says softly, rubbing himself on my tongue but not sinking deeper.

I hum, moving forward, but Teddy gives my hair a little tug, pulling my head back.

"Nuh-uh, doll. I want you just like this. A wet mouth for me to use how I please. At the pace I please."

My cock throbs, everything in my gut tightening in the best sort of way. *God, yes, that.*

"You were up early," he says, tilting my head back enough that I have to sink my ass to my heels to keep in line with his dick, the move elongating my neck. "Which means I have plenty of time to enjoy myself." He hums, as if in thought. "I think, for now, I'll have you keep me warm... Just. Like. This."

He punctuates his point by slipping the end of his dick into my mouth. My lips wrap around him in an instant, and he holds there, his fingers sliding from my hair to my face. Much to my surprise, he angles his cock to the side, pressing it against the inside of my cheek. When he rubs my cheek—rubbing the tip of his cock in the process, like he wants to feel himself embedded in my body—I damn near combust.

His response is a purr. *"Good doll."*

My cock throbs, mouth pooling with saliva as Teddy circles his thumb. His grin turns downright lethal.

"So fucking gorgeous," he says in a low growl, tapping my cheek. Tapping his *dick*. "My babydoll. Don't you dare come before me."

The words have barely sunk in before Teddy straightens out, his hands cradling my head as his cock sinks deep inside my mouth. He stops once he hits the back of my throat.

"Fuck, that's perfect," he croons, and *holy fucking fuck.* He's not even thrusting. He's just *waiting*, like he really does want me warming his dick. Like he wants to stay inside of me for as long as he possibly can.

My moan is muted around Teddy's dick as the man starts to retreat. I don't even have time to bemoan the loss before he fucks my face again. And again. And *again*, each glide painstakingly slow, each one ending with my mouth and tongue cradling his cock for good, long seconds. When I manage to relax my throat enough for him to keep going, he slips fully to the root and stalls. Wild approval flashes in his eyes as I hold his entire cock in my mouth and throat. Through blurry vision, I could almost swear his expression morphs to one of tenderness, but then the tears spill out of the corners of my eyes, and Teddy pulls back, gifting me with breath.

My lungs heave, my cock so hard it hurts. Could I come like this? It damn sure feels like it.

Teddy traces my lips with his thumb as the end of his dick rests in my mouth. "Beautiful, doll. I didn't know you could do that."

I doubt Teddy wants to hear about the countless hours of diligent practice it took to obliterate my gag reflex and learn how to deep throat like a pro, so I don't say anything at all. I hum around him, asking for more.

Please, give me more.

He does, slipping into my throat again, his hand raking through my hair as the seconds tick by. "Is this better? Are you satisfied now that my cock is buried in your throat?"

Yes. God, yes.

"Would you be more satisfied with my cum on your tongue?"

Fuck.

"Don't you dare touch yourself," he says when I move to do that very thing. "Your orgasm is *mine*."

I squeeze my eyes shut, my cock jerking, my balls tight. Teddy retreats, and I suck air in through my nose, saliva dripping down my chin as he pets my hair, his fingers raking through the strands again and again.

"Open your eyes, sweetheart."

I do, and his approval shines loud and clear.

"Suck, babydoll."

I've never sucked a dick faster. I work his cockhead with my tongue, cheeks hollowed as I suck him in heavy drags like the most perfect lollipop. Precum hits my tongue, and I groan, working him over harder, desperate to get him off. To be what he wants. What he needs.

"Fuck, yes, doll," he praises, lighting me up inside. "You're perfect. Fucking perfect. Look how gorgeous you are with my cock in your mouth."

Yes. I'm yours. Please. Yours.

Teddy's grip tightens in my hair, and he holds me in place as his hand returns to his dick. He strokes the base of it as his cockhead sits nestled in my mouth. "Suck me while I come, babydoll," he all but growls. "I want my taste on your tongue. I want you to remember it all day today and tomorrow and the next. I want you to remember *exactly* what you do to me. I want you to remember that you're *mine*."

My eyes nearly roll up as Teddy starts to swell, unloading down the back of my throat. I *can* taste him, and I try to keep him there in my mouth, but swallowing becomes a necessity. He groans through his release, his hand stroking his cock until he's good and finished. He doesn't move from my mouth, even then, and I tongue his slit, my pulse hammering wildly as the taste and feel and smell of him surrounds me.

When Teddy finally pulls from my mouth, he lowers to the floor in front of me. Hand on my cheek, eyes pinned on mine, he takes my cock in hand.

"You're gorgeous, babydoll. Perfect. Come for me now."

It's over embarrassingly fast. Two strokes and I'm coming across Teddy's bare chest and stomach, my hand on his shoulder for support. He grips my chin, tugging my face up and kissing me soundly as he works every last drop from my cock. I feel like I've been hit with a live wire, like electricity is still snapping and crackling through my veins. Teddy's tongue soothes me, soft and minty sweet, as my body jerks with aftershocks.

I've never been so utterly wrecked from giving a blowjob before, but everything with Teddy is *more*. The way he takes control... It doesn't feel like Teddy's only goal is bossing me around. He does that, sure, and I'm fairly certain that's part of the enjoyment for any Dom. *For me, too.* But more than that, it feels like every single thing he does is to make me feel good. And he's said as much to me before, but I'm not sure I truly understood it until right this instant.

He gets off on *making me feel good*. He really, truly does. And that control he wields would mean nothing if I didn't get pleasure from handing it over.

I get it now, why he said the submissive partner isn't powerless. Because I hold a lot of power in our relationship, don't I?

It's a startling realization.

Teddy's thumb strokes my cheek as he gentles our kiss. I lay my forehead on his shoulder, breathing, my thoughts tumbling around.

"Okay, sweetheart?" he asks gently.

I nod against him, reaching up and wrapping my arms around his shoulders. He hugs me back, and for a moment, we stay that way, embracing on the bathroom floor.

When I finally feel like I can move again, Teddy helps me up and back into the shower. We wash off quickly, and I'm quiet as we move around one another, Teddy getting ready for his workout, me getting dressed for my day. I catch him eyeing me more than once, but I give him reassuring smiles that he returns.

I don't have time for a big breakfast, but I grab a piece of toast and drink some juice. Teddy is just sitting down at the weight bench when I head his way. He pauses as I straddle his thighs and settle in his lap, a curious smile quirking his lips.

"Thank you, Daddy," I say quietly.

Teddy's eyes flare wide, the smirk falling off his face as he watches me closely. There was no tease in my voice, not this time, and he could hear that. He knows I wasn't joking.

He swallows, hands bracketing my neck, thumbs coming to rest on either side of my jaw.

"Yeah, doll," he replies, voice hoarse.

Maybe it wasn't a confession of my feelings *per se*. Maybe I'm still working on that. Working through the conviction that I'm not too much for this man. That, unlike the others, I fit with Teddy in a way that feels lasting and right. And he fits with me.

But that word means something to Teddy. And I can see it in his eyes; he knows it means something to me, too.

I can't say for sure what was missing in my past relationships. If there was *one thing* I was searching for. A single key. But fuck, Teddy sure unlocked something in me all the same.

I kiss my husband chastely, just a press of lips, and then I lift off his lap. When I leave for work, the memory of his taste stays with me.

Just like he wanted.

Chapter 27

TEDDY

"Knock, knock."

Scott looks up from his desk, a smile dimpling his cheeks. "Hey, Teddy. Come on in. Shut the door if you want."

"You sure that wouldn't start rumors?" I ask, leaving the door open as I step inside his office.

Scott snorts. "None I haven't heard before. So what's up? You have an update on Phillip's case?"

"I do," I say happily. "The landlord settled."

"Well, that's great. No drama is good drama."

I huff a laugh, but he's not wrong.

"I think I saw Phillip heading into the library earlier," Scott says. "Should we see if we can catch him?"

"Sure."

Scott and I head toward the community center's library-slash-study space. There aren't any younger kids around at this time of day, but a few older teens are stationed at computers, and some of the private study room doors are closed. Scott points over to the back corner, where Phillip is sitting in a chair with headphones in. He looks up as we approach and tugs out the earpieces.

"Uh, hey," he says, sitting taller.

"Hey," Scott replies, taking a seat across from the teen. I do the same as Scott asks, "Mind if we talk in here? It's good news."

Phillip nods. "Yeah, sure."

Scott waves a hand my way, giving me the floor.

"Your landlord agreed to pay you back for the excess rent he collected," I tell Phillip, pulling the check out of my bag. "I have it here. Plus your security deposit."

Phillip blinks at the check I hand him. "Really? That's it?"

"That's it," I confirm.

"But that was so...*easy*," the teen says.

"That's why we keep this guy around," Scott teases, clapping me on the shoulder.

I shake my head, although there's a smile on my face. "Sometimes it *is* that easy. Not all lawsuits go to court."

"Well, thanks," Phillip says, looking a little shell-shocked. "I didn't think anyone would care, and I just... Thank you, guys. For everything."

"Of course," Scott says gently. He notches his head at the sketchpad in Phillip's lap. "Schoolwork or fun?"

"Both?" the teen answers with a small laugh, flipping around the paper so we can see the beginning stages of his sketch. It's the outline of a human, the proportions on point. "It's for a class, but I like to draw, so..." He shrugs.

"Are you an art major?" I ask.

He nods.

"I can tell," I say. "That's really incredible."

"Thanks," he says quietly, setting the pad back on his lap. "It's been...tough? I mean, classes and working. It's hard to find time for both."

I hum. "You know, I have a friend who got his art degree while working a full-time job. I bet he'd be happy to talk to you about what worked for him."

"Really?" he asks. "I don't want to be a bother."

"You wouldn't be, promise. Alex would be happy to help. Let me give him a call. If you have a minute?"

Phillip nods, and I pull out my phone. Scott shoots me a smile as I get up and step around our seats. Alex answers swiftly.

"If it isn't my favorite Teddy Bear," he says before clicking his tongue. "Actually, my *third* favorite Teddy Bear. Sorry, Teddy. My men come first."

I huff a laugh. "Third place is fine. I have a favor to ask."

"Ooh," Alex says. "*Intrigue*. What can I do for you?"

"I have an eighteen-year-old with me who's working on his art degree. He's trying to find balance between classes and his job."

"Who is this teenager, Teddy? Do you have a love child I'm unaware of?"

"Not mine," I say, shaking my head. "It's a long story. Would you have time to talk to him?"

"Of course, Teddy boo. Call me back via video so I can chat with him properly."

"You're wearing clothes?" I double check.

He scoffs. "I will be once the video connects."

With a chuckle, I end our call and reconnect via video chat. Once Alex is onscreen, I walk back over to Phillip and Scott and hand my phone to the teen.

"This is my friend, Alex. Alex, this is Phillip," I say, giving introductions.

"Hi, boo!" Alex says excitedly.

Phillip stares, mouth slack and cheeks rapidly flushing. "Uh, hi."

Looks like Phillip might have a thing for pretty twinks. I give him some privacy and retake my seat.

Scott nudges my shoulder as Phillip tells Alex about his coursework. "You're good at this," Scott says.

"What's that?"

He shrugs a little. "Being compassionate. Helping without being asked. If you ever need a job, let me know. You'd have one here."

"Doing what?" I ask curiously.

"Any number of things. Organizing events, fundraising, helping the kids. There's always work to do."

I hum.

Scott checks to make sure Phillip is still engaged with Alex before asking, "Kipp doesn't mind your job?"

I snort, a smile curling my lips. "No. He rather likes it. He's even come to the studio with me."

"Well, honestly, that's great," Scott says. "You two seem well suited."

"Yeah," I say. *We're perfectly suited.*

If only our marriage was real...

"Thanks again," Phillip says, his words catching my attention. "I really appreciate it."

"You bet, sweets," Alex replies through the phone. "Call or text anytime. I'm happy to help."

The teen mumbles out another thank you before handing my phone back. "Wow," he says.

Yep. Alex tends to have that effect on people.

"All set?" Scott asks.

Phillip nods. "Yeah. Thanks again."

"Anytime," Scott answers, standing. "You know where to find me if you need anything."

I say my goodbyes to Phillip, and Scott and I head from the library. As we reach the front of the building, Scott stops with me.

"Think about what I said, okay? We'd be lucky to have you here, Teddy."

"I'll consider it," I tell him, meaning it.

He gives me a nod, and we part ways. I'm just sitting down in my car when my phone rings. I assume it's Alex, calling back for details about how I know Phillip. But it's not. It's my grandma.

"Allô?" I answer, a frown on my face. She doesn't usually call this early in the day.

"Mon chéri," she says simply. "Your Papa had an accident."

"Maman, what happened?" I ask, pulse starting to race.

She makes a soft sound. "Nothing major. He slipped on the path outside the garden. Hurt his hip. It's just a deep bruise, not a break, but he'll be on bed rest for a few days. I wanted to let you know."

"Should I come?" I ask, already making plans in my head.

"No, mon chéri. We'll be fine."

I shake my head, the roll in my gut telling me *I'm* not fine. "I'm coming."

"Théodore," she says gently.

"Please, Maman."

It's been over half a year since I've seen them, and if there's one thing I know for certain, it's that life can be short. My grandparents aren't young anymore, and maybe a bruised hip isn't the end of the world, but I'd never forgive myself if I didn't take the chance to visit when I could only for something worse to happen down the road. My grandparents are the only family I have left. I don't want regrets when it comes to them.

"Okay, mon chéri," my grandma says at last. "I'll make up the spare bedroom for you."

"You don't have to do that," I tell her, even though I know she will regardless.

"We'll see you soon," she says. "Bisous."

"Kisses."

We end the call, and I sit in my vehicle, eyes closed as I simply *breathe*. It's okay. Just a bruised hip. But I'm still going.

I turn on my car and dial Kipp. The call connects via my vehicle's Bluetooth, and Kipp's happy voice surrounds me.

"Hey, Teddy. I'm glad you called."

"Yeah?" I ask, pulse kicking up again for an entirely different reason.

"Yeah. You go first. What's up?"

My mood plummets. "I need to take a short trip to Canada. I'll be gone for a few days, a week tops."

"Oh," he says. "Are your grandparents okay?"

"Debatable?" I say, pulling out into traffic. "My grandpa hurt his hip. I just... I really need to be there."

"I understand," Kipp says softly, and my chest squeezes tight. It's such simple support, but it means the world. "When are you leaving?"

"As soon as I can book a flight. Will you be all right?"

He snorts a laugh. "Teddy. I've been taking care of myself for a long time. I *am* an adult, you know."

"I know. But I'm still allowed to worry."

He makes a soft sound. "Hopefully, I can catch you before you leave. But if I don't, just... Have a safe trip. And say hello to your grandparents for me."

"I will," I answer. So many other words sit at the tip of my tongue. *I'll miss you. I fucking love you. Keep the bed warm for me.* But I don't say any of them. "Um... Did you have something you wanted to say when I called? You said 'you go first.'"

"Oh," he says. "Nah. It can wait."

"You sure?"

"Yep."

"Okay," I say.

"'Kay."

We both chuckle.

"See you when I see you," Kipp says.

"Yeah. Bye, sweetheart."

There's that soft sound again. "Bye, Teddy."

Hanging up feels like the worst thing, but I do it and focus on getting home. Once there, I book a red-eye out of Las Vegas that'll land me in Quebec tomorrow morning. I call Jerome, too, making sure he can adjust my upcoming schedule. It's not a problem, and with the next several days clear, I pack my bag.

It's just after five o'clock when the door flies open and Kipp rushes in, looking adorably windblown like he was running the whole way here.

"I made it," he says triumphantly.

I can't help but laugh in a disbelieving, giddy sort of way as he strides right over to me, hands landing on my face and blue eyes meeting mine. There's longing in that stare. *Longing.* Even though I'm right here.

Kipp kisses me without a word. It's sweet. And it's hungry. Kipp's tongue tangles with my own, him taking from my mouth without pause. He pushes me back toward the couch, and the moment I sit down, he follows, straddling my lap. He doesn't let go of my face, and he doesn't stop kissing me. Not for a good, long while.

When he finally pulls back, he's breathless. "How long do we have?"

"Ten, maybe fifteen minutes."

He nods. "Fifteen minutes."

And then he's kissing me again. We stay that way, Kipp on my lap, his hands holding me tight and mine holding him close, and we simply...kiss. It's not about getting off. It's not about getting to something else. It's comfort, plain and simple. And the fact that Kipp seems to need it as much as me is a balm on my soul, reassuring and soothing in one.

As soon as I'm back from Canada, we're going to talk. I'm going to ask Kipp to be mine, properly. And assuming he says yes—because he has to say yes, doesn't he?—we're going to do this for real. Him and me, for real.

It's a wonderful, terrifying thought.

"I need to go," I mumble against Kipp's mouth, every piece of me wishing I could stay. And yet I know it's only a few days. A week at most. And then I'll be back.

Kipp nods against me, his forehead on my own. "Okay."

A thought occurs to me. "Do you want me to plug you before I go?"

He jolts slightly. "For the whole week?"

I huff a laugh as he squirms, cheeks flushing. "For tonight."

He licks his lips and nods.

We head to the bedroom together, and Kipp drops his pants without preamble, scooting up on the mattress and presenting his ass. I groan, almost regretting this. *Almost*. I pet his ass cheek before lubing up my finger.

As I stretch him open, I talk.

"I want you to keep this inside all night, okay? You can remove it if you need to, but put it back in. When you go to sleep, imagine it's me. That I'm here with you. Inside you. And in the morning, you're going to wrap your hand around your dick, fuck yourself with the plug, and come for me. Can you do that, doll?"

He nods against the bedding, moaning as I ease the plug inside his ass. It settles beautifully, the base peeking out like a dirty little secret just for him and me.

I give his ass cheek a kiss before helping him upright. *Fuck it.* "I'm going to miss you," I say, unable not to.

The smile he gives me is soft and warm. "I'll miss you, too."

I ease out a breath. "Okay. Gotta go."

Kipp nods, pulling his briefs and pants back on, and I make a quick stop in the bathroom to wash up. At the door, Kipp gives me one last long, lingering kiss. And then I go, my suitcase in hand and my heart divided in two.

It's just a few days. A week tops. No time at all.

And yet leaving has never been harder.

Chapter 28

KIPP

Cooking with a boner is not my favorite thing.

I'm hyperaware of the plug as I move about the kitchen, making myself a simple dinner of pasta with red sauce. Plus a chicken breast because Teddy keeps a lot of protein on hand.

Protein. Dick. Teddy's dick.

Ugh, stop it.

I adjust myself as I open the oven to remove the chicken. The plug shifts, and *ungh, God.* Blowing out a breath, I stand, my dick tenting my jeans obscenely.

"This is all your fault," I tell Teddy, even though the man isn't here. He's likely at his gate by now, ready to board the plane. "You're so mean and wonderful, and I miss you already. And you're not mean at all. I'm sorry I said that. I'll probably say it again because I like teasing you. And *fuck*, I'm carrying on an entire conversation with someone who isn't even here."

A knock at the door saves me from myself.

"Just a minute," I call loudly, willing my erection down. *Fucking hell.* When I'm fairly sure my dick won't be the first thing greeting my guest, I head to the door.

My smile slips when I see Antoni waiting in the hall.

"Hey, Kipp," he says softly, giving me an uncertain smile.

"Um. Antoni, right? What are you doing here?"

He nods. "Can I come in and explain?"

"No. I don't think so. We can talk right here."

He looks surprised by that answer, but his smile never falls away. "Fair enough. So, uh…" He huffs a laugh. "This is going to sound odd. But, um, I wanted to make sure you knew what you were getting into with Theo."

An uncomfortable tingle slithers down my spine. "What do you mean?"

"How long have you known him?" he asks.

"Over a year and a half."

"And did he ever tell you he's worth millions?"

What. The fuck.

I keep my mouth shut, and Antoni's lips purse, his expression screaming, *you poor thing.* "I didn't think so," he says evenly, "considering you live *here*."

The hell is wrong with this place? It's nice.

Antoni rolls onward. "Theo plays the martyr really well, Kipp, but he's not a nice man. It took me years to see it. You should get out now while you still can."

"Uh-huh," I say, edging back, but Antoni takes a step forward, his hand on the door.

"Please," he says. "I don't want to see you get hurt like I did. Did you sign a prenup?"

I grit my teeth, not about to give anything else to this man, but he must be able to read it from my face because his brightens.

"You're entitled to that money, Kipp. Whether you stay married or get divorced, half of it should be yours."

"I don't need his money."

"You will once you leave," he pushes.

I shake my head, but Antoni plows on, crowding into my space.

"I know what he's like. And at first, it feels good, right? It feels like the best thing in the world, letting him take care of you. I never thought he'd change. But he *did*."

My pulse hammers wildly, and I take another step back, wanting out of this interaction, but Antoni follows me, the tip of his boot inside the apartment now.

"It was small things at first," he says. "Spanking me harder. Pushing my limits. Not listening when I said no. Cameron got me out of there. He saw, and he saved me."

I shake my head. "You're lying."

"He's a good manipulator, Kipp," he says, nearly mirroring what Teddy himself told me of Antoni. "He'll hurt you eventually."

"You need to go."

"*Please* listen to me."

"Go. Now," I say firmly, trying to close the door.

Antoni steps back, but he doesn't remove his hand. "If he sells his shares, he's worth millions. That money is yours, Kipp. Don't forget that."

Having said what he came here to, Teddy's ex backs away and turns, disappearing down the hall. I shut the door, my pulse thundering heavily, every single part of me wishing I could hear Teddy's voice in my ear, soothing me, saying it's okay, that I'm fine, that *we're* fine.

I call him on instinct, but he doesn't answer. He must be on his plane already.

With a sigh, I sink to the floor, wincing when the plug jostles. I thunk my head back against the door, my dinner in the kitchen probably cold by now. It doesn't matter.

Fuck.

There's no doubt in my mind Antoni is full of shit. Well, not about Teddy being worth a lot of money. I already knew that. Teddy told me as much before, albeit indirectly. It wasn't hard to put two and two together when he said he had majority shares of a company worth at least seven figures. Probably more than that now.

So yeah, I know Teddy is theoretically rich, even if all that money isn't in his bank account. But the part about him being abusive? Bullshit. Complete and utter crap.

My chest *aches* knowing *that man* is the one who hurt my Teddy. Antoni *is* a good liar. His voice and expressions screamed sincerity, but I know Teddy. We might not have been married or, *hell*, on regular speaking terms until recently, but I *know* that man. I know his kindness. His caretaker instincts. I know his laugh and his smile and even the way he thinks.

I know his heart.

I know he'd never hurt me.

Antoni and Cameron want those shares. They want full control of the company because right now, Teddy holds a cleaver over their heads. He'd never let the blade drop, but *they* don't know that. He could cut them off at the head any time he wants. He's too good for that, of course, but the potential is there.

Assholes.

Part of me thinks they deserve to suffer. They deserve to live in worry after what they did to Teddy.

But part of me wonders if Teddy is only torturing himself, keeping that last tie to his past and the people he once loved. Would it be better for him to just...let it all go?

Not having the answer, I pick my sore ass up off the floor and reheat my dinner. I eat alone at the table, but the picture of that quaint street in Quebec greets me from the wall. Pretty soon, Teddy will be there. I wonder which house is his grandparents'.

Next to that canvas is another in black-and-white. It's a pond with geese and a few ducks. Two little boys sit at the edge of it. I never asked, but now I wonder if that's Teddy and Cameron. They're turned away from the camera, so I can't see their faces. But it would make sense. The clothes look dated.

I ache all over again, wishing Teddy were here but knowing he's heading to exactly where he needs to be. I ache for his betrayal, too. For what he lost. He didn't deserve that. Doesn't deserve to *still* be going through it. And they definitely don't deserve him.

With dinner finished, I watch TV for a bit, the throb in my ass blooming back into pleasure as the minutes pass. I squirm on the couch, knowing I won't touch myself or relieve the building tension. Not yet. When I go to bed, I shoot a quick text to Teddy for him to find once he lands.

Me: Thinking of you.

I fall asleep imagining Teddy is inside me. And in the morning, I come with his name on my lips.

Whoever said "distance makes the heart grow fonder" was an asshole. It's *true*. But it sucks. It's only been two days, and I already feel like a moping, sad sack of a human being who can't function without their one true love in their arms.

Goddamn it. I've turned into a fictional teenage heroine.

The thing is I went from barely speaking to Teddy to *living* with the man. To seeing him every single day. To expecting him to be there in the mornings when I wake up and in the evenings when I come home to decompress. He became part of my routine, something I could depend on. And now he's gone, leaving a big, warm, vanilla-scented gap in my day.

I don't like it. I miss him. And texting hasn't been enough.

I still need to tell him about Antoni's visit, too, which has been grating at me like a sliver in my toe. But you don't drop a *hey, your asshole ex showed up to sabotage our relationship and fuck you over* at someone via text. Not that we even have a relationship. Not officially. We're just husbands. Who fuck. And kiss. And who maybe have feelings for one another.

"My life," I groan.

When my phone rings, I nearly fall off the couch in my haste to reach it.

"Hello?"

Teddy chuckles. "Hey, Kipp."

"Sweet Jesus, your face," I whisper, staring at the man I haven't seen in two days. He's smiling at me, all handsome and bearded and looking like he smells good. And *fuck*. "I miss you."

His smile softens. It looks like he's outside in front of his grandparents' garden. "I miss you, too, sweetheart."

I try not to whimper.

"Are you wearing my shirt?" he asks.

"No comment," I say primly, smoothing the material over my chest. "How's it going over there? How's your grandpa?"

"He's doing as well as can be expected," Teddy says, running a hand through his hair. "He's still on bed rest for another day or two but is griping about it. It's a good sign."

"I'm glad he's okay," I say seriously. "Do you feel better? Being there?"

"Yeah," Teddy breathes. "I'm glad I came. I think I would have regretted it otherwise."

"I get it."

"You doing okay?" he asks. "Eating enough?"

I snort. "Yes, Daddy."

Teddy's lips twitch.

Fuck, those lips.

Clearing my throat, I ask, "Does it bother you when I joke around like that?"

"You mean calling me Daddy?"

"Well, yeah. Because I know you said you like it, but there was only that one time where..." I peter out, cheeks hot, and Teddy smiles. I'm pretty sure he knows I'm referring to the time I said it seriously. "But I've never called you that when we're, you know..."

"Having sex?" he asks bluntly, uncaring about potential eavesdroppers.

"Yes, when we're having sex," I say loudly. "Cripes, Teddy, I was trying not to scar your grandparents if they were near."

"They're not," Teddy assures me, chuckling softly. "It doesn't bother me, Kipp. I don't need you to call me Daddy when we're fucking. And as you've so often told me, you tend to use humor to deflect. I suspect saying it in jest is easier for you, as it takes the weight off while still allowing you to use the term, and that's okay. I like what we are, and we don't need to follow some formulaic guideline when what we have works for us. I know you trust me when we're together, and that's all I need. It's all I ask for."

"Well shit, Teddy."

He gasps. "Watch your language, Kipling Delaney Lavoie. There are old people about."

I fall into laughter, my eyes a little teary in a way I suspect has nothing to do with Teddy's joke.

"Honestly, Kipp," he says, a gentle but serious expression on his face. "Even if you were to never say it again, I wouldn't be disappointed. I never could be when I have you."

My breath catches, and I pray Teddy can't see the way my lip wobbles. I feel ridiculous having such a visceral reaction to those words, but I think he truly means it. And coming from a family whom I've done nothing but disappoint, the idea that I couldn't let down Teddy is a remarkable thing.

He makes me feel solid. Secure. The only other time I've had that is with Niko. But I never felt for Niko what I do for the man who wears my ring.

"Thank you, Teddy."

"Mhm. Now tell me, what've you been getting up to?"

"I, um... Ah, crap." I rub my hand over my eyes before blurting it out. "Antoni showed up the night you left, and I'm fairly certain he's the devil."

"Wait, what?" Teddy asks, eyes going wide.

"Ugh," I groan. "Antoni showed up here. I answered while your plug was in my ass—thanks for that, by the way—and he went on to tell me what a horrible person you are and how I should convince you to sell your shares and then divorce you for your millions."

I cringe as I finish, the whole thing sounding even more ridiculous when I say it aloud.

Teddy blinks at me in shock for a moment before cursing loudly.

"The old people," I whisper.

"What the actual fuck," Teddy growls.

"I know, I know," I say calmly. "But Teddy, obviously I don't believe a shitty word out of that man's mouth. I'm not going to sue you for your millions. I mean, you're a *lawyer*. Like I'd even have a chance."

He stares at me blankly.

"Not that I would in the first place!" I add quickly. "I don't want your money. Or to divorce you. I don't want any part in something that would hurt you. I never want to hurt you."

"Kipp," he says softly.

"And I don't believe for one second you'd ever hurt me, either, despite what Antoni claimed. He..." *Fuck.* "He said you were abusive, Teddy. I thought you should know that. Even though it's the most ridiculous bullshit I've ever heard in my life. That man has a special spot in hell waiting for him, let me tell you."

"He seriously said that?" he asks, scrubbing a hand through his hair.

"Yeah," I answer softly. "But it's okay. I don't believe him. No one who knows you would believe him."

He shakes his head, looking so distraught I can feel it in my chest. "Thank you for telling me, Kipp."

"Of course," I reply, my nerves rolling over for a second. "Teddy, can I ask you something?"

He nods.

"Why are you holding onto those shares if you want nothing to do with the business?"

He's quiet for a moment before he answers, the lines of his body taut. "Because I earned them. I built that business from the ground up with Cam. I worked *hard*, and then I lost it all. After everything we went through together, I lost my brother and my boyfriend and my job, all at once. But they didn't get to take my hard work away from me, too."

"Okay," I say softly, trying to keep my voice soothing and calm in the face of Teddy's obvious ire. "But they can't erase your achievements, Teddy. Not ever. And couldn't you do something with that cash? Something good? You could fund a whole fleet of pro bono lawyers for kids who need them or, I don't know, start a scholarship program for up-and-coming law school students. I just think you're hanging onto the last tether that ties you to a painful part of your past, and maybe you'd feel a little lighter if you cut the cord."

He huffs, shaking his head. "It's not about the money," he says hotly, kind of missing my point. "It's not."

"Okay," I say placatingly. "I'm sorry. I didn't mean to make you upset, and I'm not trying to push you. I just..." *I care? I want what's best for you?* "I'll let it go, sorry. It's not my business."

"It's fine," Teddy grumbles, but clearly, it's not. I pushed a button I should have left alone. Right on the heels of giving him news of his meddling ex, I did the same thing—meddled.

"I'm sorry," I repeat.

"Stop apologizing, Kipp. You did nothing wrong."

Sure feels like it, though. "Okay, well..."

"Sweetheart," he says, and my gaze snaps to his. "You did nothing wrong."

I blow out a breath and manage a nod.

Teddy rubs his forehead, looking off to his left. "I should go. I'm taking my maman to the market."

"Of course. Go. I'll talk to you later."

Teddy's gaze meets mine for a long moment. "You okay?"

I nearly huff a laugh. Me? If anything, I should be asking Teddy that. "I'm fine. Go on," I say lightly.

He gives me the ghost of a smile. "Talk soon."

"Yep."

Teddy's face disappears, and with it, all the warmth leaves my body.

Fuck. Way to screw things up, Kipling.

God freaking damn it.

Chapter 29
Teddy

"Okay, mon chéri?"

"Of course," I tell my grandma.

She gives me a scrupulous look. It's been a few days since my video call with Kipp, and I can't get past the feeling that I screwed up. I should have been gentler with him, not barked when I know Kipp is sensitive to that sort of thing.

Damn it, I need to see him. I need to hold him in my arms and assure him we're okay. That I'm not mad at him. It's Antoni and Cameron who keep wriggling their way back into my life and messing shit up.

I pull my phone from my pocket while my grandma stirs the soup she's making.

Me: How's your day, sweetheart?

I drum my fingers while I wait for a reply. It doesn't come quickly.

"Still heading back tomorrow?" my grandma asks.

"Yeah," I answer. "Unless you need me to stay?"

"Pft," my grandpa says, hobbling slowly into the room. "I am not an invalid, Théodore. It has been nice to see you, but I am perfectly capable of taking care of myself."

"I never said you couldn't," I reply, not pointing out the fact that, for a couple days, he *did* need someone to take care of him. He'd only wave me off. "I'm glad I came home. I love you both."

My grandma pats my shoulder. "And we love you, mon chéri. Now, are you going to tell us what's going on between you and that nice young man before you go? Or shall I keep guessing?"

I huff a laugh, sitting at the table as the smells of herbs and chicken perfume the kitchen. Maman sits next to me while Papa prepares himself a cup of tea.

"It's complicated," I start with, "but I like him. A lot. We kind of accidentally got married a month back and have been almost dating ever since?"

My grandpa sets his spoon against the side of his mug, his expression more befuddled than anything. "Is that how kids do it these days?"

I snort. "No. Only us."

My grandma gives my arm a tap. "But he likes you, too, yes?"

"I think so," I tell her. God, I hope so.

She nods. "You'll bring him next time you come."

My smile is so wide, I can't even temper it.

"Now tell me about this wedding," she says. "Are there pictures?"

As I pull out my phone, it chimes with a text.

Babydoll: Today has been fine. Are you still getting back tomorrow?

Me: Yeah. I'll be home around 8.

It takes a few seconds for a reply to come through.

Babydoll: Okay. See you then.

I sigh. It's not the warmest response, but I'll fix it as soon as I'm home. For now, I open up my photos and show my grandparents the two pictures from our wedding. Not for the first time, I wish I could remember that night. I wish I could remember saying *I do.*

It feels like I'm vibrating as I walk the last few steps to my front door. It's only been six days since I saw Kipp in person—since he kissed me goodbye—but it feels like a lifetime ago. My trip put more than just physical distance between us, and I'm anxious to rectify that.

It's quiet as I slip my key in the lock and push open the door. "Kipp?" I call lightly.

He appears from down the hall, coming into the living area slowly. "Um, hey."

Christ, he looks nervous, like he's waiting for a blow. It damn near breaks my heart that I'm the cause of that. "Hey," I say softly, stepping toward him.

"Welcome home," he says, flashing me a smile that misses the mark.

"Kipp," I say gently, stopping in front of him. I slide my hands up into his hair, and his eyes feather closed before snapping open again.

"Look, I'm sorry, okay?" he says quickly. "It wasn't my place to pry, and I owe you an apology for that. I forget, sometimes, that we're not actually..." He waves his hand in the scant few inches between us. "You know."

"You have nothing to apologize for," I tell him again. "I'm not mad, sweetheart."

His lips purse, like he doesn't quite understand. "Wait, what?"

"I'm not mad," I repeat. "And I handled that conversation poorly. *I'm* sorry."

His face goes through a complicated roll of emotions. "Well, I don't know what to do with that," he all but huffs, reminding me of a disgruntled kitten. I refrain from telling him so, fairly certain it wouldn't be appreciated right now.

"Did you want me to be angry with you?" I ask, stepping closer. Close enough to feel the heat of him at my front.

"Well, no," he says. "I just...expected it."

God.

"Kipp, I don't think I'm capable of true anger when it comes to you. You're quite possibly the sweetest man I know, and all I could think about these past few days was coming home to you. I wanted to hold you and kiss you and be with you again. I couldn't stop missing you."

"Really?" he asks hopefully.

"Really."

"I mean, it's kind of ridiculous, though, isn't it? It wasn't even a full week," he says, lips inching closer to mine. "I shouldn't want you this much."

My heart beats fast, fingers still caught in Kipp's hair.

"It doesn't make sense," he mumbles, blue eyes meeting mine before dropping to my lips.

"Sweetheart," I breathe.

Kipp doesn't reply. He just crashes his mouth into mine.

He moans into the kiss, as if he can't help it, his lips pillow-soft and sweet and feeling like home. It's such a *relief*, having this man at my fingertips, tasting his desire on my tongue, that I don't hold back. I let him taste every ounce of my returned desire for him, tightening my hands in his hair, holding him in my grasp as I take and take and *take*. He goes pliant under the onslaught, the tension draining from his body as the two of us stumble through the room toward the couch. Kipp hits it first, his ass landing on the back of the sectional, his hand traveling down to cup my hardening cock.

I have just enough sense to pull back before things get too heated. "Kipp, wait."

"What?" he groans, pulling me back in, nipping at my lip and rubbing me through my jeans. "Want you."

"I know, but *fuck*, hold on," I manage to get out, forcing a few inches between us. "We need to talk. About us."

He makes a disapproving sound, his lips shiny and red, hair disheveled and eyes swinging between my own. "We talked already. You said you missed me, and I missed you. *God*, how I missed you. Isn't that enough? I don't want to talk anymore, Teddy. I want you to spank me and fuck me and *own* me. I want you to *keep* me. Is that too much to ask?"

My pulse hammers, my mouth opening in shock.

"What do I need to do?" Kipp nearly whines. "Need me to repeat my safeword? Bananas. Now fucking wreck me, *please*. I need it."

He reaches for me again, but I grab his hand. "Kipp."

"*No*," he says, the one word panicked. "I want you to fill in that place that's been empty, Teddy, because no one else, least of all me, seemed to know what was missing until *you*. You showed up, and you made me feel whole, and you can't take that away. You can't. You make me *happy*. You make all the doubt quiet. You make me believe happily ever afters could be possible for a guy like me. So, *please*. Please don't ask me to leave you. Please don't make me."

Kipp's wide, blue eyes ping between my own, and I stutter a breath, tugging him to me until there's absolutely no space left between us. His hands grip my shirt, face tucked against my chest, and I hold him tight as his back heaves beneath my palms.

"Kipp," I breathe, my heart squeezing in a mixture of joy and aching regret that I avoided this conversation for too long. "I'm not asking you to leave. I won't."

"I don't want to, Teddy," he mumbles against my shirt. "I'm not ready to lose you."

I shush him, kissing his hair. "Sweetheart. When I said I want to talk about us, I meant the opposite. I... I don't want to keep pretending we're married."

Slowly, he leans back, meeting my gaze with wet eyes. "We *are* married."

"You know what I mean," I say softly. "I don't want to pretend this isn't real, Kipp. That I don't love you and you don't have feelings for me, and all of this—all the nights together and laughing and *fucking* and goddamn moments where you're in my arms just like this—that it doesn't mean something more. This isn't fake. You and me, it's not a lie. I can't pretend otherwise anymore."

Looking dazed, he shakes his head. "You love me?"

"I do. So fucking much. I love you, Kipp."

He opens and closes his mouth. "But I'm such a mess."

I huff a laugh, my eyes stinging. "My mess," I say, bringing my palms to his face and kissing him lightly. "My husband. My chéri. My beautiful, perfect babydoll."

His fingertips dig into my chest, forehead coming to rest against my own. "*God*, I love you, too, Teddy. And I'm so glad we got drunk married. Because if we hadn't, I don't think we'd be here. And I really like it here."

"Yeah?" I croak out.

"Yeah. I'm quite possibly the luckiest guy in the world to have landed you. I think it was the neon shooters. Went straight to your head."

I chuckle hoarsely as Kipp lifts his face, his lips brushing my own.

"I do," he says. "I want this, too. No more pretending."

I kiss his cheek, his forehead, his lips, my hands shaking until Kipp steadies my wrists.

"Now would you please fuck me?" he asks quietly. "I want you to show me I'm yours. I want you to prove it."

I blow out a breath before hoisting Kipp over my shoulder. He yelps happily, his hand slipping down under my waistband and grabbing my ass. He doesn't let go until I toss him onto the bed, and then he watches me hungrily as I shuck my clothes. Naked, I grab his ankle, tugging him to the edge of the mattress. His breath hitches, but he groans as I flip him onto his stomach and tug his feet to the floor. Reaching underneath him, I undo his jeans quickly, pulling the material down with his briefs. Kipp lifts his foot free, widening his stance as I spread his ass cheeks, and then he grabs the comforter, moaning as I drop to my knees and tongue his ass.

"*Fuck, fuck*," he chants, pushing back against my face. The *thwack* against his ass cheek rings through the room. Kipp's moan quickly follows. "*Teddy.*"

I hitch up his leg, sliding his knee onto the bed so he's wide open for me. "Keep it there," I tell him, diving back in.

Kipp groans long and low, the most gorgeous sound. He reaches back and grabs under his knee, keeping his leg in place as I loosen him with my tongue. Once I'm able to spear it inside of him, I grab the lube.

"You want it hard tonight, babydoll?"

"Yes. God, *please*," he says.

"You want me to show you who you belong to?"

He groans, pushing against the fingers I slip inside his ass. "*Yes.*"

"You want me to keep you?" I ask, pumping into him, my other hand pressing indentations into his ass cheek.

He hiccups a breath, tightening around me before loosening again. "Please." It's a whisper, and I kiss his ass cheek, adding a third finger.

Once Kipp is a mumbling, incoherent mess, I pull my fingers free and roll on a condom. I maneuver him onto his back before hefting him up into my arms. Kipp's eyes go wide as I spin us, sitting on the bed with Kipp in my lap.

"Ride me, babydoll. Show me how much you want me."

Kipp curses, fumbling below himself for my cock. Holding it aloft, he sits down, taking me into his body with a wild groan, his head tossed back. I sink my fingers into his hair, holding him in place as his ass comes to rest on my thighs.

"Squeeze me," I tell him.

He does, eyes half-lidded, hands on my waist.

"Now move."

Kipp leans forward, his head dropping beside mine as he starts to ride my cock. He loops his arms over my shoulders, finding purchase, and I grab his ass, feeling the sway of him, the jiggle as he moves up and down. His body fits me like a glove, hot and tight and perfectly slick, and as soon as Kipp finds a rhythm, I bring my hand down against his ass cheek hard.

He jolts, his cock bucking against my stomach as he groans.

"Don't stop," I tell him. He picks up his pace, body sinking over me again and again. "You want me to spank you and fuck you and *own* you?"

"God, yes," he whispers.

I slap his other cheek, and Kipp cries out, but he doesn't stop moving.

"*Fuck, fuck, Teddy.*"

"You want me to prove that you're mine?" I ask, giving him another slap.

He moans, his hands scrambling at my back, his ass flexing under my fingertips.

"Words," I remind him.

"Yes, yes," he says, voice quiet and already half-slurred. "I want..."

"What do you want?"

He squeezes tight around me when I give his other cheek another slap, his rhythm faltering. "I want you to take me to that hazy place, Teddy. I want to be good for you."

"You're so good for me, sweetheart," I tell him, pulling him off my cock.

He objects for half a second, but then he groans as I shift him face down on the bed. Sitting beside him, I run my hand over the pink on his ass. I slide my fingers down his crease, teasing over his hole, and he shifts up, trying to take me inside his body. I pull away.

"I'm going to take you right up to the edge, babydoll. But you're not going to come. I want my cock inside you when that happens."

"*Fuck*, yes," he breathes, rubbing his erection against the sheets. "Anything you want. *Please.*"

"Gorgeous," I mutter, bringing my hand down on him hard.

He groans, the sound eaten by the mattress, and I do it again. I gentle the hits quickly, giving his body time to release those endorphins that will leave him floating. It's about prolonged impact, not causing maximum pain, and when Kipp starts to mellow, his body going lax, I know we're there.

"Beautiful," I praise, running my palms over his skin, slapping him lightly. His moan is soft and sweet. I could make him come like this, I know I could, but I slip a finger inside his body, rubbing, coaxing.

His answer is a whine, and I roll him onto his back. "Teddy," he breathes.

"I've got you," I tell him, notching against his entrance. The glide inside him is smooth, and I wrap his legs around my hips before bracing over his body, lips at his cheek. I kiss him there and on the other side, too. His nose. His lips. He blinks up at me, crossing his heels over my ass and urging me closer.

The first slam of my cock inside Kipp's body has him moaning, his head thrown back. I give it to him hard, knowing each slap of my hips on his sore ass will send him higher. His legs don't fall, but he's utterly boneless beneath me, completely lost in his submission. I vow then and there that I will *always* treat him as the precious gift he is.

I know Kipp won't last long. And I don't try to delay the inevitable. We have our whole lives to do this over and over again, don't we? We have all the time in the world.

I bring my lips to Kipp's ear as I fuck him delirious, telling him how good he is, how beautiful, how perfect and gorgeous and *mine*. He takes everything I have to give him, and when I feel his ass clamping down on my dick and hear the little *oh, ohs* coming from his lips, I take his mouth, wrap my hand around his dick, and stroke. It's all over from there. Kipp floods the space between our bodies, his cum on my hand and our stomachs and our chests. I stroke him through it, my own orgasm detonating like an expertly timed bomb. I jerk against him as I come, grinding shallowly, trying fruitlessly to push my cum as deep into his body as it will go. One day, maybe soon, we can do that. If Kipp wants to. I have a feeling he won't be at all opposed to wearing my mark inside his body.

When my ears have stopped ringing and I've come down from my high, I let go of Kipp's dick and kiss him softly. His lips meet mine, a slow, lazy press. He's still out of it, and I pull carefully from his body to dispose of the condom. He mumbles incoherently until I'm draped back over him. I hold him tight, careful to keep pressure off his reddened ass. I just hold him and kiss him and murmur affectionate words as he drifts in the clouds.

They've done studies on impact play and subspace. The same stress hormones that rise in Kipp's body during a spanking lower in mine. That stress reaction is needed for his body to dump those feel-good endorphins that allow him to reach nirvana. But for the Dom, for *me*, spanking is calming all on its own.

I feel nothing but calm and contentment as I hold Kipp in my arms. And I know part of it is the natural physical response to what just happened. But a big part of it, I'm certain, is Kipp. My husband. The man I tried so desperately not to love. I've never been happier to have failed.

"Teddy?" Kipp mumbles, shifting slightly.

I lean back to give him space. "Okay?"

"Yeah," he says quietly, blinking up at me. "So good."

I kiss his nose lightly. "You were perfect, babydoll."

"Yeah?" His smile is sweet, and I kiss that, too.

"Yes. Perfect and mine."

"And you mean it, right?" he asks. "I'm yours?"

There's that calm. That contentment. "Yeah, sweetheart. You're all mine. And I'm yours."

He sighs, the sweetest sound. "Drunken weddings for the win."

I huff a laugh, squeezing my husband tight. "Drunken weddings for the win," I agree.

Chapter 30

KIPP

I've been walking through my day in a bit of a haze. I felt a little low waking up this morning for no reason I could discern, so I told Teddy. He rubbed lotion over my ass, held me, made me breakfast, picked out my clothes, showered with me, dressed me, and held me some more.

It felt nice, if maybe a bit over the top. But I wasn't about to complain, and the process seemed to help Teddy feel better about me leaving for work. He's texted about twenty times over the morning, including the most recent string.

Teddy: Okay, doll? You have lunch, right?

Teddy: Let me know if you want me to bring you anything. Happy to stop by.

Teddy: You're gorgeous. Not sure if I told you that yet this morning.

He has. Several times.

I chuckle as I text him back.

Me: I'm fed and doing fine. You're gorgeous, too.

Teddy: Love you, sweetheart.

Ah, shit. And now I'm crying. Fucking hell.

Me: Love you, too.

"Hey, Kipp. Everything all right?" Carly asks, a worried look on her face as she stands in my doorway.

I wave my hand quickly. "I'm actually fine, despite the tears. Sorry. You need something?"

She gives me a gentle smile. "Just a reminder, actually. You haven't filed the paperwork to adjust for your plus one status. HR needs that for taxes and such."

"Oh, right," I say, having completely forgotten about that. But now that Teddy and I are staying married, I *do* need to fill in that paperwork. My stomach flips over, a burst of giddy energy making me laugh. I add a mental note to change my last name officially, too. To truly become a Lavoie. "Yeah. I'll get right on that."

Carly grins at me, probably wondering why I'm giggling like an idiot. "He seems like a total sweetie, by the way. You should have him stop by again. We barely got a chance to chat the last time he was here."

Right. When he rode in on his white-horsed chivalry to bring me home because I was as sick as a dog. *Such a gentleman.*

"I'll do that," I tell my boss. "Thanks, Carly."

"You bet."

Carly gives my door a tap before walking off, and I relax into my chair, feeling a welcome twinge in and on my ass. The reminder of Teddy's palm on my skin has me tearing up again. Not in a sad way. Just because I miss it. I miss *him.*

I wipe my cheek. *Stupid hormones.*

Midafternoon, I take a break and head outside to call Niko, excited to give him the good news about Teddy and me. If he's filming, it'll go to voicemail. But he answers on the second ring.

"Hey, Kipp. What's up?"

I promptly burst into tears.

"Shit, are you okay?" he asks.

"Fine. *Fuck*. All day. I'm a mess."

"What's going on? Where are you?"

"Work," I explain, taking a seat gingerly on a patio seat out behind the building. Traffic is quieter back here, and there's no one to overhear my conversation. "Honestly, I'm fine. I just, uh... Teddy spanked me into heaven last night, and I've been a little off ever since. It's *fine*. He's been looking after me. Apparently it's a thing that can happen? I'm new to this sub stuff. But hey, good news! Teddy and I are in love now, and we're going to stay married, and I'm pretty sure I want to propose again, but like the proper way? What do you think?"

"That..." he says slowly, "was a lot of information to take in at once. Okay, you guys talked?"

"We did," I say on an exhale. "We're good. Same page. All the feelings."

"Okay," he says with a chuckle. "That's good. And you're staying married?"

"I mean, yeah. Maybe it's fast for that sort of thing, but it doesn't make sense to get divorced when we'd probably end up right back here eventually. I love the man. I don't want to divorce him, not even for a few months."

"Well, awesome. If you get proper-married, can I be your best man?"

"Duh," I answer.

"Shit, Kipp. You found your guy."

"I know," I breathe. "And he's so fucking hot. Hell, Nik, have you seen him? Stupid question, I know you have. You guys have fucked, for Christ's sake. Which, again, hot. But we're not going to talk about it. Or the fact that I've watched it. Hey, the three of us have all had sex with each other. Isn't that kinda weird? The only ones who haven't fucked are me and Dixon."

"Kipp. Gonna stop you right there."

"Yep, lips are being sealed. Topic closed. Moving on."

He huffs, and I'm pretty sure he's shaking his head. At least, I assume he is. "The spanking?"

"*Ohmygod*," I say. "I'm such a spank slut now, you have no idea. The first time was like, *whoa, is this good?* And then, *oh yes, this is very good.* And now it's like, *fucking spank me, Daddy—*"

"Kipp!"

"Yep."

Niko sighs, but it sounds like laughter. "I'm really happy for you, brother. And I'm always here if you wanna talk. Have your folks been any more supportive? Or Vaughn?"

"No," I answer. "But I think I'm going to call. Try one more time."

"You sure?"

"Yeah. I was thinking about how Teddy dropped everything to visit his grandparents when his papa got hurt. And, in a way, my family did that for me. They *did* come, even though that visit sucked. And... I don't know. Maybe that means something."

"Just be careful," Niko says.

"I will. I'm not afraid to stand up for myself anymore."

"That's really good, man. Those spankings must be toughening you up."

I snort. "Pure bliss, bro-friend. You don't even know."

"Don't you dare give Dixon any ideas," he says. "That man would be insufferable if I let him spank me."

"Yeah, no. Can you imagine?"

He chuckles. "You doing okay, though?"

"Yeah, truly, I'm good. Talk later?"

"You got it. See ya."

After hanging up with Niko, I stare at my phone for a long while before dialing my mom. She picks up on the fourth ring.

"Hello?"

Her tone is somewhat hesitant, and I can't blame her. I haven't been the first to call in years, and our last conversation wasn't the best.

"Hi, Mom. Do you have a minute?"

"Sure."

"I just... I wanted to apologize for how our last visit went. I know things between us have been strained for a long time, and there are topics we don't see eye-to-eye on. But you guys made the effort to come see me because, in your own way, I think you care. And I appreciate that."

"Thank you, Kipling," she says quietly.

I blow out a slow breath. "That being said, I like who I am. I like my life and am proud of my sexuality, and I'm married to a man. Those are simple facts. And if you guys can't support that, there shouldn't be more visits. It hurts, more than I can properly convey, to hear you tell me I'm wrong as a person. That you believe I'm going to hell. I'm open to talking, to maybe even getting together, but not if you can't find it in your heart to accept me for who I am. That's a deal-breaker for me."

I can hear my mom breathing over the line, the both of us quiet in the aftermath of my short speech. Finally, she says, "Your father won't accept it, Kipling."

"No, I don't expect he will. And you?"

Another pause before she says, "I don't know."

"Fair enough," I answer, my eyes stinging. It's not that I expected otherwise, I'd just...hoped.

"I'll talk to your father and Vaughn," she says. "But if you don't hear from me..."

She doesn't finish her sentence, but it's clear enough. If I don't hear from them, then that's it. It hurts more than I want to admit, the finality of that statement. This is my mom. The woman who raised me. The woman who loved me in her own way, and I loved her in mine.

But I deserve better than the treatment they've given me. I know I do. Words can hurt just as much as fists.

I want to believe everything will work out in the end. That she, if not my father and brother, will open her heart and her mind enough to see that there's no shame in loving a person of the same gender. There's no sin in it.

But I know things don't always work out that way. And there's a chance this is it. That this is goodbye.

The right decisions aren't always the easy ones, are they?

"I wish you well, Mom," I finally say.

"You, too, Kipling."

And then she's gone. Just like that.

Fuck.

With a deep breath, I head back inside and finish the rest of my workday in the same sort of haze I started it in. A little teary-eyed. A lot floaty in the wrong sort of way. It's not until I'm packing up my things that a text comes through from my brother.

Vaughn: Seriously, asswipe? You're trying to cut us off? We're the only family you've got. You're stuck with us.

I sit back down as I type out a response, not leaving any words unsaid this time.

Me: No, I'm not stuck with you. You're a bully, Vaughn. You're mean to me because it makes you feel good. You don't have to agree with my life, but if you can't speak to

me with the respect you would show any human being, then I'm going to block your number. I deserve to be treated with decency. And if that's not something you can offer, then no, I don't need you. I have other family.

My heart races as I wait for a response, but one doesn't come. I take that as a good sign, sticking my phone in my pocket with shaking hands.

Shit. This day.

The trip home passes in a blur. I drive the speed limit. Stop when it's appropriate. Park my car. Pass the doorman and say hello. Ride the elevator up to the third floor. Open the door.

Teddy looks up from the couch when I step into the apartment, his smile slipping. "Kipp?"

I don't stop. I walk right over to him, dropping my bag on the way, kicking off my shoes. I climb onto his lap as if I'm not a nearly thirty-year-old man who's too old for such things. I sink down onto Teddy's warm thighs, nestle my face in the crook of his neck where his spicy vanilla scent surrounds me like a cocoon, and I let myself be vulnerable.

"Daddy."

His arms come around me instantly, warm and safe, his hands protecting me from the world at my back. "Yeah, baby-doll," he breathes. "What do you need?"

"Hold me."

"Anytime you want," he says, hands smoothing across my back. He rubs circles over my shirt, kisses my temple, murmurs sweet words into my ear. He's there for me, the way so few people in my life have been.

It's easy to convince yourself you shouldn't be sad about certain things. Because other people have it worse. They get kicked out of their homes for coming out of the closet. They work jobs they hate and barely make rent. Maybe they have an abusive partner. Maybe they're living with chronic pain. There's always *worse*, and I haven't had a bad life. Not by a long shot. I'd even say I've enjoyed myself maybe more than most.

But that doesn't mean I haven't been lonely. It doesn't mean I haven't been sad at times because of that empty space in my chest reminding me of what I was missing.

Teddy saw me trying to fill that void with another night of bad decisions and too much alcohol. He stepped in, and maybe it led to us getting hitched without either of us remembering. But I refuse to count that among one of my bad decisions. It was quite possibly the best.

"Teddy," I say quietly.

He hums. "What is it, sweetheart?"

"Would you re-marry me?"

He stills, but I rush on.

"Maybe it's too early to be asking, but I don't care. You already told me you don't want a divorce, and *no take-backsies*," I say quickly. I ease out a breath before going on. "I just... I want you to know I don't regret it. I'd do it again. I *want* to do it again. The right way. I want that."

When Teddy doesn't say anything, I lift my head. His gaze is unbearably warm as it meets mine, his expression making it clear exactly what his answer will be.

"Yeah, Kipp," he says softly. "I'll marry you again."

"Really?" I ask, my tension unspooling.

"Believe it or not, I've always been yours," he says softly.

Damn it. There go my eyes again, leaking like a faucet. "Then why did you ignore me?" I ask, the words coming out before I can stop them. "In the beginning, why'd you stay away?"

Teddy swears, and I almost regret asking. My emotions and insecurities are getting the better of me today, and maybe I shouldn't have brought it up.

But then Teddy's hands are in my hair, tugging gently, and all of that fear dissipates, just floats away under the reassurance of his touch.

"I was never ignoring you, Kipp," he says, voice cracking. "I was all too aware of you, and that scared me."

"Because of Antoni."

"In a way," he answers, his fingers massaging my scalp. My eyes slip closed. "It was hard to trust after everything that happened, and I knew you were someone I could fall for. I was scared to. Not that it stopped me in the end."

"But I'm just a doll, Teddy. Are you sure you don't want a real boy?"

The both of us freeze as my words settle. Teddy's lips twitch.

"Oh my God," I groan, dropping my forehead to his shoulder and snorting a laugh. "I'm living my very own kinky fairytale."

Teddy chuckles with me, hands rubbing my back again. "Kipp," he says seriously.

"Yeah?"

"I'm not scared anymore, okay? You're exactly what I want. And I know you won't hurt me. I won't hurt you either. You're safe with me."

And that, I believe wholeheartedly. So I lift my head, and I kiss my husband. And when we go to bed at night, limbs tangled, I fall asleep knowing my family just got a little bit bigger.

Chapter 31
TEDDY

"Oh my God, oh my God, oh my *God*."

"Are you going to be like this the entire time?" I ask Kipp, grinning as he does a little shimmy.

"Yes, I am, Teddy. Because it's Bring Your Kipp To Work day. My favorite fucking day."

"Try to behave," I tell him, opening the door to the studio.

He snorts.

Well, that bodes well.

"Kipster!"

Aaand, here we go.

"Alex, my *man*!" Kipp replies.

As my husband and coworker embrace like long-lost lovers, I head toward Studio 1.

"You've sure been visiting a lot," Alex says, the pair following after me. "Thinking about expanding into the porn industry?"

Kipp snorts. "Nah. I'll stick to voyeurism, thanks. Besides, Teddy wouldn't like it. He doesn't share his doll."

There's a beat of silence before Alex goes, "*Daaamn*. Teddy Bear. Teddy. Hey, hey. *Daddy*."

I keep my amusement firmly hidden. "Yes?"

"That's hot as fuck," Alex says. Kipp blushes but looks pleased. "You can thank me now." Alex waves his hand in a *gimme* gesture.

"Thank you?" I ask. "For what?"

"For setting you two up," he says proudly.

"Um, I think that was Niko," Kipp says.

Alex squawks, the three of us passing through the doorway into Studio 1. "What? No, it wasn't. I was *constantly* pushing you two together. Right, Teddy? Back me up."

I shake my head as Kipp says, "Yeah, but Niko is the one who invited me to the party bus that night. *Sooo*, sorry. I think he gets credit."

Alex stutters for a moment before spinning away. "Adonis!" he yells, storming toward the folding chairs where our coworkers are congregated.

Niko's head whips away from his conversation with Dixon, eyes flaring wide. "What did I do?"

As Alex lays into Niko, I grab Kipp's arm to keep him from veering toward the table of bagels. "Not until after," I tell him.

He pouts. "But..."

"You want Jerome to yell at you?" I ask, leading him to a couple empty chairs.

He shudders as he takes a seat. "God, no. That man makes me feel like a schoolboy, and not in a good way."

I snort as Nathaniel walks into the room, followed by Jerome. "All right," the latter shouts. "Seats."

Everyone scrambles, performers and crew alike, except for Nathaniel, who stays at Jerome's side, a clipboard of notes in hand. Jerome's eyes sweep the room before pausing on Kipp. He raises a brow but doesn't say a word about him being here.

When Nathaniel hands Jerome the clipboard, our boss starts the meeting. "Let's get right to it. I'll be hiring some new talent soon."

Ears perk at that.

"With a few of our colleagues having left recently, including Malibu and Himbo, and with Dix informing me he'll be wrapping up in a year or so—"

Jerome doesn't get another word out before Alex shouts, "*What?*"

"Oh Lord," Dixon mumbles.

Alex makes an unintelligible sound.

"As I was saying," Jerome says loudly, giving Alex a pointed look to hold it for now, "I'll be scouring for new talent and opening up auditions. Expect some new faces around here soon."

Kipp raises a hand, and Jerome eyes him dubiously.

"Yes?" our boss asks slowly.

"How do auditions work? Not asking for myself, but I'm curious. Is it like"—Kipp mimes jacking off, ending with what I assume is an explosion of cum—"or do you have them read Shakespeare or something?"

Jerome simply blinks as Nathaniel fields the question, Alex snickering behind us. "It's essentially a combination of the two," the assistant producer says. "We assess comfort when it comes to nudity and performance, as well as gauge acting talent with a scene partner. No Shakespeare, though. Anything else?"

Kipp shakes his head. "Nope. Cool, cool. Thanks."

Nathaniel nods, and Jerome gets back into our meeting points. He covers which recent videos were the biggest hits on our site, and what that means moving forward. He mentions an awards ceremony coming up, and he congratulates Bill on his anniversary. The cameraman fields well wishes as the meeting comes to a close, and Alex beelines right for Dixon.

"Let me explain," Dixon says evenly.

"Explain what?" Alex counters, hands on his hips, his tiny body practically vibrating with anger and what I suspect might be a good dose of sadness. "Explain why you didn't tell us first?"

"I only told Jerome earlier today. I was getting there," Dixon replies.

Alex doesn't look pleased, but he does deflate a little. "You're seriously leaving us, Grumpy Bear?"

"I'm leaving the studio, not *you*," Dixon says as Niko squeezes his leg in support. "It's time for me, small fry. It won't be for at least another year, but I'm looking into other job options. I'm ready to be done."

Alex huffs before wiping at his face. "Damn it," he mutters, unceremoniously climbing onto Dixon's lap and wrapping the bigger man in his arms. "I'm going to miss you."

"Is it going to be like this for the next year?" Dixon asks, sounding resigned. He pats Alex on the back twice.

"You bet your ass," Alex replies. "Expect hugs, random showerings of affection, and plenty of *we love yous*. I'll be shoving so much happiness down your throat, you'll choke."

"Joy," Dixon deadpans. Niko smacks a kiss on his cheek, not even hiding his amusement. Dixon looks about as excited as one might expect from an upcoming enema patient.

Kipp gives me a small nudge, pointing over to the bagel table. "Now?" he whispers.

I snort, giving his hand a tug as I stand. Kipp looks extremely excited as we reach the breakfast buffet. He slathers cream cheese on a salt bagel, promptly falling into discussion with Marco about how heavy the booms are, if he can test holding one, and how Marco keeps up concentration if he gets a boner while filming is underway. Emil steps up on my other side, debating his choices before choosing a poppy seed bagel.

"Hey," I greet. "How's the new place treating you?"

Emil flushes, adjusting his glasses. "Good. Yeah, it's great."

"Something going on there?" I ask, curious why he looks either guilty or excited or both. "Meet a cute neighbor, maybe?"

"Um." He blinks before huffing a short laugh. "Something like that."

I don't have time to prod further before I hear Chase, a guy who works here part-time, ask Kipp, "So you guys open? I'd love to take you out."

"Oh," Kipp says, a gentle smile on his face. "No, totally committed to this guy. Thanks, though. I appreciate it. You're super hot. I'm just a love-one-man kinda dude."

Chase nods, accepting that easily, but I see Alex freeze out of the corner of my eye. My lips twitch as he comes over.

"Kipp," Alex says calmly. Much too calmly. "Did I just hear you say you love Teddy?"

Alex's eyes swing between the two of us as Kipp smiles.

"Well, yeah," Kipp says. "I wouldn't have asked him to marry me a second time if I didn't."

Unable to help myself, I tug Kipp to my side and kiss his temple.

Alex gawks before throwing his hands in the air. "Why does no one *tell* me anything anymore?"

"It just happened," I assure Alex, chuckling at his put-out expression.

"Wait," Alex says, tone shifting into excitement. "Does this mean we're having another wedding?"

"At some point, yeah," I say, checking in with Kipp.

"Definitely yes," he says, nodding.

"Dibs on flower girl," Alex shouts. "Motherfucking dibs." He points a finger around at the others gathered nearby, as if anyone would dare fight him for it.

"All yours," I tell him, snorting.

"Well, shit, you know what this means?" Alex says.

I'm almost afraid to ask, but Kipp beats me to it. "What?"

"Engagement party!" Alex declares.

Oh boy.

"Everyone," Alex yells. "Listen the fuck up. Engagement party this Friday for Teddy and Kipperoo. Mark your calendars. I'll bring the dicks."

Kipp perks up at that. "Oh, could you get me another dildo crown? I lost my last one."

"You bet, sweets," Alex says, a mischievous glint in his eye I don't much care for. "I'll get you the most glorious crown of penises you've ever seen. And Teddy Bear." Those eyes swing my way. "I'll bring something extra special just for you."

I have a feeling I'm going to pay for not giving Alex the news about Kipp and me the moment we shared our *I love yous*.

Ah well. So long as Kipp keeps smiling at me the way he is now, the price will be well worth it.

When I step into the coffee shop where I told Cameron and Antoni to meet me, they're already waiting. They have matching looks of unease on their faces, and I could head right over, be nice, and set their worries to rest. But I walk up to the counter first, ordering myself a drink.

Kipp gave me a huge hug this morning when I told him what I was planning to do. I think it helped, hearing what he had to say about my past. It let me gain some much-needed perspective. Because Kipp was right.

I *was* hanging onto the pain of what they did to me. I'm done with that.

Coffee in hand, I head to the table. Cameron and Antoni stop talking the moment I near, and they wait, silent, as I take a seat across from them.

"Thanks for coming," I say.

Neither quite knows what to make of that. They exchange a brief look before Cameron says, "Of course. Are you finally willing to sell your shares?"

"Yes," I say, knowing by their mutual wide-eyed shock I've managed to surprise them.

"What's the catch?" Antoni asks.

"There is none," I say. "I'm going to sell them to you for market value, not a penny under, and you're never going to contact me again. Not me. Not Kipp. You're going to leave us alone."

Antoni and Cameron exchange another glance, the both of them unusually quiet.

"Did you have me followed?" I ask, unable to let my curiosity rest. I told myself I wasn't going to engage—that I was going to get in, lay out my terms, and get out—but I have to know. "Is that how you knew where I lived?"

"Theo," Antoni says, using his soothing voice.

"No, don't you dare act like I'm being irrational. I didn't tell either of you where I moved to. But you knew. And you knew exactly when to catch Kipp alone. You had someone watching me?"

"Yes," Antoni admits, voice quiet but not ashamed.

I shake my head. *Unbelievable.* "I never did anything to either of you," I hiss. "I was a good brother. A good boyfriend."

Antoni makes a sound in the back of his throat. "You kept me at arm's length, Theo. You wouldn't let me into your life."

"You mean I wouldn't give you access to my money," I counter. He doesn't deny it. "And that gave you the right to fuck me over?"

Antoni looks away, blinking at the window.

"And you?" I ask my brother.

He shrugs. "It wasn't personal, Theo. It was business."

"That—" I have to take a breath so I don't explode. I'm not an angry person—I'm *not.* But these two bring it out in me.

I think of Kipp sitting at home, waiting to hear how this meeting went. I think of him telling me how proud of me he is for letting these two men across from me go. I think of his lips as he kissed me a temporary goodbye. And I think of the way he told me he'll be there for me the moment I get home.

My heartbeat is calmer when I speak. "You made it personal in the worst way. I'll sell my shares. Lavoie & Lavoie will belong to you. But make no mistake—I'm not doing it for *you.* This is it. As soon as it's done, no more contact. You leave me and mine alone, or I *will* come for you. I'll tell everyone at the company the truth, whether or not they choose to believe it. And I will make you regret reneging on your word. Got me?"

The both of them nod, and Cameron says, "Deal."

With that one word, it's done. My brother doesn't care about losing me. He just wants the business to be his. He always did. And Antoni? He's just happy to have someone around to fund his life. He found that someone in Cameron.

I hope they're happy together.

I call Scott when I leave the coffee shop, a good heaping millions richer yet lighter than I've felt in a long time. He picks up as I'm walking to my car.

"Hey, Teddy. What's up?"

"So, I have this idea," I tell him. "What would you think about expanding the center?"

Scott makes a curious sound. "I'm listening."

As I give Scott a shortened rundown of events on the drive home, there's a feeling of rightness in my gut. No, I never cared about the money, not the way Antoni did. I didn't care about the prestige, like Cam. But there's a whole lot of good I can do with the curveball I was thrown. And I'm glad Kipp helped me see that.

When I get home, I find my husband in the kitchen, looking as if he's getting ready to make something for lunch. I don't hesitate to head his way, wrapping my arms around him as Kipp makes a garbled sound against my neck.

"Okay?" he asks, squeezing me tight.

I nod, finding his cheek and kissing it. And then his nose. And then his smiling lips. I drag my hand to the back of his neck, squeezing. "I really love you," I tell him.

The way his face softens is better than anything money has ever bought me. "Yeah?"

"Mm. I love your optimism. Your generosity of spirit."

Kipp sighs, smiling. "I love your kind heart. And the way you feel when we're like this. You really are a teddy bear."

I huff a laugh, kissing his neck. "I love the way you blush sometimes. And how you're never afraid to let me know what you're thinking or feeling."

His fingers tighten on my back. "I love how sure you are. You make me feel grounded. Like I belong."

"You do," I say, easing back and cupping his face. "You belong here with me."

He nods, eyes glassy. "I love you, Teddy. And I promise I'll do whatever I can to make you happy."

I huff the smallest of laughs, tilting his head back. "That'll be an easy promise to keep."

"Yeah?" he asks, eyelashes fluttering.

"Mm," I answer, kissing him ever so gently. "All you have to do is be yourself, Kipp, and I'll be happy."

His hands slip to my lower back, tugging me in as close as possible. "Then I guess we're stuck, huh?"

"Stuck?" I ask.

His lips quirk before brushing against mine. "Yeah. We're stuck being happy for the rest of our lives. *Oh nooo*," he whispers.

I shake my head, a grin on my face. "You're such a little shit, aren't you?"

"Maybe," he says, grinding against me. "What are you going to do about it?

"I can think of a few things, doll."

Kipp laughs as I hoist him over my shoulder. It's a sound I'll never get tired of.

Not for the rest of our lives.

Chapter 32

KIPP

"So here's how this is going to go," Alex says, staring down every single person in our group one at a time. "There will be no hands. No assists from your neighbor. No slurping from the top. You wrap your mouth around that tip, and you suck it back and swallow. Got it?"

"Pretty sure we all know how to do a blowjob, pint-size," Niko says from down the table. He holds up his arms to deflect the massive dildo Alex chucks his way. "Shit, that thing was *huge*."

"Big dick energy!" Alex shouts over the noise of the club. "Okay, ready? Three. Two. Blowjob!"

In unison, we all bend down to grab our shots. I have to remove my huge, glittery gold dick crown first, lest I take out half the table. With that hazard out of the way, I grab on to my shot glass with my mouth and tip the liquid back. It goes down smooth, the whipped cream giving the drink a creamy aftertaste. Alex cheers and claps as we set our shot glasses back down, and Teddy slides in close.

"Not too much, all right?" he says at my ear. "I can't fuck you later if you're unconscious."

A thrill rushes through me. "Are we sure about that?"

He groans, a vibration I can feel against my side. "Behave."

That voice makes me very much want to find out what would happen if I *don't* behave, but then I catch sight of Teddy's shirt and have to stifle my laugh. Teddy rolls his eyes at the reminder of what Alex made him wear—a t-shirt with Alex's own face and the words, "Who's your Daddy?" Teddy was *not* amused when Alex shoved it over his head while standing atop a chair, but he hasn't taken it off.

I think he loves his coworkers more than he admits. They're not just friends. They're family.

"I'm going to grab a couple waters," Teddy says.

"I'll come with," I tell him, sticking my hand in his back pocket so we don't get separated. It has absolutely nothing whatsoever to do with feeling up Teddy's glorious glutes. Not even a tiny bit. Nope.

The lights strobe overhead as we make our way to the bar. We're in the same club we visited on our party bus tour the night Teddy and I got married. It's like nostalgia in the weirdest way. Even weirder is that the chapel is right across the street. You can see it from the door.

What would have happened if Teddy hadn't approached me that night? If I hadn't joined the celebration in the first place? Would we still be veritable strangers, moving around each other but never touching? Or would we have ended up here at some point regardless?

I'd like to think we would have made it to exactly where we are, one way or another. The idea of not having Teddy as my husband is like a painful stitch in my side. The man burrowed his way into my life and—dare I say it—my heart in such a short amount of time, and now, I can't imagine being the Kipp

I was before him. The one who was aimless and feeling alone. The one who ached as if something was missing.

He was. Teddy filled that missing space inside my chest.

Teddy's hand slips to my lower back as we sidle up to the bar, a gentle reminder of his presence. It's crowded and noisy, but my husband's thumb rubbing over my shirt makes it feel as if we're in a world all our own.

When the bartender comes our way, his eyes widen. "Holy shit," he says, gesturing between the two of us. "It's you guys."

"Uh," I manage as Teddy, more eloquently than me, says, "What about us?"

"You were the two that got hitched out back!"

Teddy and I exchange a look.

"You know about that?" Teddy asks.

The bartender turns to his coworker, saying something before waving us around the bar. Teddy and I follow the guy outside, where it's quieter.

"I wanted to get this to you, but you guys left before you gave me a phone number," the bartender says, producing his own phone from his back pocket. He unlocks the screen, clicks a few times, and then flips the device our way. A video is playing.

My heart does a swooping hop inside my chest as the Teddy onscreen drops to one knee, the two of us in the back alley behind the bar.

"Kipp," video-Teddy says, his hand holding mine as I stand in front of him, a blue dildo crown on my head and my other hand over my mouth. "I don't know if I believe in love at first sight, but the moment I saw you, I knew you were mine. My heart longed for yours, and it hasn't once stopped. Maybe this is fast, but I can't let you get away. Not when it feels like I'm finally right where I'm meant to be. So if you truly want me to keep you, I will keep you and care for you for the rest of our days. Because I'm yours, too. I always have been. Would you marry me?"

"Holy shit," video-me says, apparently in as much shock as real-me is. "That was the most romantic thing I've ever heard, dude. Of *course* I'll marry you. Are you kidding me? Where do I sign?"

The image wobbles after that, but video-Teddy stands and swoops me into his arms before it cuts out for good.

I turn to my husband, who's blinking at the screen.

"You asked *me*," I whisper.

He opens his mouth, seemingly not knowing what to say.

I assumed I was the one who asked Teddy. I always thought it was me who roped him into a spur-of-the-moment Vegas wedding. Because of course it would have been. I'm not exactly known for keeping out of trouble.

But the whole time, it was Teddy. Teddy asked *me*.

"I'm going to suck your dick so hard later," I inform him.

The bartender laughs.

"Neither of us remembers this," I explain to him, in case it isn't obvious. "We couldn't remember what happened that night."

"No shit?" he says before nodding down at our hands, where two gold wedding bands glint in the light. Mine fits perfectly now, thanks to the resizing I had done earlier this week. "But you're still together?"

"Yeah," Teddy says, seemingly having regained his ability to speak. "For good."

"That's some sappy shit right there," the guy says. "Well, I'm glad I caught you two while I was taking out the trash. Want me to send the video your way?"

"Please," I answer, giving him my number. My phone pings a moment later, the video now ours to rewatch again and again. "I have *got* to show this to Alex."

Teddy groans. "I'm never going to hear the end of this."

"Nor should you," I say, both of us following the bartender back inside, where sound picks up. "That was the pinnacle of romance, drunkenly declared or not, and it shall be treasured forever. I'm watching it at our wedding redo, on every anniversary, and anytime I'm sad."

"You guys need anything before I get back to work?" the bartender asks.

"Water," Teddy tells him.

He nods and walks behind the bar. Teddy turns to me, his hands going to my ass and tugging me tight to his body.

"I'm glad I asked," he says, lips near my ear. "I'm glad for every single thing that happened that night. And I'd do it again, drunk or not."

My heart thumps wildly as I lean back, meeting Teddy's gaze. "It's kind of perfect, don't you think? You asked me once, and I asked you once. It's like, I dunno...maybe we both really like each other or something."

Teddy's lips twitch. "Only maybe?"

"Maybe definitely."

"And just *like*?" he adds, nipping my ear.

I groan, a sound that's lost to the club. "Maybe love."

"That's better," he rumbles, turning as the bartender returns with our waters. Teddy uncaps mine, handing it over, and I guzzle it down. "Shall we dance?" he asks.

My gaze pings down to Teddy's shirt, and I cringe. "Maybe that can go first? I really don't want to get a hard-on against Alex's face."

Teddy raises an eyebrow. "And how, exactly, would your hard-on be reaching my chest?"

I huff. "I don't know what kind of dance moves we'll be doing, Teddy."

He shakes his head, but he does tug off the shirt, sticking it in his back pocket and revealing his much classier button-down.

I raise an eyebrow, and Teddy rolls his eyes so hard I worry for his brain. But then he proceeds to cuff his sleeves up to his elbows, giving me the most perfect view of his forearms, and all is right in the world.

"That's the stuff," I sigh.

Grabbing my hand, Teddy leads me onto the dance floor, where a few of our partygoers are already enjoying the evening. Without a word, he tugs me against his body and guides me in a close-quarters salsa. There's a wide smile on my face as we move, hips grinding together. When he spins me in a tight circle, I laugh, my body brushing his chest before he tugs me back in.

I lose myself for a little while in Teddy's arms. It's just him and me, dancing a rhythm of our own. He's sexy as sin as his hips roll and his feet lead me through the moves. But he's also sturdy. He's a guiding hand, the heat at my back. He's a softly smiling face and the gentle brush of beard hair against my cheek. He's vanilla and spice and the most resilient person I've met.

He's comfort. He's home. With him, everything quiets. Everything stills.

I think love is different for each person who experiences it. For me, it's peace. It's not wild or chaotic or the thrill of freefalling. It's the hand in my own holding steady and the knowledge that my bed will be warm tonight because of him.

Of course, it doesn't hurt that the man in said bed will likely fuck me unconscious as soon as we get there. I suppose that's just a perk of having a dirty-as-fuck Daddy Dom for a husband.

"What's so funny?" Teddy asks, hauling me close.

"I really don't think you want to know the inner workings of my head," I tell him, grinning wildly. "It's a very horny place in there."

He snorts. "As if I didn't know that already."

Good point.

"I need to use the bathroom," he says. "You okay for a minute?"

"Please," I say, scoffing. "I'm twenty-nine. I can handle myself."

He gives me a smirk, a kiss on the cheek, and then heads off the dance floor. Seeing Dixon and Niko close by, I make my way through the throng of people to join them.

"Hey!" I practically shout.

Niko gives me an up-nod, waving me in.

"Dixon, we've never had sex," I say to Niko's beau.

Both men still before Niko shakes his head. Dixon narrows his eyes.

"I'm not offering," I make sure to add, lest Dixon murder me with his gaze. "Yeesh. Just stating facts."

"Coming over Sunday?" Niko asks me.

I nod, feeling a little odd now that I'm dancing by my lonesome in front of Niko and Dixon as Dixon very blatantly grinds against Niko's ass, his hands on the front of Niko's jeans. "Uh, yeah," I say. "Is Teddy still invited?"

"Of course," Niko says. "You know everyone is dying to meet him."

Oh, I'm well aware. All four of Niko's sisters have been hounding me endlessly. The sweet little buggers.

"Do you think we should warn him or let the vultures—"

"Hey," someone cuts in, voice close to my ear. "Wanna dance?"

Turning, I find a cute twink eyeing me blatantly. "Oh, thanks, but my Daddy wouldn't like it."

The guy's eyes widen, his smile slipping. I can tell he doesn't know whether or not to take that comment seriously, which, honestly, makes it all the more fun.

"No, really," I go on. "He'd spank me if he found out." *He wouldn't.* "And honestly, I'd enjoy the hell out of that, but I don't wanna make him mad."

"I, uh..." the guy sputters.

An arm slips around my middle, Teddy's scent enveloping me as the newcomer's gaze pings over my shoulder.

"That's my husband," Teddy says coolly.

Oh, shit.

The guy backs away as my body rolls in a shiver. I turn my face so Teddy can hear me. "That was hot as fuck, hubby. Do it again."

Teddy tugs me back against his crotch, his voice low and for my ears alone. "You're *mine.* My husband. My precious babydoll. Isn't that right?"

Fuuuck.

"Yeah. Yep. You know, I never realized I was into the whole 'rawr, me caveman' thing until you," I tell him.

He huffs a laugh at my ear, hands winding around me as he starts to sway. For a second, I swear I hear him humming that song we first danced to. Content in his arms, I let him pull me along for the ride.

"So, I was thinking," he says after a moment, hands distracting me as they move across my stomach and hip. "I always had this idea that a mountain wedding would be nice."

I bark a laugh. "You did, huh?"

"Mhm," he says, spinning me around chest to chest and pulling me close again, my feet following his, his hand holding mine as we move. "What do you think? Nice mountain backdrop. Something romantic but understated. Pink flowers maybe?"

"White," I say. "Definitely white."

A smile curls his lips. "White flowers. You, me, our friends, our families? I think it sounds kinda nice, don't you? And maybe, someday soon, we could even get that puppy you always wanted. I'd really like that. Starting a family with you."

My heart lopes happily inside my chest as I stare at the man I love, who's waiting for my answer. The future he's promising isn't one I have any desire to pass up. In fact, it sounds like all the things I've wanted for a very long time.

I lean my cheek against his, feeling his warmth. Inhaling his scent. "Yeah, Teddy. Sounds pretty damn perfect to me."

Epilogue

Kipp

Three Years Later

It takes me a moment to process what I'm feeling. One minute, I'm dreaming about marshmallows taking over the city, for some odd reason. I'm fighting them—because of course I am—and then I'm rolling around in them. And then one is sucking my dick? It's all very confusing.

All I know is I'm suddenly awake, the dream wisping away like spun sugar, and I'm horny as *shit*. There's a hand clasped around my erection, and—

"*Oh, God*," I moan.

"Yes?" Teddy checks, his cock already buried inside of me. He's thrusting his hips shallowly, lighting me up as I arch back into him.

"Yes, yes," I say quickly, giving him the reassurance he needs. This isn't the first time Teddy has literally fucked me awake, but we have a system.

First, there's the plug I put in before we go to sleep. Not only is it a clear signal to Teddy that I'm up for action in the middle of the night, but it keeps me stretched and ready so he can sink inside my body without waking me to prep.

Second is the verbal confirmation the moment I'm lucid. Teddy needs that most, and I have no problem giving it.

He lets go of my cock to curl his fingers around my own, his weight pressing me into the mattress.

"Do you know how much I love this, doll?" he asks, his cock sinking deep. "Do you know how much I love knowing you're mine any goddamn second of the day?"

I moan against the pillow, not capable of anything else. My dick is hard and leaking, the friction against the sheets torture because it's not enough yet perfect for keeping me right on the cusp.

"Let me hear you, babydoll. I want to know exactly what I do to you."

I turn my face, letting Teddy hear the sounds I'm making. Not that it's a hardship giving the man what he wants. Teddy ruts into me harder, forcing me up the bed.

"Every time you go to sleep with that damn plug in your ass, I can hardly stand it," he says, voice hoarse and choppy with his breaths. "It's like trying to shut my eyes before Christmas."

I huff a laugh, groaning as Teddy grinds and grinds and grinds against my ass. "Are you saying... I'm a present?" I ask, my own voice breathy, even though I'm barely doing a thing.

"You are *mine* to play with," he nearly growls. "That's what I'm saying."

Fucking fuck.

"Yours," I agree heartily.

"Now I'm going to fuck you until I come," he says, chest gliding against my back as he returns to those long, punishing thrusts. "And then I'm going to plug you up while my cum is still in your ass, and I'm going to suck you down my throat. Got it?"

I groan something unintelligible, my balls drawing up.

"Don't come until my lips are around your cock, sweetheart."

Fuck, fuck.

"Teddy," I moan out.

He lets go of my hand to circle my cock, squeezing the base tight enough to stop my impending orgasm. I try to thrust against his hold, but the bite to my shoulder has me stilling in an instant.

"*Ah, God,*" I mutter, the mix of pleasure and pain a wild turn-on. I know he would have slapped my ass if he'd been able, but with the way he's lying half on top of me, one hand on my cock, he couldn't.

I don't mind the bite.

He releases my shoulder, pressing a kiss there afterwards. "Who do you belong to?" he asks.

"You," I breathe.

"And who makes you come?"

"You do," I gasp out.

"That's right, babydoll. So be good and take what I give you. Every single second of it. And then, once I'm done playing with what's *mine*, I'll make you come."

I nod frantically against the sheets as Teddy holds my cock in a vise grip. He's fucking me so hard, I can feel every inch of him. Every glide of his dick inside my body. The way his balls slap my skin every time he bottoms out. The grunt he lets out that tells me just how far gone he is.

It's intoxicating, all of it, and I surrender myself to the feel of him over me and around me. The feel of my husband holding me tight.

"Love you," I moan.

That seems to do it. Teddy jerks, his seed spilling inside of me in bursts I can feel, along with the swelling and twitching of his cock. I squeeze around him as tightly as I can, and he groans, his hair tickling my neck as he pants against my shoulder. He fucks me shallowly a few more times, enjoying the *slick* of his cock through the cum he left inside me.

We ditched the condoms shortly after our second wedding. I haven't regretted it once.

Teddy lets go of my cock as he slowly pulls out of my body, taking his time, watching, I assume, as his cum trails out with him.

"Enjoying the view?" I ask cheekily.

I never did say I was *good* at behaving. Frankly, I think Teddy likes it all the more.

"It's a gorgeous sight," he retorts, the end of his cock leaving me in a wash of cold air. Teddy's fingers run around my rim, pressing shallowly inside before I feel the unmistakable end of the plug. He slips it into my body easily, giving it a wiggle that has me groaning. "Do you like keeping me inside of you, doll?"

"Love it," I slur.

Teddy rolls me to my side and slips down in front of me. I look down just in time to see him giving me a wicked grin. And then he tucks his arm over my hip, tugs me in close, and swallows my cock.

My shout fills the room, my hand flying to Teddy's head as I struggle to calm my hips. Teddy holds me in place, his head bobbing up and down as he controls the pace, which is so damn fast it leaves me dizzy.

"I'm gonna come," I mumble. *Holy shit.* "Gonna come."

He pops off my dick just long enough to say, "Good baby-doll. Come down my throat." Then he's back on my cock, his hand slipping between my ass cheeks and pressing the plug.

I'm off like a rocket. I shoot down Teddy's throat as he sucks me dry, his lips and tongue feeling like the best sort of heaven.

How this man is capable of controlling my strings with a few choice words or touches, I don't think I'll ever know. I swear he understands me better than I understand myself. But you won't hear me complaining about it. I love the way he takes control. The way he takes care of me.

"Thought you were a marshmallow," I mumble sleepily.

Teddy pops off my cock with an obscene sound, sliding up the bed to kiss me. I moan into his mouth as he shares my taste, his hand gripping my hair tight. He gentles his hold after a moment, his kiss slowing. "A marshmallow?" he finally murmurs against my lips.

"Mm," I answer eloquently, already slipping back under. "C'mere. Lemme squish you."

He chuckles as I wrap my arm and leg around his body, plastering myself against his front. "Don't forget, we have brunch with Niko's family in a couple hours."

"Shh," I tell him, stuffing my face against his chest and giving him a pat. "Sleep now."

He presses a kiss to my head, and I float away.

"Mon chéri, look at you. So handsome," Teddy's grandma says, giving me a smile through our video call. I can practically feel her small arms around me, even though it's been months since our last visit.

"Hi, Grandma El," I say, waving. "It's good to see you."

Cub, needing to get in on the action, clambers over my lap, tilting his head back and forth as he stares at the screen, likely trying to figure out how one of his favorite people is inside my phone.

"And hello, little chiot," Grandma El says, using the French word for *puppy*, even though Cub is two and a half now and nearly bigger than me.

I had no clue the tiny ball of brown fur we adopted from the pound would turn out to be partially Bernese Mountain Dog. Luckily, Cub is as sweet as he is big and rarely ever causes a problem.

"Aren't you looking so handsome?" Grandma El coos.

Cub preens, wagging his tail. I push his butt out of my face as Teddy's grandpa appears onscreen, taking a seat next to his wife. "Is that Kipp?" he says.

I wave from around the ball of fur.

"Ah. Hello, Kipp. Did you try that tomato sauce recipe I sent?"

I huff a laugh as Teddy shakes his head from within the kitchen. He's putting away the remnants of our dinner. "I did. Thanks for sending it. It was delicious."

Grandpa Luca looks pleased. "Where is our Théodore?"

"Right here, Papa," Teddy answers, sitting beside me and Cub, just inside the frame of the video call.

"Happy anniversary," Grandma El says.

"Thanks, Maman," Teddy replies, his arm coming around me as Cub licks his face.

Technically, it's our *second* third anniversary. I keep track of both. There's the anniversary of our first marriage—the kinda, sorta, definitely accidental one. Even though neither Teddy nor I remember it, it still counts. It's what brought us together, after all.

Then there's the anniversary of our quote-unquote *real* marriage. The one we had in front of our family and friends exactly three years ago in the fall at Red Rock Canyon. It was a gorgeous night, the temperature a little cooler and the sunset casting a beautiful glow over the red rocks. We had white flowers, the mountains as our backdrop—just like I always wanted—and everyone we loved was there, including Grandma and Grandpa Lavoie.

Neither Cameron nor Antoni were invited, of course. And no one from my immediate family came. In fact, I haven't heard from any of them in years, apart from a couple unpleasant texts from Vaughn before I finally blocked his number. It's okay, though. I have a wonderful family of my own with Teddy, his grandparents, our sweet Cub, the Adamoses...heck, even my work crew and the wacky bunch at Elite 8 Studios.

I wouldn't trade any of them for the world.

Teddy and I spend a good while catching up with his honorary parents. We'll see them again shortly for Thanksgiving. Christmas this year will be spent at Mama Adamos's house.

"We'll let you two enjoy the rest of your night," Grandma El says. "Bisous."

"Kisses," Teddy and I reply in unison.

As the call ends, I give Cub a good scratch. His tongue lolls out, doggy breath fanning over my face. "You know what time it is," I say excitedly to Teddy.

His lips twitch, but he stops my hand as I reach for the remote. "I thought we could do something a little different this time."

"But..." I pout. "Our videos, Teddy. We always watch our videos."

"Trust me?" he asks, standing and holding out his hand.

Trusting him—*always*—I grab on.

Cub whines at the door as we leave, but Teddy tells him to stay. "Your daddies will be back soon," he assures our fur-son. I about melt.

After closing the door, Teddy leads me down the hall, and, much to my surprise, to the stairwell. We take the stairs up, not down, and Teddy opens the door to the roof. I momentarily falter, having trouble comprehending what I'm seeing.

"Teddy..."

"I thought we could watch the videos up here tonight," he says, setting a brick against the door to hold it open before leading me toward the projector screen that's on top of the roof.

"Where did... How..."

I can't seem to figure out what question to ask, but Teddy explains, "I borrowed the projector from Scott. As for the rest of it, well, that was me."

My mouth hangs open as I take in the roof of our apartment building, which Teddy has transformed into some sort of romantic outdoor theater. There are bunches of white flowers set up along the perimeter, more flower petals blowing gently over the concrete, two chairs with cushions in front of the screen, and a bucket between them with half-melted ice and a bottle of champagne. He must have crept away while I was finishing our dinner, the sneaky man.

"Shit, Teddy," I mumble.

"Come on," he says, a soft smile on his face. We take seats, and Teddy cues up the first video. The one where he proposed.

I can't help but laugh as I watch Teddy's short speech for what must be the hundredth time. "How were you so eloquent while drunk?" I wonder aloud.

"Talent," he says, winking at me and handing over a glass of champagne.

Our wedding day is next. The one in the mountains. It starts off with some video footage of the prep we did that day: Teddy getting ready with a whole bunch of rowdy porn stars, me with Niko and his sisters. Even though we watch it yearly, it never gets old.

I twine my hand with my husband's as we sip our champagne.

The ceremony is next, although it wasn't official. We were already married by that point, but this was us doing it right. Doing it with intention. Scott is the one who officiated.

When Teddy sold his shares of Lavoie & Lavoie, he sunk a big part of the money he gained into helping expand the LGBTQ+ community center. He works there several days a week now, having cut his hours back at the studio, and, of course, he still takes on pro bono cases whenever they pop up. As for Scott, he's become a good friend to us both, and he even helped me convince Teddy to wear his Aquaman costume again for Halloween last year.

The man was so hot, he had to pull me away to a private room during the middle of the party because I couldn't stop groping him. The subsequent spanking-slash-fuckfest was memorable, to say the least.

"Oh, this is my favorite part," I tell Teddy as our onscreen doppelgangers walk down the aisle, hands entwined and the mountains in front of us. The sun was already beginning to set, the same way it is now. Teddy's hand squeezes mine in real time as we watch our vows in silence. I mouth along, having them memorized at this point.

"Kipp. When I was young, I had this idea in my head of what I wanted my life to be. Family was important to me, and I wanted to create one of my own. To add to what I had. When I met you, I could see it. I could see us cooking in the kitchen together or lying down to watch TV. I could see us sharing a home, a life, our hearts. I was scared to go after that dream, but you broke through my fear, and not a day goes by that I'm not thankful for that."

I wipe my face, chest squeezing tight as past-Teddy continues to speak.

"When I think of my future, I think of you. You, me, the family we've created. I think of jogs through the neighborhood and dancing with you next to the couch. I think of all the little alongside all the big. Most of all, I think of loving you. It's been a privilege to call you my husband. And if you'll accept my hand once again, I promise you, I won't ever take the future you and I are building for granted. I love you, Kipling Delaney Lavoie. And I want to spend the rest of our lives with you by my side."

Teddy squeezes my hand again, pulling my chin around to give me a kiss. "Love you," he mutters.

I nod, my eyes welling as past-me starts to speak.

"Teddy. Goddamn it, I'm going to mess this up. You were so perfect, and here I am, already swearing and going off-script."

Our guests chuckle in the video as real-Teddy snorts beside me.

"Okay. Here's the thing. I love you a lot. Like, it's hard to put into words. When you're a kid, you see couples who kiss or hold hands, and you think 'oh, that's love.' And when you get a little older, there's sex and everything gets more complex than that. And holy fucking shit, I'm talking about sex in our wedding vows."

More laughing from our guests. I groan, slumping in my chair.

"But... No matter how much you look at romantic love from the outside, you can never understand what it means until you live it. Until you feel that swoop in your chest that's unlike anything you've ever felt before. Until you realize it's about more than holding hands and kissing and sex. Love is unique. It's not the same for any two people. For me, love is you. It's the way you make me feel. It's the way I feel for you. Teddy... I love you so much. It's big, and it holds me safe, and I want you to know—I'll hold you safely, too. Your love is safe with me. Theodore Maxwell Lavoie, I would be honored to become your husband. Again. I'd do it ten times over. Although, really, let's just do it this once. Who knows what I'd say next time."

I huff a laugh, watching happily as Scott leads us through our *I dos.* "Never gets old, does it?" I say.

Teddy's eyes are warm as he takes my champagne flute, setting it aside. "No, it doesn't. Dance with me?"

"Right now?" I ask, a grin on my face.

Teddy gives me a gentle tug. "Right now."

I let Teddy pull me to my feet, and he immediately guides me close, his hand in mine, his other on the small of my back as we sway together in a slow-moving salsa. Our first dance starts onscreen, past and present colliding, and music floats over the rooftop as the sky turns a hazy shade of pink reminiscent of the mountains. I sigh, laying my head on Teddy's shoulder, the heat of him warming me through.

"My salsa-dancing, dog-dad, Daddy-Dom, French-speaking Canadian with horrible taste in maple syrup," I mumble happily. "You're quite a mouthful. Literally. You know that?"

Teddy chuckles, his chest shaking against mine.

"Say something for me in French?" I request.

He hums, spinning us around. "Mes goûts en matière de sirop d'érable sont bons, ma p'tite patate."

I shiver a little. "Sexy as fuck. What did you say?"

"My taste in maple syrup is fine, my little potato."

I bark a laugh. "My life with you is going to be interesting, isn't it?"

"Are you saying it's not already?" he asks.

"No, it definitely is," I reply, lifting my head so I can see his face. It's such a good face. Soft brown eyes. Warm smile. My lovely Teddy. "I mean, look at all this." I wave a hand around the rooftop for emphasis. "It's wonderful. I just mean... The life I have with you feels right."

"Yeah?" he says softly. The song in the video has ended, but Teddy keeps his hand in mine, moving us to a silent beat.

"Yeah," I answer seriously. "Teddy, you've never once tried to change me. We both know I'm a bit of a chaotic mess, and honestly, I don't think I could be different even if I tried. But no matter what I say or do, you just smile and kiss me sweetly. You *embrace* me, and yet you keep me grounded, too. There aren't enough ways to say thank you for that."

Teddy tucks his face against mine, our cheeks brushing together. "Your thanks is in the way you love me, Kipp."

"God, Teddy." I blow out a breath, chest oh so tight.

"Will you promise me something?" he asks.

"Anything."

"Don't ever stop being yourself," he says softly, leaning back and turning us in another slow circle. "That's the man I fell in love with. He's the one I want. You. Just you, Kipp. Every single piece of you."

And what do I possibly say to that?

"I promise," I answer.

Teddy's lips twist into the gentle smile I know so well. And as the sky sinks into night and the Teddy and Kipp of three years ago toast to many years together, I hold my husband in my arms, knowing there's nowhere else I'd rather be. And no one else I'd rather be with.

My hubby? Yeah. Turns out he's the one. The absolute love of my life.

How freaking lucky am I?

The End

About the Author

Information about Emmy Sanders and her complete list of works can be found on her website. Subscribe to her newsletter, join her Facebook reader group, Emmy's Enclave, and connect via email or social media:

www.emmysanders.com

Find online:
www.facebook.com/emmysandersmm
www.instagram.com/emmysandersmm